Anne felt consciousness returning

Then a fuzzy awareness of something warm and heavy covering her body. She turned, and a bolt of pain shot through her head.

An elusive memory teased at her, then disappeared like a tendril of fog. She'd been injured, but the details eluded her. The only thing she knew for sure was that her temple throbbed and there was a rough scratchiness against her face.

Fighting a wave of dizziness, she willed her eyelids open....

And discovered that the scratchiness on her cheek was the curiously gentle rasp of a man's five o'clock shadow—a man who was lying on top of her!

Dear Reader,

Be prepared to meet a "Woman of Mystery"!

This month, we're proud to bring you the start of our new, ongoing WOMEN OF MYSTERY program, designed to bring you the debut books of writers new to Harlequin Intrigue.

Meet Judi Lind, author of *Without a Past*.

When Judi was eight years old, she was so absorbed in reading a Nancy Drew mystery that she failed to notice when the library closed and she was locked in the huge building. She still loves books with an element of suspense, and by publishing her first Harlequin Intrigue novel, she has realized a lifelong dream.

We're dedicated to bringing you the best new authors, the freshest new voices. Be on the lookout for more "WOMEN OF MYSTERY"!

Sincerely,

Debra Matteucci
Senior Editor & Editorial Coordinator
Harlequin
300 E. 42nd St., Sixth Floor
New York, NY 10017

Without a Past

Judi Lind

Harlequin Books

TORONTO • NEW YORK • LONDON
AMSTERDAM • PARIS • SYDNEY • HAMBURG
STOCKHOLM • ATHENS • TOKYO • MILAN
MADRID • WARSAW • BUDAPEST • AUCKLAND

For Peg Sutherland, who believed in this book
and offered wonderful words of encouragement
when I most needed them

ISBN 0-373-22260-2

WITHOUT A PAST

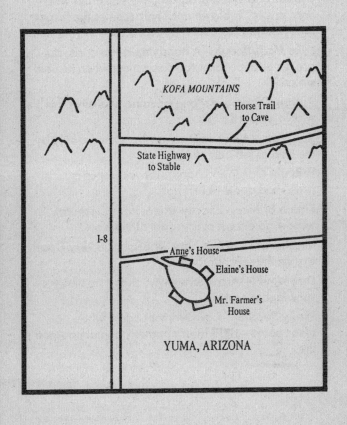

KOFA MOUNTAINS

Horse Trail
to Cave

State Highway
to Stable

I-8

Anne's House

Elaine's House

Mr. Farmer's
House

YUMA, ARIZONA

CAST OF CHARACTERS

Anne Farraday—Supposedly safely hidden in the witness relocation program, she's terrified when her "cover" is blown and she becomes the target for the notorious assassin, Scorpion.

Luke McCullough—A handy man in a crisis, but are his appearances too convenient when trouble strikes?

Auggie Riczini—As long as Anne was alive, his life was in jeopardy.

Scorpion—A hired assassin who's known only by the bodies left behind.

William Gardner—Anne's former fiancé is presumed dead—but *is* he?

Elaine Bittner—Exactly where does the merry widow go almost every night of the week?

Mr. Farmer—A neighbor who keeps a very close eye on the neighborhood.

Dan Nevill—An attorney who shows up under a very feeble pretext.

Wally Spears—A government agent who disappears—right after another attempt on Anne's life.

Prologue

The dark man with cold, dead eyes leaned forward and scrutinized the burly younger man on the other side of the wire mesh "cage." August Riczini, aka The Boss, and head of Baltimore's foremost criminal syndicate, watched his subordinate squirm like an insect pinned to a specimen board—still alive, but doomed to a certain slow death.

When he spoke, his voice held the icy menace of an Arctic night. "Boy, we must take care of this ... problem ... immediately. Do I make myself understood?"

The mob lieutenant nodded mutely. The responsibility for this mission was his alone. No one had to tell him the penalty of failure. "It's already been taken care of, sir."

"Oh? I was under the impression our 'problem' was still very much with us. Then I've been misinformed."

"What I meant to say was that the problem is being taken care of right now."

"Now? Today?"

"I...I'm not sure, sir. Scorpion has been on the scene for quite some time."

The Boss's cold eyes glittered with a deadly light. "What's the hold up then?"

"Your orders were not to do anything about the girl until you gave the word."

The Boss stood up and leaned toward the metal grill until his face was only inches from his second-in-command's. "Well, I'm giving the word now. I don't like the accommodations in this federal hotel. Understand?"

"Yes, sir."

"Good. My arraignment is tomorrow. No doubt I'll be bound over for the preliminary hearing—we can't do anything about that. The lawyer'll handle it—I pay him enough. But if that woman appears on the witness stand, Perry Mason couldn't get me off. *Capisce?*"

The younger man nodded his understanding. The Boss wanted the hit activated—now. "I'll place the call right away."

The Boss's fist slammed the plastic counter. "No, dammit! I want you to *go* out there and personally make sure Scorpion takes care of our witness."

"But, sir, I haven't done fieldwork in years."

"It'll come back to you. I'm not taking any chances. Since I left in the middle of the last trial and hid out in South America for nearly two years, it's not likely that the Feds will let me out on bail again. They're still a little ticked about that."

"I understand, sir. But Scorpion's always worked solo. The last time anyone was sent in to assist, his body was found four months later—in several different garbage dumps."

"Then you'd better make sure Scorpion doesn't know you're on the scene. I've been assured that one of our 'problems' will give us no more trouble," The Boss continued. "I want *you* to make sure our other witness is dispatched with the same ease. Got it?"

"Yes, sir," the younger man answered. The jail smell was starting to get to him. Some people hated the smell of hospitals—he couldn't stand the peculiar odor of a prison. Antiseptic, sweat and fear. He'd spent two years in one of New Jersey's finer facilities—and he didn't intend to ever go back.

He was thankful when his boss waved his hand in dismissal.

But Riczini's glacial voice caught him before he made his escape. "Don't forget...don't forget to make sure, make *very* sure that it looks like an accident."

Nodding once more, the mob lieutenant fled the confining visitors' room. Outside, he leaned against the car and wiped moisture from his face.

The Boss wasn't thinking straight. Interfering with Scorpion was asking for trouble. No one—cop nor wise guy— had ever seen the killer's face and lived to give a description. Now The Boss was sending *him* into the field to make sure Scorpion was doing the job right.

Might as well sign his own death warrant. He sighed. Orders were orders; and like it or not, Muldaur knew he would be taking the red-eye flight to Arizona.

Most men quailed before the mob lieutenant's size and power. He was unawed by man, beast or God. Only the Boss intimidated him. And that intimidation, that weakness, ate at Muldaur like a festering cancer, reminding him of his mortality.

Unable to accept his fear, he looked for someone else to blame.

That woman.

Yeah.

She was the one who made The Boss so crazy. The one person who jeopardized his own freedom. Well, he wasn't going back to stir. Not on account of a blabby woman, anyway. He'd soon fix her. Her death had to look like an accident, but it could be a real slow, painful accident, couldn't it?

Chapter One

The doorbell shrieked in the stillness.

Anne Farraday tried to push away the sound, to keep it from disturbing her sleep.

It pealed again.

Fighting consciousness, she clung to the warmth and softness of her bed, the caress of blankets tucking themselves around her, cocooning her from the outside world. That strident sound was trying to steal her comfort.

Anne's left hand, which she was using to shove aside the insistent bell, met resistance; and she heard the extra pillow hit the floor. Oddly enough, it was the soft plop of the down pillow that brought her fully awake. She sat up, the cool air causing her to shiver. Her diaphanous shorty nightgown did nothing to protect her from the chill of the Arizona night.

"Elaine, this is too much," she moaned, still groggy, as she groped her way across the room and into the hall, not bothering to turn on the light.

Elaine Bittner had recently rented the house next door. A widow, Elaine had shed her mourning clothes to become a social butterfly. Anne just wished the woman would remember her house key. This was the fourth time in as many weeks she'd come for the spare key she'd given Anne.

The doorbell blared again.

"I'm coming!"

In the darkness, Anne bumped into the lamp on a small table in the entry hall as she hurried to the door. The bell kept ringing as she steadied the lamp, then turned it on, her irritation mounting with each peal.

"Elaine, I'm going to... hurt you, " she muttered, biting back an angry oath. Anne hated being awakened in the middle of the night.

Grumbling under her breath, she pulled off the chain lock and threw open the door with her right hand while her left fumbled for the outside light switch. But as she opened the door, Anne silently cursed the burnt-out bulb she had neglected to replace. The only illumination on the porch was the meager result of reflected streetlights.

"Really, Elaine..." Her words died as she stared at the towering male figure on her front porch.

The faint light behind him afforded only a silhouette of a strapping masculine body. He stood a few feet back on the porch, shielded from the faint illumination of the table lamp. His face was hidden in the shadow of a broad-brimmed Stetson. But even in the darkness she could discern a tenseness in his posture like a tightly coiled rattler ready to strike. She tried to slam the door, but his booted foot stepped onto the sill.

Instinctively, she took a step backward until the hard edge of the hall table pressed against her thighs.

"Wh-what do you want?" Her voice was hoarse and tinged with suspicion.

He moved toward her, just a fraction, but enough to cause Anne to reach behind her back, searching for a possible weapon. Touching a round, hard object, she clutched it tightly, taking comfort in the small defense it offered.

He stepped forward into the soft light.

The tendrils of her sleep-fogged mind took him in and told her she must be dreaming. Though his face was contorted in a scowl, its intensity was somehow offset by his silver-flecked eyes.

He was intriguing, but Anne wondered why she had to dream up a man who looked so angry. Must be the result of some repressed guilt.

But even as she looked at him, his expression changed. The anger faded from his eyes as he stared back. He seemed surprised. After a hushed moment, he thumbed the rim of the Stetson to the back of his head, releasing his thick, glossy black hair.

Then, without warning, he grinned sheepishly. That cockeyed grin transformed his face from attractive, if forbidding, to the most incredibly sexy countenance Anne had ever beheld.

The man was drop-dead gorgeous.

Although his hair was darker and his eyes lighter, he had an Indiana Jones tinge of the adventurer about him. The tiniest aura of danger. Excitement.

"May...may I help you?" she managed to murmur.

"Uh...I," he stammered, and cleared his throat. He had those thick, incredibly long eyelashes that only men are blessed with; and those lashes were fluttering now, threatening to dust his cheekbones. "Uh...I, uh, don't know how to..."

Oh, Lordy, all this and shy, too. If this was a dream, brought on by her long-suppressed hormones, she didn't want to wake up. But in case he was real, she smiled encouragingly.

"Ma'am, I need to get into your backyard."

Why? she wondered mildly. This dream seemed so real. A luscious fantasy, spun of moonbeams and silken bedclothes.

"Lady," he prodded, his voice more confident now, "I've got to get into your backyard. I rang your bell because I didn't want you to hear me prowling around back there and take a shot at me."

Anne blinked with confusion. Her fantasy was supposed to whisper sweet secrets, sweep her off her feet. Swash-buckle her, for crying out loud.

"Lady!" His mood changed again and his quicksilver eyes snapped with impatience. "My horse is in your swim-ming pool."

Without waiting for her response, he stepped into the doorway, stunning her with his breath-stealing presence.

She stared at him, unbelieving. This wasn't making sense. Her visitor was no dream; he was real and she was awake. Her mind was beginning to clear.

His story was obviously a feeble invention made up on the spur of the moment to gain access to her home. What his motivation might be she didn't know, and that made her even more nervous. Her fingers found the thin batiste fab-ric of her nightie and twisted a knot. Suddenly, Anne re-membered her immodest attire.

Too unnerved to act rationally, she continued to stare while she backed up, convinced in her stupor that distance would make her flimsy gown longer and thicker.

He seemed to take her movement as permission to enter, and crossed the threshold. Taking one long-legged stride into the hall, he gave a cursory glance to the right, then turned into the living room.

"I'll go through the house," he said. "I just stumbled on the rocks around your flower bed."

He paused and raised a thumb toward the kitchen. "This way?"

Anne nodded mutely, more bemused than frightened. Her mind couldn't accept the possibility that anyone with that haphazard grin would want to harm her. Besides, he'd stalked by her with barely a glance.

No, she didn't think her physical safety was in jeopardy.

A cool desert breeze filtered in through the open door. The chill seemed to free the final cobwebs of sleep that had been clogging her brain. She must be insane, letting a stranger into her house in the middle of the night.

She of all people. When she'd entered the federal Witness Relocation Program, she'd been warned repeatedly about trusting strangers. In the past two years she'd hardly spoken to anyone except her customers, and lately, the next-door neighbor.

But one good-looking man shows up at her door and she throws aside all caution.

There was no rule that only good guys were that gorgeous.

Her heart thudded at a sudden crashing noise from the back of the house. She leaned against the door frame, giving in to the weakness that suddenly threatened to buckle her knees. As abruptly as her wobblies appeared, they vanished in a white-hot flash of temper. She was angry at her unwarranted trust of this pale-eyed stranger. The way she had stood, unresisting, while he strode through her home as if he owned it!

Suddenly, her wild Irish temper flickered, then burst into flame. She may have been momentarily stunned by that good-looking cowboy, but not any longer.

Anne stormed into the bedroom for her bathrobe. This bozo was out of here. Now.

Moonlight sifting through the venetian blinds spotlighted the telephone on her nightstand. She *should* call the police. It would serve him right. Even as she extended her hand toward the receiver, she knew she wouldn't. After all, she had opened the door; he had entered with her implied permission. If the police came, questions would be asked. Maybe too many. She could take care of this herself.

Anne thrust her arm into her faded blue chenille robe. Now her infamous temper was bubbling over like lava from Mount Vesuvius. The nerve of that guy. He'd caught her half-asleep; no wonder she'd behaved like a moonstruck fairy dancing in la-la land. She'd just go out there and show Wild Bill Hickok exactly whose house this was.

Anne marched back down the hall, trying to get her left hand through the bathrobe sleeve. She shoved firmly but her hand wouldn't pass through the narrow cuff. Anne looked down in impatience. She was still clutching the "weapon" she had taken from the hall table. An apple from the fruit bowl. Good thing he *hadn't* attacked her. She frowned in frustration as she stuffed the piece of fruit into her pocket.

Pausing by the kitchen door, she inhaled deeply to summon the reserves of her courage. She still had some residual worry that he might be a burglar employing an elaborate ruse to gain her confidence.

The sliding glass door to the patio was open when she entered the kitchen. Judging by the salty language filtering through the stillness, Wild Bill was having his own problems. Anne scampered across the cold tile floor to the patio door and stared across the inlaid brick area surrounding the pool.

Wild Bill didn't look so dangerous now. In fact, he looked pretty pitiful.

He was in the water, the sleeves of his red plaid shirt dripping wet. A fleece-lined, leather vest was draped across a lawn chair, where he'd apparently tossed it in his haste.

Anne moved a little closer to the edge of the swimming pool and slanted disbelieving eyes on the tableau taking place there. True to his word, the man was trying to lead a glistening black horse to the steps at the shallow end.

The sleek beauty had its own ideas. No sooner would the man pull the reins than it would jerk suddenly, tossing its would-be captor back into the water. The acrid smell of chlorine stung Anne's nostrils as waves splashed over the coping.

She knew very little about horses, but there was something about the insolent posture of that equine head that warned this was a high-spirited creature. Was it the light, or was there really a mischievous gleam in those liquid brown eyes?

But there was nothing playful about the man. His determined expression and the hard muscles straining against his shirt displayed his serious intent. Anne felt a twinge of sympathy. He had his work cut out for him.

They were in waist-high water, near the middle of the pool where the footing began to slope sharply. The animal's hooves scraped the plaster as it tried to maintain its balance.

Although he was speaking softly, Anne could tell the man was becoming more frustrated as the words muttered between his tightly clenched teeth became increasingly more colorful.

A wide grin split her face. She couldn't help it. She knew her "burglar" wasn't finding much humor in his predicament, but from where she stood, the man and his steed looked like actors in a slapstick comedy.

"Dammit!" His sharp yell sliced the air as he was shouldered beneath the surface again.

Anne pressed her hand to her mouth, trying to smother another chuckle.

He turned and glared at her for a second, then growled, "Couldn't you do something more constructive than stand there and laugh?"

Water dripped from his pitch-dark hair. His Stetson lay on the back of his head, a sodden mass. Even so, there was enough menace in his face to cause her to choke back her laughter.

She did want to help, but nothing in her experience lent itself to any reasonable suggestions. "How about if you got behind and pushed?"

He merely snarled in response.

"You certainly react well to pressure," she observed.

He ignored her sarcasm, but she felt a surge of satisfaction as his Stetson slid off his head and drifted across the pool. One look at his stormy face, however, convinced her to refrain from making any further observations.

The horse reared again, this time liberally dousing Anne with chlorinated water. She shivered and pulled her worn robe tighter. She had become so engrossed in the spectacle she hadn't realized how cold the night air had become. She felt a stab of pity for the man in the pool—he must be freezing. In fact, both combatants looked battle-weary.

"Here, let me help." Anne leaned over and took the leather straps from his hand while he calmed the horse.

His voice was quiet, reassuring. His firm tanned fingers gently stroked the animal's muzzle. "C'mon, Bounty, that's a girl."

The animal responded by whinnying softly and nuzzling the man's shoulder. He took the reins from Anne and tried once again to guide the horse back to safety. Bounty shook her elegant head, once more thwarting his efforts.

Anne reached down and stroked the velvety muzzle. Bounty turned toward her, snuggling against the fleeced robe as if to absorb Anne's body heat.

Poor thing was chilled to the marrow, Anne thought. There had to be a way to lead her up the steps. Why couldn't it be a dog, she could lure it out with a bone.

Bounty nickered halfheartedly and nudged the robe again.

The apple! The horse could smell that darned apple. Anne retrieved the "weapon" from her pocket and held it up in front of Bounty's muzzle.

The horse lifted a foreleg onto the first stair and lunged forward.

"Atta girl," Anne murmured, then stepped backward, speaking softly, urging the animal toward the fruit. Slowly, one step at a time, Bounty followed the temptation and mounted the shallow stairs.

The man stood, knee-deep in water, a look of stunned disbelief on his face. Shaking his head in wonder, he watched as the horse emerged from the pool.

With a chuckle of delight, Anne presented the "bait" to Bounty who made quick work of chomping it, mushy bits of pulp flying from her mouth.

Anne glanced at the man, expecting to see a congratulatory smile. Instead, he was back in the center of the pool treading water furiously, arms and legs churning like an electric mixer gone wild. Evidently, he had decided to retrieve his hat as it now lay, limp as a deflated beach ball, on his head.

The moon had reached its height, clearly illuminating his expressive features. His eyes were downcast and his chin jutted in consternation. She smiled at the scowl creasing his forehead. He looked like a small boy who had struck out with the bases loaded. No wonder her instinct had been to trust him.

With a couple of strong strokes, he swam to the side of the pool. He stopped and angled a contemplative gaze at her. For an instant, their eyes locked and a shudder of awareness rippled through Anne's body. Suddenly, her skin felt too tight to contain her thudding heartbeat. His silvery eyes were compelling, almost hypnotic in the magical glow of the desert night.

Every sound was amplified. The faint rattle of wind tossing tumbleweeds across the barren dirt. The rustle of night creatures foraging in the open landscape. She was caught in a trance, bound by an unfathomed sensual awareness. Anne wanted to turn away, run inside.

The force of his eyes held her in place.

Finally, with a supreme effort, she forced her glance down, away from his arresting features only to focus on the vee of damp hair peeking above the top button of his red plaid shirt.

Then, as if to release her, he turned away. His movements were fluid, graceful as he reached above his head, slowly clasping the edge of the concrete coping. Gracefully his powerful arms gradually lifted him onto the deck.

Anne watched, mesmerized, as his long strides carried him toward her. He could have been a comical sight: soggy Stetson drooping over his forehead, water sloshing out of his boots. But there was nothing laughable about this stranger.

His pewter-gray eyes were glazed with a dangerous fire. His tall, lithe body moved like a jungle cat. There was a stealthy look about him—the look of a hungry predator.

Her eyes followed the purposeful economy of his movements as he stopped at the lawn chair and retrieved his vest. In a disarmingly boyish gesture, he mopped the moisture from his face with the lamb's-wool lining.

Anne gasped, her amusement frozen on her face.

On the lawn chair where it had been concealed by his discarded vest, a black leather holster glimmered in the bright moonlight.

He was carrying a gun.

Chapter Two

Luke McCullough glanced over at the woman huddling at the edge of the pool. One look at her white, frightened face, her huge brown eyes, and he knew that he'd lost her.

A moment before she'd been laughing, good-naturedly enjoying his plight. Then her warm brown eyes had chilled into frosty Fudgsicles. Slowly, her laughter had tightened until her face froze in alarm.

Following her gaze, Luke looked down and spotted the object of her fear. The gun! Of all the stupid oafs...why hadn't he remembered it was there? Civilians tended to get twitchy around firearms. This could ruin everything. He snatched the weapon and wrapped his vest around it.

"Uh, look...don't be afraid. I can explain." His mouth was working faster than his brain. For the life of him, Luke couldn't think of a feasible explanation.

The woman—Anne, he remembered from her dossier— started backing away from the pool coping. So transparent were the expressions flitting across her face, Luke could almost read her thoughts. She was only seconds from running for the telephone.

He couldn't allow her to call the police, but if he physically attempted to stop her, he would never gain her trust. The thing to do was to distract her. Fast.

"Please wait. If you'll help me get the horse dried off, I'll explain everything."

"J-just leave," she murmured.

"But I can't ride her home yet. She'll catch pneumonia."

A flicker of indecision sparked in Anne's eyes.

Ah, a softie for animals. Probably the type who wouldn't care if *he* froze to death but would consider it inhumane to let the horse shiver for even a few minutes.

Luke thrust home the advantage he instinctively felt he had. "Horses hardly ever recover from pneumonia. She'd die if I rode her now. You wouldn't want that would you?"

Anne shook her head. "I . . . I just want you to go."

"And I will. As soon as she's dry. Look, if I had wanted to hurt you, I had the perfect opportunity while we were alone in the house."

She frowned, assessing the truth of his words.

She was swaying. He could feel her resolve melting. Luke pressed his last argument. "I'm harmless, I promise. How could you not trust a man who's dumb enough to let his horse wander into a swimming pool?"

The expression on her face remained inscrutable.

He flashed that winning smile, showing a hint of dimple on his left cheek. "Please? Just lend me a blanket. I'll wipe her down and be out of here before you know it."

Anne chewed her lower lip while she considered his request. "All right. Under one condition."

"Anything. Name it."

"I hold your gun until you leave."

"No way am I giving it to you or anyone else."

"Then obviously you're a man who can't be trusted. Honest, law-abiding citizens don't carry sidearms. Even in Arizona. I'm going into the house. If you're not out of my yard in one minute, I'm phoning the authorities."

Anne turned on her heel and stalked across the patio toward the kitchen.

Luke watched the resoluteness in her step. Nothing in the report warned him about Anne Farraday's determination. This whole operation was in danger of crumbling before it got started. Luke blew a damp strand of hair out of his eyes. He only had a few minutes to come up with an explanation that would salvage this mess, but his first priority was to stop her from phoning the locals.

Grimacing at being forced to hand over his gun, he nevertheless knew it was the only option he had. Besides, he had the advantage of knowing everything quantifiable about one Anne Farraday, and he was reasonably certain that she wouldn't shoot him with his own weapon. At least not yet. "Okay," he yelled, pulling a 9-mm automatic from his shoulder holster, "you win."

Anne turned around and eyed him suspiciously. "And you'll explain everything after we get the horse dry?"

"I said I would. Here." He dangled the gun by the trigger guard. "Take this and bring me a blanket. And be careful, it's loaded. See, this is the safety, and it's on, but—"

Anne walked back and grasped the weapon by the checkered handle. "I know what a safety is," she said, "and I know how to turn it off as well as on. Just don't try anything."

Try anything? Not likely, Luke thought. He didn't like the sure way she handled firearms.

AN HOUR LATER, Bounty was dry and resting quietly in the shelter of the cottonwood tree in Anne's front yard. It had taken most of Anne's blankets and several towels to dry man and beast. Not to mention the quilt off her bed to cover the horse while she and the man talked in the kitchen.

Although her unwelcome guest seemed appreciative of her efforts, no doubt she'd be the one hauling all those damp linens to the heavy-duty washer at the laundromat tomorrow. Make that today, she thought, glancing at the clock on the microwave.

Anne poured two steaming mugs of decaffeinated coffee and set them down on the kitchen table. She would have rather had the real thing but still entertained hopes of catching a few hours' sleep.

Once seated, she patted the hard security of the gun in her robe pocket. She waited while he stirred his coffee, but once she had his attention, she pounced. "Okay, you're reasonably dry and I fixed you coffee, which wasn't in our bargain, by the way. So now, talk."

Luke blew on his coffee and sipped. "Mmm, good."

"Look, mister...what is your name, anyway?"

Luke looked up in surprise. Having studied her abbreviated subject file in intimate detail for the past three days, he felt he had known her for years. He'd almost forgotten that she didn't have an inkling about his identity. He had to proceed very slowly.

"Hey, I'm sorry." He stuck out his hand. "Luke McCullough. And you're...?"

Anne clasped his hand lightly and introduced herself. It was nearly two-thirty in the morning; these pleasantries seemed inane. She wanted this man to finish his coffee and leave. *After* he told her what he was doing, armed, in her yard.

"So tell me, Mr. McCullough—"

"Luke," he interjected.

"All right, Luke. Why were you wearing a gun? Isn't that being in possession of a concealed weapon?"

"Uh-uh, only if you don't have a permit, which I do."

"Which doesn't tell me much—unless you happen to have your permit with you?"

He grinned, stalling for time. He had figured out the rudiments of a cover story, but didn't have all the details down pat yet. "Look, I said I'd tell you, and I will. Just let me start at the beginning, okay? I'm a very orderly person."

Another lie, but a minor one, in Luke's opinion.

Anne sighed. It didn't look as if she was going to get back to bed, after all. This was a stubborn man. He may have temporarily given up his weapon, but he was going to proceed at his own pace. Well, she could at least prod him a little.

"So, to what do I owe the pleasure of your nosing around in my yard at one o'clock in the morning? Out for a bedtime stroll? Or a little breaking and entering?"

He stretched back, resting the kitchen chair on its rear legs, using the time to hone the weak story he'd invented while she made the coffee.

Luke blew into his mug and looked up, treating Anne to a lopsided grin. "I'm a bit of a night owl. So's Bounty. We were just out enjoying the moonlight."

"How did you end up in my yard?"

Luke scratched his head, as if puzzled. "Actually, it was kind of strange how that happened."

"I'll bet."

Ignoring her sarcasm, he continued, "We were just about ready to turn around and head for home when I thought I saw someone looking in your window. I'd heard that a young widow lived here alone and I was a little worried."

"Being a good Samaritan and all?"

Luke frowned. She wasn't buying this story. And he thought it sounded pretty good. Shoot, he'd have believed it himself. Anyway, there was nothing to do but plunge on with the yarn he'd started.

"Yes'm. That's right. Anyway, I left Bounty in the front and went on around to the side where I saw him. I'm pretty sure somebody was there—your gate was wide open. I walked all around your property. Whoever it was must've lit out. But when I got back to the front, Bounty was gone."

Most of that was true. Sort of. Actually, Luke was checking out the lay of the land. The subject—Anne—wasn't his primary responsibility, but he always made it his job to study every conceivable aspect of an assignment.

Since few people parked their cars on the quiet street, he'd opted to ride Bounty the short distance to the subject's home. If anyone noticed him, he'd look like one of the locals out enjoying the desert evening.

Luke hadn't seen the agent assigned to cover the Farraday woman, but he *had* seen a man-size shadow lurking in the low shrubs by the side of the house. He'd left Bounty near the gate while he circled around to approach unseen from the rear.

The intruder must have spotted him, anyway. No one was near the window once Luke rounded the corner. He'd looked over the fence just in time to see a tall, lanky figure leading the horse across the patio. Before Luke had had time to react, the man had smacked Bounty on the flank and she bolted, knocking Luke off his feet as she galloped right into the deep end of the swimming pool.

Not bad for a spontaneous diversion. By the time Luke got to his feet, he heard the squeal of tires as a car sped away.

At that moment, his primary concern had been Anne, so he'd opted for ringing her doorbell.

He just wished he'd gotten a good look at the prowler. Instinct told him it was Scorpion—casing the setup. No one had ever seen the assassin close enough to give an accurate description.

The intruder would be back, if Luke's information was correct. Before he could decide his next move, however, he had to get a handle on the situation.

"So," he continued with his spur-of-the-moment invention, "when I saw Bounty'd gone for a moonlight swim, I ran around to your front door. You know the rest."

Anne shook her head in disbelief. That was the most ridiculous story she'd ever heard. She didn't know what Mr. McCullough had really been up to, but she'd bet a week in Tahiti it wasn't as innocent as he made out.

Finishing the last of her coffee, Anne carried the mug to the sink. Turning around, she leaned against the counter and studied her visitor. "Before you leave, I think there's one small detail you should explain."

"Oh, what's that?"

"Even if you have a permit, why carry a gun while you're out for an evening ride? And don't try to tell me it was to fight off coyotes."

He felt the steadiness of her eyes on his face. For a moment, Luke allowed his gaze to be captured by hers. Eyes, dark like melted Belgian chocolate, stared evenly at him. While her bearing was feisty, sparked with bravado, there was a hint of sadness in those telltale eyes.

He shook his head. He hated dealing with civilians. They were so straight-ahead, trusting. Through years of dealing with thieves, assassins and spies, Luke had donned a healthy coat of cynicism. Civilians such as Anne exposed him for what he had become—a caustic observer. Not really experiencing life but watching and disapproving from the fringes.

Luke rose to his feet. "Actually, it's nothing so dramatic. I always carry one. The nature of my work."

Anne blanched. The only people she could think of who carried guns in the course of their employment were cops and crooks. If he was a police officer, he would have said so straightaway.

That only left one alternative.

Carefully masking her emotions, she turned back to the sink under the pretense of rinsing her coffee mug. She felt movement behind her and sneaked a glance over her shoulder.

Luke had gone to the patio door and was looking out toward the pool area.

Quickly, Anne pulled the gun from her pocket. Keeping a wary eye on him, she removed the clip and laid the empty weapon on the counter.

Turning on the faucet to camouflage the faint clicking sound, she flicked the bullets into her palm and slipped them into her robe pocket. With a nudge of her elbow, she pushed a spoon into the sink at the same moment she shoved the empty clip back into the weapon. Not an instant too soon, she noted, as Luke turned from the sliding glass door.

"Well, I kept my end of the bargain," he said. "That's the whole story. Can I have my piece now?"

His words confirmed her suspicions. Criminals called a gun a "piece." She'd heard them do it often enough on television.

With a trembling hand, she returned the gun.

If only he would just take it and leave before he noticed the missing bullets.

Chapter Three

Luke unhitched Bounty and led her back onto the road. They walked a few paces before he pulled the tired animal over to the curb. He *should* go home and get some sleep. His assignment wasn't to watch the woman. Luke was here to intercept Scorpion.

Yet, his well-honed sixth sense made him unwilling to leave the subject's premises just yet. The very air was electric, humming with tension. If Scorpion decided to make the hit tonight, Luke intended to be on the spot. He glanced around, looking for the optimum surveillance position.

The quiet street was lined with small, Spanish-style adobe houses. Across the road from Anne's home was a large vacant field. While the rugged landscape offered ample vantage points from which he could watch unseen, Luke knew that same advantage was afforded the man who had been in Anne's yard. He finally decided he would be best hidden from curious eyes by a stand of scrub oak trees. Crossing his arms against the frigid early-morning air, he watched the quiet house.

One by one Anne's lights went out. He leaned against a sturdy trunk and waited. Years of experience told him the man he had seen wouldn't be back so soon, but he'd been fooled once tonight and didn't intend to let it happen again.

Was the intruder the assassin Scorpion? Or some hapless burglar? It was a coin toss.

He hadn't expected Scorpion to take action against the Farraday woman so soon. He would have thought her former employer, William Gardner, would be the primary target. After all, Gardner was the key witness—the one who could put The Boss away for a long time. Anne's testimony was only supporting evidence.

Interesting woman, this Anne Farraday.

The report he'd received certainly hadn't painted as complete a picture of her as he'd thought. For one thing, her file photo would've made a passport photograph look glamorous. It didn't give a clue of the woman's rather... piquant... beauty. Nor did the biographer capture her curious mixture of naiveté and healthy cynicism. Luke's directions had been to keep her in the dark, unaware of possible danger. He seldom questioned orders, but he was the one out here in the field dodging her pointed questions.

Of course, he was free to modify his orders as necessary. He had this peculiar reaction to Anne Farraday. Something about her made him want to pull her onto the back of his horse and get her safely out of town. Yet, he had nothing concrete to support his intuition. Was he being influenced by the vulnerability he sensed beneath her facade of boldness? If so, he had indeed been in the field too long. Had he forgotten the first rule drummed into his head all those years ago? Don't empathize or become involved with the subject. Ever.

If Luke lost his objectivity, it could cost him his life.

A shudder that had nothing to do with the cool morning air swept through his body. A memory, fresh as yesterday, flooded his mind. The time when he'd lost his perspective and lost Glenna, the only woman he'd ever loved.

There was no comparison between Anne and Glenna. Yet, Anne's gaze had held a disarming softness that made him want to shield her from harm. Protect her. Luke shook his head in disbelief. He was getting soft. Too soft. Maybe too many years in the field had, indeed, taken their toll.

Brushing aside the painful memory, Luke pulled his attention back to the present and his misgivings. For now, he would maintain the status quo; but it would be easier to gain her cooperation, if not her trust, by being straight with her.

Smothering a yawn, he hunkered down against the rough bark of a cottonwood tree and continued his watch.

When the first pink shadows of dawn faintly lightened the horizon, he rose with a groan. His back ached, and his eyes burned with fatigue. Surveillance sure had been easier a dozen years ago when his body was younger, more flexible.

Maybe he should just get out of the business and take some cushy desk job. Although he couldn't imagine himself stuffed into a suit every day while he fought the rush-hour commute. No, Luke needed space. Freedom. He'd be lousy in an office.

He wondered if thirty-six felt this old to civilians. Probably. Unmarried, Luke couldn't imagine the rigors of stretching a budget, nursing sick babies and coping with the worries of adolescents. He had enough to worry about just managing his own life. Still, one day, he wouldn't mind planting rosebushes and pulling crabgrass on weekends—if the right woman came along.

Of course, in his job most of the women he encountered were junkies, thieves or hookers. Certainly not many he'd want to take home to Mother.

Luke's ruminations were interrupted by a shadow passing behind Anne's front window. He moved a little closer.

He ducked behind a stand of eucalyptus trees just as her front door opened. Anne stepped out onto the stoop. The previous night's events must have made her nervous—even from fifty feet away, Luke could see her cautious expression as she scrutinized the yard, even looking beneath shrubbery and behind her car. Apparently satisfied no one was hiding on her property, she gave a last glance down the street, bent over and turned on the sprinklers.

Sparkling jets of water danced over the front yard, shimmering silver and gold in the growing sunlight, casting her auburn tresses in a fiery glow. Luke's breath caught as she cocked her head to the side, running splayed fingers through her heavy sheaf of hair. For a brief instant, Luke again flashed back to another time. Another woman. One who had had that same mannerism.

Glenna. Luke shook his head, as if to shake away the intruding memory. He couldn't think about the past. It was dead and buried. Like Glenna. Funny, he thought, for the first time in ten years, he couldn't bring Glenna's image to mind. Try as he might, his imagination kept conjuring a picture of a lovely redhead with flashing dark eyes.

This job had taken his past and his future. Now it was stealing his memories.

He rubbed his weary eyes with the back of his hand. *Come on, McCullough, no more self-pity.* He had a job to do and nothing was helped by dwelling on ancient heartaches.

Deliberately pushing his errant thoughts to the back of his mind, he concentrated on Anne Farraday.

Across the road, Anne turned to go back inside, then stopped and looked around again as if sensing his watchful presence. He ducked behind the covering shelter of a clump of gangly ocotillo cactus.

After a moment, she went indoors. Across the street, Luke distinctly heard the slam of the night bolt being thrown. She was a very careful lady now that her suspicions had been aroused.

Another yawn forced its way out of his mouth. He had to get some rest. If trouble started, he wouldn't be much good if he was out on his feet.

Besides, he reasoned, there was really no need to keep her under surveillance during working hours. Unless she deviated greatly from her normal routine, she'd soon be heading for her bookstore where she rarely left before six. Later in the afternoon, he could pick up the watch again, if necessary. At least he could phone headquarters and get an update.

"C'mon, Bounty, old girl. Let's get you home."

With a weary sigh, he mounted the horse and headed back to his borrowed house a half mile away. After wiping down, currying and feeding Bounty, he dragged his body in the front door.

Stopping only to splash cool water on his face, Luke staggered into the bedroom, took off his gun belt and boots and threw himself onto the bed. Within moments he was fast asleep—unaware of the red light blinking furiously on his telephone answering machine.

ANNE HADN'T SLEPT WELL. Her sleep had been interrupted by wild dreams of horses swimming in her pool. A crazy man also figured in her dream. He held an unloaded gun, and his features were indistinct except for his eyes, which looked as though they had been dipped in sterling.

She'd pummeled her pillow and turned over. The dream had faded only to reassert itself moments later. Finally, when dawn peeked through the gap in the venetian blinds, Anne gave up and got out of bed.

In the kitchen, she flipped on the coffeemaker and looked out the sliding patio door. The pool surface was still, the deck clean and dry. Could she have dreamed last night? No, the two empty mugs on her drainboard and the weight of his bullets in her robe pocket told her that her night visitor had been real.

Shaking off a sense of foreboding, Anne went out to turn on the lawn sprinklers and see if the morning paper had arrived.

The moment she stepped onto the porch, she felt the presence of another, unseen person. Watching her. She drew back, close to the safety of her front door, and studied her surroundings.

Not a breath of life stirred on the silent street. Another desert dawn had just arrived, painting the sky with its pastel palette of golds and pinks. How silly she was being, looking for bogeymen in her yard on this serene morning. It was all Luke McCullough's fault—with that ridiculous story about a prowler.

Anne frowned. If Luke had made up that tale, who was he really? And why had he been skulking around her property? Why did she have this sudden sick feeling that his appearance was somehow related to the events of her past. That dreadful past that had caused her to change her name and flee to this desert wasteland.

No! She had to stop thinking every man on every street corner was watching her. Waiting for her to make a mistake. The past was over. She was safe in her new life. The taint of the past couldn't touch her here.

This morning, looking through the sanctuary of bright light, last night's events no longer seemed so fraught with danger. Anne was usually a good judge of character, and Luke felt…right…somehow. Besides, if he meant her harm, why ring her doorbell and leave when she told him to? None of it made sense.

At any rate, there was no prowler in the bushes this morning. No newspaper, either. She was up awfully early.

With a sigh, she turned back toward the house.

Just as she opened the door, Anne felt another tingle along the back of her neck.

She looked again around the silent neighborhood. Glancing at the house next door, she thought she saw a brief movement in Elaine Bittner's bedroom window, the one that faced Anne's house.

She watched for a moment. There was no further sign of movement in the house next door. No doubt Elaine had heard her moving around outside and looked out the window for a moment. That was probably why Anne had felt she was being watched.

What had brought on this sudden display of nerves, Anne wondered as she went inside. She was safe now. The past was behind her.

Just the same, she bolted the front door before she went into the bathroom for her morning shower.

ANNE RINSED her cereal bowl and poured her second cup of coffee. She felt nervous. Restless. The image of quicksilver eyes followed her everywhere. And that lopsided grin. Cute. Definitely cute. So were skunks, she reminded herself, but you didn't get too close to one.

And that's how she had to think about Luke. He was probably a con man or a thief. At best, he was a cute skunk, and if she had a lick of common sense, she'd stay far, far away from Mr. McCullough.

Determined to put him out of her mind once and for all, Anne went back outside, turned off the sprinklers and brought in the morning paper, which finally arrived.

She settled down at the kitchen table, glancing through the headlines, she idly wondered why she even subscribed to the newspaper. Reading it was depressing—riots in Africa, attempted coups in South America, family of four killed in an auto accident. The news never seemed to vary, only the names of the victims.

With a sigh, she folded the paper in half and started to toss it aside when a small headline on the back of the news section caught her attention: KEY GOVERNMENT WITNESS KILLED IN BOATING ACCIDENT.

She hated stories like this. Since she herself had entered the government's Witness Relocation Program two years ago, it seemed she was always reading about a witness who had died in some vaguely described "accident." It made her worry about her own safety.

The article wasn't lengthy, just a single column perhaps six inches long. When she finished it, the newspaper dropped from her suddenly cold fingertips. The dead witness wasn't just an unknown name, another statistic. The "accident" victim had been her former employer and fiancé, William Gardner.

The article only briefly mentioned his role in the trial of organized crime czar August Riczini, more commonly known as The Boss. Mostly the article played up the fact that Gardner had gone undercover and had been living under an assumed name in Bangor, Maine, these past two years. He'd been killed when his speedboat exploded three miles out at sea. The cause of the explosion was still under investigation.

The article ended with barely concealed speculation that The Boss, or one of his henchmen, was responsible for the alleged accident.

Anne rubbed her forehead with a trembling hand. Could they have tracked William down? Was she, too, in danger? The questions flew into her mind, but Anne couldn't face the answers. She only knew she felt sick to her stomach.

William Gardner hadn't been an evil man, just a greedy, immature one. If he hadn't doctored the books and tax returns for Riczini, she would still be Annette O'Toole of Baltimore, employed as Gardner's accountant while she worked toward her C.P.A.

No, by now they would probably be married, living in an upscale suburban house, driving matching Volvos and working on the appropriate two-child family William had planned. That life had been Anne's future before her fiancé had taken Riczini's bribe. And that had ended Anne's dreams.

Had the mobster somehow found out William's new location and murdered him? A ripple of fear coursed through her body. Whatever the real cause of William's death, she was now the only living witness to Riczini's crooked financial transactions.

A cold dread quivered through her stomach. She was the last witness. The last person who could put Riczini away for life. If he had been responsible for William's death, she would be next on his hit list.

Anne knew she couldn't just sit around and wait for an "accident." She had to find out what had really happened to her former fiancé.

She willed her shaky knees to carry her to the wall phone, and stuck a tremulous finger in the dial. Though she hadn't called this particular number in over two years, her subconscious dredged up the numeric sequence and brought it to the forefront of her mind.

After four rings, a familiar voice, now weak and tinged with grief, answered. "Hello?"

A sudden lump lodged in Anne's throat, rendering her speechless.

Barbara Gardner, William's sister, barked into the receiver. "Hello? Who is this?"

Anne chewed on her lip, taking comfort in the pain. Finally recovering her voice, she pulled the instrument closer to her lips. "Barbara? It's me, Annette."

The phone wires hummed with the strained silence.

"Barbara, are you there?"

"Yes, I'm here. And you have some nerve calling here, Annette O'Toole."

Ignoring the contempt in the other woman's voice, Anne plunged on. "I just read about William. What happened?"

"If you read the paper then you know—a boating accident."

The derision in Barbara Gardner's voice made it clear what she thought of the "accident."

"But you listen to me," Barbara continued, her tone an icy finger of accusation. "This is your fault, do you hear? Your fault! You killed my brother as surely as if you'd planted that bomb yourself."

"Bomb! The paper didn't say anything about a bomb."

"Sure, the old cover-up. Accidental explosion. Bomb. Same difference. Oh, they made sure it would look like an accident. But it was a cover-up. You should know all about cover-ups, shouldn't you, Annette? He loved you. How could you betray him like that?"

Anne held her silence. The truth spoke for itself. She'd tried many times before to explain to William's family why she'd been forced to turn him into the authorities, but no one had wanted to listen. Just like William had refused to listen when she'd begged him to go to the FBI himself.

He'd refused flatly, unwilling to believe that his luxurious world, built with the bloody money of drug czars and mobsters, could crumble around him.

But Anne had known the end was coming. Her heart had cried out in anguish when she'd returned his engagement ring. Tears streaming down her cheeks, she'd begged him one last time to go with her to the FBI.

William had turned on his heel and stalked out the door.

The next day, federal agents had busted into his office and arrested him.

Anne shuddered, remembering the look on William's face when the FBI agents, brandishing search warrants, had stormed into the accounting firm.

Knowing it was futile, she nevertheless tried again to reason with the older woman. "Barbara, please listen to me. I had to do what was right. It was the only chance we had!"

"Sure," Barbara sneered. "I suppose convincing him to testify was another one of your attempts to *save* my brother?"

It was useless to try again to explain. "Barbara, I just wanted to say that I was sorry your brother was killed. It was a boating accident, surely you can't hold me responsible for that, too?"

"Accident!" Barbara Gardner screamed. "If you believe that, you're more naive than I gave you credit for. Why don't you come back for the funeral if you're so sorry? It should be loads of fun. Of course, there won't be a casket, or a burial. There wasn't enough of William's body left to even recover, did you know that, Annette?"

"Barbara, please. Try to understand—"

"Understand? I understand that this is all your fault! You caused my brother's death by making him a walking victim. He's been waiting for two years for those gangsters to kill him. I guess poor William's wait is finally over. Now, maybe, *you'll* have to start looking over your shoulder."

Anne shook her head. It had been a mistake to telephone. Barbara, like the rest of the Gardner family, blamed her for everything. They wouldn't accept the truth: that

William had eagerly agreed to testifying for the prosecution—in return for immunity.

Anne understood their feelings. She, too, had been betrayed by his duplicity. How had she been so naive for so long? Closing her eyes to the evidence and accepting his lies, his half truths?

"Barbara, whether you believe me or not, I *am* sorry about your brother's death. I just wanted to tell you."

There was no forgiveness in the other woman's voice as it blistered the phone lines. "You *should* be sorry. My brother trusted you. We all trusted you. You ruined his life and now you've killed him."

Anne broke off the other woman's tirade by dropping the receiver back on the hook. William Gardner had been the beloved, change-of-life only son. His three older sisters and middle-aged parents had spoiled him rotten. He'd grown up believing he was immune from any consequences of his behavior. For a long while, Anne had deluded herself, hoping that someday he would mature, but, of course, he hadn't.

It was that basic immaturity, more than malice, that had caused William to think he could go into business with hardened criminals and come out unscathed.

Anne sat back down at the table and dropped her head into her hands. Did they think that her life hadn't been ruined, as well? There was nothing left of the person she had been.

Like William, Anne had agreed to appear as a prosecution witness. Of course, she hadn't been involved in any actual money-laundering, but she had been a witness to some unusual office practices regarding Riczini's accounts.

In the end, when the attorney general's representative had convinced her that her life would be in jeopardy regardless of whether or not she appeared in court, Anne had agreed to corroborate William's statements.

They had gone on the witness stand and testified. That had been the last time she had seen William and his family.

The sad part was that their efforts were in vain. The Boss had jumped bail during the trial. Only a couple of his minor gang members had actually been sentenced and imprisoned. Even so, Anne had been given a new identity, a new job and set up in a new location—Yuma, Arizona. Sometimes, especially during the scorching summer heat, she wondered if the criminals in jail might not have received the better bargain.

Although, to be honest, she was getting used to Arizona's arid climate, and the people were certainly friendlier than city dwellers. Still, she was no longer able to pursue her dreams of becoming a certified public accountant. The relocation officials warned it would be too easy to find her if she were in a state-licensed profession.

So the government set her up with a small bookstore, and she slunk out of Baltimore like a fugitive in the night. Two years later, here she was.

No one in the world, other than government officials, knew her true identity. Anne hadn't many relatives, so that part hadn't been so hard. Except for her mother. Anne wondered if she'd ever be able to see her again. She hadn't realized how close a bond she had with her parent until that tie was abruptly severed. They still communicated from time to time by telephone, and letters were channeled through a mail-drop in Colorado, but other than those brief ties to her past, Anne was cut loose in the world.

She had never felt so alone as today.

Imagine, William Gardner dead.

Suddenly, she remembered Luke McCullough and his improbable story. What if he was an assassin hired by Riczini? Anne trembled at the thought of how easily he had gained entry to her home. But if Luke *was* one of Riczini's hired guns, why hadn't he killed her last night?

Or was he biding his time, setting up another "accident"?

She toyed with the idea of closing the bookstore for the day, but decided that if she was home with time to worry, she'd go crazy. So in the end, Anne clipped the small article about William Gardner and tossed the rest of the paper in the trash. It was probably just an accident, anyway.

But the icy chill stalking up her spine warned her otherwise.

THERE WERE STILL a couple of hours to kill before it was time to open The Book Nook, so Anne decided to expend some of her nervous energy cleaning house. Doing ordinary household tasks like running the vacuum, changing sheets and polishing furniture sheltered her mind from the fear that lurked in its corners.

When the house could stand no further tidying, she still felt charged with an electrical current and looked around for something else to do.

Deciding to sweep the patio, she went into the backyard. Next door, Elaine Bittner was watering her plants. Anne walked around the pool deck and leaned over the wooden fence separating the properties.

"Hi," Anne called. "Was that you I saw moving around so early this morning?"

Elaine turned off the hose and joined Anne at the fence. "Can you believe it?" she asked in her deep, husky voice. "I heard strange noises all night and never got back to sleep properly. Did you hear anything?"

Anne smiled ruefully. "Did I ever. Elaine, I'm afraid to tell you what happened last night for fear you'll think I've been hitting the tequila bottle."

"You're kidding—quiet little Anne Farraday had an adventure?"

"I guess you could call it that."

"Well then, tell all. Every juicy crumb."

So Anne told her about her late-night visitor, deleting only the fact that Luke McCullough was a *very* attractive man. Elaine was adept at jumping to farfetched conclusions without any help.

When Anne finished, she asked, "So, what do you think—prowler or Samaritan?"

Elaine ran her fingers through her thick, shaggy blond hair. "What a story! Was this guy good-looking? No, don't tell me—I'd rather have my fantasies. How come nothing like that ever happens to me?"

Anne smiled. "Are you kidding? I've never met a woman who has so many male admirers."

"Yeah, but they're all old fogys. No tall, dark, mysterious strangers."

"I didn't say he was tall *or* dark."

"I told you—leave me my fantasies."

The women chatted for a few more minutes before Anne glanced at her watch. "Ouch! I've got to run."

BY NOON, Anne decided she had done the best thing by opening The Book Nook. Business was brisk and she was only able to take a few minutes for lunch.

When she turned the Closed sign around at five o'clock, she was bone-tired and ready for a quiet evening, but hours of paperwork awaited her. Anne had found out the hard way that owning your own business meant frequent eighteen-hour days.

Still, working all day had realigned her perspective: William Gardner had died in an accident. Sad, but one of those things. She'd long since gotten over the heartache of realizing that William never really loved her. He loved himself too much.

Too bad she couldn't send flowers, but there was no way to do it without leaving a trail for someone to follow. The relocation agent had told her to never, ever think she was one hundred percent safe. Never, he said, leave a trail. She'd already taken a horrible chance in telephoning William's sister.

What if someone had been listening on the lines? She had no doubt that Riczini's accomplices would have the means to tap the Gardners' telephone. Anne thought back over their conversation, then breathed in relief. No, she hadn't said anything that might give away her location or new identity, but making that phone call had been a foolish thing to do, nonetheless. She'd have to be more careful. More alert.

After less than an hour of working on her bookkeeping, Anne threw in the towel. Her mind simply wasn't on her business. Already she'd made three simple errors. The paperwork would wait until tomorrow.

She was getting paranoid, she thought ruefully as she pulled the seat belt across her body. Still, she squeezed her eyes shut and gritted her teeth in dreadful anticipation as she turned the key in the ignition. In the movies, the criminals always wired the car bomb to the starter.

Relief washed over her as the engine started smoothly.

William's death had shaken her more than she wanted to admit. How melodramatic could she get, looking for bombs under her car?

She couldn't help casting a nervous glance over her shoulder before engaging the gearshift. This morning she'd been sure someone was watching her. Satisfied that no one was hanging around, Anne pulled into the slow-moving traffic.

Ten minutes later, she turned her trusty Toyota Celica into the driveway. She pulled up to the garage, exited the car and walked down the sloping driveway to her mailbox.

A white sedan, with rental plates, was parked across the street. The setting sun dazzled her eyes, and she could only make out the silhouette of a man sitting behind the wheel.

Why was she so nervous all of a sudden? The car door opened, and a tall, sturdy virile torso emerged. The man loped across the road.

Déja vù. The first time she had seen Luke McCullough, he was silhouetted against the streetlight.

Anne had no doubt that it was he. What she didn't understand was that little thrill of anticipation that raced through her body when she recognized him.

Not wanting to seem anxious, she turned her back and made an elaborate show of unlatching her mailbox.

A fraction of a second before she plunged her hand into the metal container, she heard a strange, clicking noise coming from the inside of her mailbox.

Her heart lurched. She tried to scream but the sound froze in her throat.

"Oh, dear God," she screamed, at last finding her voice, "Luke, duck! I think it's a bomb!"

Anne felt a pair of strong masculine arms wrap around her waist and she was thrown to the pavement. At that moment, the world went black.

Chapter Four

Anne felt consciousness returning.

A soft, swirling cloud filled her brain, like smoke from a distant fire. She was wrapped in a cottony cocoon, safe and swaddled. Then a fuzzy awareness of something warm and heavy covering her body lured her focus away from the softness.

She turned, and a bolt of pain shot through the side of her head.

Raising her hand from her side, her fingertips found and explored a healthy goose egg. What the—?

An elusive memory teased at her, then disappeared like a tendril of fog. While she had a vague understanding that she'd somehow been injured, the details totally eluded her. The only thing she knew for sure was that her temple throbbed and there was a rough scratchiness against her face.

Fighting a wave of dizziness, she willed her eyelids open. As awareness settled in, she slowly took in her surroundings. She was on her back, sprawled on the hot pavement in front of her house.

But why was she lying in the street?

Anne tried to remember what could have caused her to do such an extraordinary thing, but concentrating made the lump on her temple ache furiously.

Then that strange heaviness she'd felt earlier shifted slightly. Anne turned her head and gasped in astonishment. Luke McCullough was lying on top of her!

The scratchiness on her cheek was the curiously gentle rasp of his five o'clock shadow. He was so close she could hear the soft rhythm of his breathing, feel the warm puffs of his breath on her cheek. Yet there was no feeling of passion; rather, she had the peculiar sensation that he was... sheltering her from harm.

How strange. Had she somehow fallen?

Shifting her gaze slightly, Anne saw her purse, lying open, its contents strewn all over the sidewalk in front of her mailbox. Her still-intact mailbox.

Anne's memory returned in a flash of blinding light. The bomb! It hadn't gone off. She was still alive.

As Luke's warm breath puffed against her cheek, a shudder of relief rippled through her. *Luke* was still alive.

But he wasn't moving. Had he been badly injured? He'd tried to save her. She had to get help for him.

Before Anne could match her actions to her thoughts, she became aware of a faint movement near the open mouth of the mailbox. Something dark. Alive.

Then, that dreadful clicking sound returned.

Anne's heart thudded in her chest. The horrible creature slowly emerging from her mailbox was almost as fearful as an explosive. She realized that there never had been a bomb, but something infinitely more menacing. More evil.

"Luke!" Her whispered exclamation and the low, ominous rattling were the only sounds on the quiet street, yet the air seemed to cry out with a thousand warnings of danger.

Luke lifted himself up from his protective position over her body, and his eyes followed the direction of her terrified gaze. The distinctive wedge-shaped head of a rattlesnake was leaning out of the mailbox opening. Its long, pronged tongue flicked through the air, tasting peril. The wicked sound of its rattles clicking against each other left no doubt that the snake was agitated. It could strike without further warning.

Slowly, deliberately—never taking his gaze off the rattler—Luke got to his feet, positioning himself between Anne and the hissing serpent.

"Take my hand." He bent over slightly and extended his arm toward her. "Anne? Come on, take my hand. But reach slowly. No sudden moves."

His voice was as hushed as a penitent in a cathedral.

Almost too terrified to move, Anne concentrated on the calm in his voice, the self-assured tilt of his head and the protective stance of his body. His quiet, soothing tone was like an ointment balming her screaming nerve endings. With each murmur his deep velvet voice reassured her, inspiring her trust. Her confidence. Although Anne's muscles felt paralyzed with fear, at Luke's urging, she lifted her hand toward his.

Then, in a kind of macabre slow motion, he clasped her hand in his own firm grip and tugged. Anne closed her eyes, clenched her teeth against the thrumming in her temple and allowed him to pull her to her feet.

"Okay, you're doing fine, Anne."

Fine? Her legs were as limp and wobbly as cooked spaghetti. Her stomach was churning; and her head throbbed as if a blacksmith were working behind her eyes, striking an anvil with an iron mallet. And this man thought she was fine?

"Listen carefully and don't make any sudden movements!" he whispered tensely, his voice melding with the anxious hissing of the rattler. "I want you to take three *very* slow giant steps backward. Careful now. One. Atta girl. Two—"

At that moment, she sensed rather than saw that the rattler had completely emerged from the mailbox and was winding down the steel post. Luke's shoulder moved slightly, allowing her a full view of the snake.

It was huge! An ugly diamondback rattlesnake, the color of mud and as big around as her forearm. Its rattles were shaking furiously as the creature quickly slithered down to the bottom of the pole. It landed with a soft plop and immediately coiled around itself, its forked tongue tasting the air as it sought the source of danger.

The reptile writhed in their direction. Horror filled Anne as she stood rooted in place, watching its approach. Then, abruptly, the rattler stopped, momentarily distracted by Anne's handbag.

A chill of revulsion raced down her spine as its ugly triangular face ferreted inside, its nasty tongue sampling her belongings. Finding nothing of interest, it climbed effortlessly on top of her purse and surveyed them with its beady, unblinking eyes.

"Come on, Anne! Hurry, step back."

Before she had time to respond to Luke's command, the rattler raised its tail high, giving them an urgent final warning. They were only about five feet from the snake, and Anne knew that a rattler could strike as far as its body length. This one looked to be six or seven feet long. They were surely within its striking range.

The diamondback reared its head and hissed.

"Run, Anne! It's going to strike!"

Needing no further encouragement, she bolted for the driveway, stopping only when she reached the safety of her car. Moving as if the hounds of hell had set upon her, Anne scrabbled up onto the Toyota's hood and turned to face Luke.

He'd drawn his service revolver and was aiming at the squirming, writhing snake. Apparently, the creature had already made one strike because it was uncoiled, only inches from Luke's booted foot. Had the angry creature already struck him? Was the treacherous venom already seeping into Luke's bloodstream, pumping its poison through his veins?

Anne looked around, hoping to spy something—some weapon—that she could use to help. If only she had a pole, even a broom. Something to push the snake away from Luke until—

"Damn!" Luke exclaimed as the rattler hissed and struck again, its fangs striking the air only inches from his leg.

"Shoot, Luke, shoot!" she screamed, wondering why he was hesitating.

"I can't, dammit," he muttered between clenched teeth.

She saw then that the snake had wound so close to Luke's feet that he couldn't get a clear shot.

Then Anne remembered. The bullets! She'd taken them from his gun the night before.

Oh, dear Lord, what had she done? Her hands clenched into fists of helplessness, she shouted, "Luke, run!" Her voice sounded shrill, like a rusty hinge that hadn't been used in a long time. She cleared her throat and tried again. "Get away—your gun isn't loaded."

If Luke heard her, he gave no indication, for his silvery eyes never wavered from the creeping reptile.

Finally, the rattler changed its course and slithered away a few inches. Luke swiveled his revolver, tracking the snake's rapid movement. Then, with eye-dazzling speed, the reptile twisted back on itself and struck again.

Like a slow-motion scene in a movie, she watched as Luke's finger slowly squeezed the trigger and a loud, terrifying boom filled the air.

Anne gasped and turned away as the rattler's head exploded in a red haze. The body twitched a couple of times, then the reptile lay still.

For a long moment, nothing moved. Not a sound broke the still-quivering silence. Then, the slap of leather when Luke reholstered his gun broke the unnatural quiet, and Anne felt her senses coming back to life.

The acrid smell of gunpowder tickled her nostrils. From the corner of her eye, she saw Elaine Bittner step out onto her front porch. From two houses down the road, old Mr. Farmer was hobbling toward them, his cane thumping out a peculiar rhythm on the scorching sidewalk.

A trickle of sweat dropped off Anne's forehead and sizzled on the Toyota's hood. A sudden shimmering heat beneath her brought her fully back to the present. August in Arizona has been likened to high noon in hell, and at that moment, Anne heartily agreed. The car hood she was perched on was blistering her thighs through the thin material of her cotton dress.

Moving gingerly, and not really sure her wobbly legs could hold her, she slid off the Toyota and took a couple of hesitant steps toward Luke.

He was leaning against the mailbox, removing one of his boots. Dear Lord, Anne thought, he *had* been bitten.

Forgetting her fear and her revulsion over the mutilated snake, she ran the few feet to Luke's side. "Are you all right? Should I call an ambulance?"

"Don't know yet. Hold my boot, would you?" He began tugging on his sock.

Anne's numb fingers accepted the dusty boot. Without thinking, she looked over at the grisly remains. Luke certainly was a crack shot. One round and the snake was smeared all over the sidewalk. Swallowing a gag, she averted her gaze and asked tentatively, "Your bullets? I mean...I uh, that is..."

Arching a black eyebrow, Luke stopped his examination of his foot and gave her a sharp look. "Yeah, *someone* must've mistakenly taken all the bullets out of the chamber last night. Good thing I clean and check my weapon every morning, or *someone* would be a sorry young woman right now."

A flush crept up Anne's neck and stained her cheeks. "I'm sorry, Luke. It's just that last night, I didn't know who you were and—" She stopped abruptly. She still didn't know who he was or how he just happened to be here at such an opportune moment.

Old Mr. Farmer thumped up at that moment, his dentures clacking noisily. He was dressed in his normal attire of dark western shirt, enormous turquoise-and-silver bola tie and red-striped suspenders. He hitched a thumb under a suspender strap and assessed Luke. "Some mighty fine shootin', young fella. You get yourself stung? Got a hanky? Need to bind off that foot. Stop the blood from circulating."

Luke examined his foot carefully, then took his boot from Anne's hand and ran his fingertip inside the leather. After a moment, he looked up at her and winked, his quicksilver eyes reflecting the late-afternoon sunlight. "Guess that old diamondback's bite wasn't quite as tough as my shoe leather. Didn't penetrate."

Mr. Farmer whistled, his loose dentures wobbling with the sound. "You sure were lucky. That's one big snake. Heck,

I've heard they can bite through a tin can if they're riled enough. Why, I recollect one time down near Tucson—"

"Anne, are you all right?" Elaine surged into the small group and interrupted the old man's story. The blond woman's normally loud, deep voice was subdued with curious concern as she wrapped an arm around Anne's shoulder. "What happened, kiddo?"

Anne shook her head, copper curls coming loose and tumbling around her face. She pointed a shaking finger toward the gruesome mess. "Somebody put that snake in my mailbox!"

"What?" Elaine and Mr. Farmer queried simultaneously.

Elaine shot the older man a silencing glance and asked, "But honey, why would someone want to do something like that? That's crazy!"

Suddenly, what was left of Anne's composure threatened to crumple as she considered the implication of Elaine's words. It *was* crazy. But it certainly couldn't have been an accident—could it?

"I...I think someone tried to k-kill..." Her voice trailed off as she turned to face Luke, confusion and fear etched plainly on her delicate features.

Quickly stuffing his foot back into his boot, he grinned nonchalantly and winked again. "Nah. Seems to me more like a schoolboy's prank. Damn kids. Probably sounded like a good idea when they did it. But it's over with now. And I think you owe me a glass of iced tea—maybe even something stronger."

"Oh, yes, certainly." She couldn't believe Luke was taking this so lightly. How many "accidents" could be so readily accepted? But of course, she reminded herself, he didn't know about the "accident" that killed William Gardner. Or did he?

Elaine cut into Anne's thoughts by patting her on the shoulder. "Looks like your tall, dark stranger has everything under control. And *I* think he's very handsome."

Anne could have cheerfully throttled her outspoken neighbor. The implication was, of course, that the two women had discussed Luke and that Anne had found him lacking. She was aware of Luke's curious eyes watching her, but she couldn't bring herself to return his gaze.

Elaine, seemingly oblivious to the discomfort her comment had caused, aimed a kiss at Anne's cheek, not quite connecting. "I've got to go, honey. Hot date tonight." She pointed a bright red manicured fingertip at the dead snake. "You are going to get...that...cleaned up, aren't you? Ugh. Disgusting."

"We'll take care of it," Luke muttered. As if to stifle further conversation, he leaned over and retrieved Anne's handbag, stuffing in two granola bars and a bruised apple that had rolled out of it.

Taking his cue from Luke, Mr. Farmer bent over and picked up a lipstick and Anne's key ring.

Elaine didn't take her leave, after all. As if fascinated by the sickening spectacle, she watched intently while the men attended to the cleanup chores.

"Women sure do carry a lot of junk," Mr. Farmer muttered, looking suspiciously at a hair pick he'd rescued from the gutter.

Luke took the items from the old man's hand and stuffed them into her purse. He started to hand it to Anne, but turned away abruptly and wiped some gruesome spatters off the shiny white leather surface on his pant leg.

Anne deliberately averted her eyes as she took the stained bag from his hands. She pulled out her house keys and vowed to toss the purse directly into the trash as soon as she got it emptied.

"Well, it looks like all the excitement's over." Elaine sounded disappointed, like a five-year-old who just opened her last birthday present.

"I guess that's it," Luke agreed, "except for the rest of the cleaning up. Of course, if you want to help—"

"No thanks! This is where I say good-night. See you later, kiddo." Elaine waggled her manicured fingers, turned away and, seconds later, disappeared into her house.

Luke grimaced at the woman's exaggerated wiggle and turned his attention to the grisly mess on the ground. This "prank" confirmed his suspicions—Scorpion was here. On the job. One of the hired killer's trademarks was that he rarely used a method more than once. A creative murderer, Scorpion employed every technique from poking his victims with a poisoned umbrella tip to adding cyanide to their mouthwash.

That was one reason the madman was so hard to catch. And made Luke's mission so difficult.

Right now, though, he had to get this mess cleaned up before other neighbors took an interest in the goings-on and telephoned the police. He didn't need that complication right now.

Pointing to the reptilian corpse, he asked, "Anne, do you have a plastic trash bag? And a shovel?"

"Yes. Of course."

Mr. Farmer stepped between them, his thumb popping a suspender strap. "Well, you jist give them to me. I'll give this old fella a proper burial." He looked at Luke and shook his head, wonder clear in his faded blue eyes. "Sure was some mighty fine shootin'. Haven't seen marksmanship like that since the big one—WWII, you know. Spent some time on an island in the South Pacific. I ever tell you about—"

"No, Mr. Farmer, I don't think you have," Anne said quickly. Then, seeing the disappointment mirrored in the old man's eyes, she felt compelled to add, "Why don't we all get together this weekend and you can tell us about it?"

"Why, that'd be real nice, Miss Farraday. Mighty neighborly."

Turning to Luke, she said, "If you'd care to check your firearms at the door, Mr. McCullough, I'll see about that iced tea."

"Mighty neighborly, Ms. Farraday. Mighty neighborly," Luke mimicked.

Anne treated him to her sauciest glare and turned and stalked to her door, uncomfortably aware of his loping stride right behind her. Ignoring his looming presence, she fished inside her purse for her house keys only to find them still dangling from her fingertips.

That small lapse bothered her more than she would have thought possible. For the past twenty-four hours, Anne felt as if her life had once again spun out of control. Since this black-haired, silver-eyed stranger had galloped into her life, everything had gone completely haywire.

She closed her eyes, mentally ticking off the peculiarities of the past few hours: a horse in her swimming pool, an unseen burglar, one sexy but very suspicious stranger, William's death and now this "accident."

Before "The Trouble," as she'd come to think of the events that followed William's arrest, Anne had led a perfectly ordered life. She liked—no, needed—structure and organization. Her dream career was to be an accountant, for crying out loud! It had taken almost two years to regain a modicum of routine in her life, and now that scant control was once more slipping away.

Anne felt... She blinked rapidly, overwhelmed at the sudden realization that what she felt like doing was bursting into tears. She hadn't cried since the trial, when William had turned away, refusing to look at her. A moment later, a kind federal agent had confided in her that right after his arrest, William had blamed everything on her. A lone tear had slipped down her cheek, in response to the ultimate slap of his betrayal.

She'd never shed another tear since that day but knew she was dangerously close at this moment. Anne hated the weakness in herself, the vulnerability that Luke's kindness had brought to light.

At that moment, the pulsing in her temple started anew with a vengeance. Then, her knees decided to give out. To steady herself, she leaned against the door frame for a moment.

"Anne? Are you all right?" Luke's voice was as gentle as the soothing fingertips he'd placed on her shoulder.

Raising a trembling hand, she knuckled away an errant tear. She wouldn't cry. Not now and certainly not in front of this virtual stranger.

But to her utter mortification, her shaking fingers couldn't manipulate the door lock and she stood, silent, while he slipped the key ring from her grasp and opened the front door.

Feeling like a small child who'd had a rough day on the playground, she allowed him to drape a forearm around her shoulder. She felt so exhausted. If she could just rest for a moment. With a sigh, Anne gave in and relaxed in the protective circle of his embrace, slanting her weary head against the strength of his chest.

LUKE LOOKED DOWN at the woman resting against him. Her face was white, her lovely brown eyes glazed with shock. Then he saw the ugly bump, swelling rapidly on the side of her head.

She was hurt! The whole time he'd been jawing with the old man, Anne had been standing quietly with what must be one hell of a headache.

Kicking the door ajar, he scooped her into his arms, amazed at the sinuous grace of her lean body, the way she melted against him. Totally trusting. Totally vulnerable.

This was exactly why he hated getting involved with civilians. For more years than he cared to remember, Luke's world had been populated with thieves, drug dealers and murderers. For a while, he'd been able to convince himself that he was doing a dirty job that everyone wanted done—they just didn't want to know about the details. But that was before Glenna. Before he'd seen the trust in her eyes fade to disappointment. Before the same filthy scum who populated his world had taken Glenna's life.

Luke bit his lower lip and pulled Anne tight against him. He didn't want to think about Glenna right now. And he didn't want to think about the sweetness of Anne's body snuggled close to his own. He didn't want to recall the quick gleam of intelligence in her eyes last night when she'd questioned him, nor the fear that was mirrored in them today.

At that moment, a resolution was born in him. He wasn't going to sit back and let Scorpion snuff out this gentle woman's life. Nothing was going to happen to this witness. Not as long as he was alive to prevent it. If he had to hire a team of mercenaries to guard her, Anne was going to be saved.

"Luke, put me down." Her voice cut into his thoughts as she protested weakly against his throat. "I can walk. Really." As if to prove her point, she squirmed in his arms, like a newborn fawn, wobbly and unsure, but ready to try.

"Shh. Give yourself a minute." As she wriggled, a loose strand of her fiery hair fell across his face. Luke breathed in, jarred by the whirling aromas of her. The clean sweetness of her hair, the flowery scent of her fragrance. She reminded him of a delicate-looking orchid he'd seen once in a nursery. Lovely to behold, sinfully aromatic and—

She twisted in his arms again and he almost lost his grasp.

"Put me down, Luke," Anne muttered, "I'm not a baby. I don't need any more help."

"Then humor my male ego." He remembered then that a horticulturist had identified that fragile-looking orchid as one of the toughest of the species. Tenacious, he recalled.

Luke shouldered the door closed behind them and carried her across the terra-cotta tile foyer. With a flick of his wrist, he sailed his Stetson through the air. It landed neatly on the hall table, next to the bowl of apples.

"I'm heavy," Anne insisted. "You're going to hurt yourself."

"I'll chance it," he said, chuckling. The woman weighed about as much as a moonbeam.

Totally ignoring her further entreaties, he crossed the living room and deposited her gently onto the sofa, propping her up with a couple of southwestern-print throw pillows.

Placing both hands on her shoulders, he gently encouraged her to lie back against the pillows. He lowered himself onto the sofa, his hip touching her waist. A gently curling strand of her coppery hair had strayed across her cheek. Unconsciously, he allowed his fingers to brush the gossamer strand from her eyes. She looked so lovely, so vulnerable.

She lifted her head from the pillows, raising to a sitting position and started to swing her feet onto the floor. "I'm okay now. I . . . I have things I need to do."

What she needed was to be alone. To work her way through this maze of conflicting emotions. One minute she was sure that Luke was all he appeared to be, kind, caring, protective. But then her common sense took over.

It couldn't be coincidence that he'd appeared in her life just when all these horrible things began happening. She couldn't allow herself to be taken in by his handsome face or his supportive words and deeds.

William was dead. She was the last witness. The woman without a past and without hope for a future. Luke McCullough had shown up out of the blue, worming his way into her life, doggedly trying to earn her trust. All the better to lure you into a false sense of security, my dear?

"Anne?"

With a start, she realized he was still seated beside her. Still staring intently with those pale eyes. He captured her gaze with his and she was lost. How could those incredible eyes hide deceit and treachery?

How could she believe otherwise?

Anne shook her head, forcing the confusing thoughts to let her be, let her rest. If she kept weighing one emotion against the other, she'd surely go insane. Biting her lip, she forced herself to answer him. "I'm sorry, Luke. Did you say something?"

"I said you should lie back. Rest for a while." His strong hands urged her back against the cushions. "I want to get some ice on that head. In fact, we should call a doctor. I think you blacked out for a minute or two."

Instead of resting against the cushions, Anne leaned forward, until her face was scant inches from his. Her deep brown eyes were heavy-lidded, and her lips were full and pouty.

A sudden surge of desire coursed through Luke. The lady looked very kissable. If he wasn't on the job...

Her long fingers touched the back of his hand, sending a charge of electricity sizzling through his body. "I didn't black out, I was suffocating. You were lying right on top of me."

His eyes flashed with a mischievous light as his mind conjured up a very different scenario, but one that still had her lush body beneath his. "I know, and it was very enjoyable. But next time, maybe we should try it indoors. Less likely to attract so much attention from your neighbors."

"There won't be a next time," she growled, her eyes narrowing dangerously. With a fierce determination, she pushed his hands away and sat up. "I only had a couple moments of wooziness. I'm not swooning, for Pete's sake!"

He looked at her in disbelief. Anne Farraday might look as fragile as a hothouse flower with her creamy skin and her finely curled auburn hair, but this woman had the stamina of one of those desert cacti that populated her front yard. And she was about as prickly.

Furthermore, she had absolutely no sense of humor! It wasn't as if he intended to... to ravish her. Well, maybe he *had* considered a minor ravish, but only if she was willing. And for that small moment, when she'd leaned forward, her moist mouth slightly open, for that one instant, Luke could have sworn she was waiting for him to kiss her.

But then she'd almost visibly retreated into herself, a cold opaque barrier covering the warmth and invitation he'd seen in her eyes only seconds before.

"How about if I run you in to town to see your doctor—I promise, I won't touch you," he added quickly when she opened her mouth and slanted her eyes in a warning glare.

"I don't need a doctor. All I need is a little breather." She dropped her head against the cushions and rested the back of her hand across her eyes. "I appreciate all you've done, but I don't need your help any longer."

Raising his hands in surrender, Luke said, "Hey, no problem. For my last great act of valor, I'll fix you an ice pack and leave you alone." He turned on his heel and stalked to the kitchen.

He found a bottle of aspirin in a cupboard over the sink. He poured a glass of water, then opened the freezer door with a jerk and yanked out a tray of ice cubes.

While he rummaged through the drawers looking for a dish towel, he thought about all the mistakes he'd made that day.

Apparently, this was his day for forming poor judgments. First, he'd been reasonably certain that Scorpion wouldn't make an attempt on Anne's life yet; not so soon after William Gardner's "accident." Events had proved him wrong there.

His biggest error, however, had been the totally inaccurate reading he'd done of Ms. Independence Farraday.

Vulnerable, hah! Delicate, yeah, sure. Defenseless, right. That woman was about as fragile as a forged-steel sword. With a tongue about as sharp.

Who needed it? Who needed her? He sure didn't.

He dumped a couple of trays directly into a dishcloth, and tied a knot in his makeshift ice pack. Still grousing, he tucked it under one arm, picked up the aspirin and water, and marched back out to the living room.

"Here," he said as he approached the sofa. "Put this on your head. Then take these two aspirin and call someone else in the morning."

Pulling her hand away from her eyes, Anne sat up and took the pills from his outstretched hand. Holding them cupped in her palm, she looked up at him, her brown eyes moist with a film of tears. Her voice was soft but clipped, almost as if she was conceding to a bitter defeat. "I . . . I'm sorry I was so . . . so cranky. It's just that I've always taken care of myself. *Had* to take care of myself."

She snatched the glass from his hand and gulped down the pills.

Luke felt his anger melting like the cubes dripping cold water down his wrist. There it was again, that flash. That brief glimpse of a woman who'd been so hurt, so... destroyed that she couldn't allow herself to trust again.

He understood that kind of pain.

Avoiding his eyes, she took the ice pack and held it against her temple with trembling fingers. She sighed deeply, closed her eyes again and dropped her head on the pillows, her cascade of copper hair spilling around her shoulders like a lacy shawl.

Drawn by a power stronger than his own will, Luke lowered his hip to the edge of the sofa. Tenderly, as if he were touching the beautiful, yet fragile wing of a butterfly in flight, his fingertips swept back her hair.

Her porcelain skin was still pale but he could see a tinge of color creeping back into her cheeks. Her dark lashes had dusted away the dark circles of fear from beneath her eyes and her enticingly full lips glowed a healthy pink. Never in his life had he found a woman so appealing. She'd instinctively reached behind all the layers of defenses he'd so carefully erected, unerringly finding and touching the real Luke McCullough.

The man who vowed he'd never love again. Never feel again. Never need again.

Anne's eyes fluttered open.

The gamut of emotions that she was experiencing flickered in her doe-brown eyes like the images on a movie screen. Luke could read them all: surprise, confusion, momentary fear, then interest and, finally, anticipation.

Slowly, gently, he lowered his head until his lips captured hers in a tremulous kiss of infinite sweetness.

Anne tasted of all the good things in life—all those wonderful things he'd been missing. His tongue sought the sweet flickering hardness of hers.

The arching of her body as her desire rose to meet his echoed the practiced and secure union of a couple who have joyously loved each other for a long time.

With a groan of passion long denied, Luke raked his fingers through the bountiful mass of her hair and urged her closer. Her questing fingers moved restlessly across his back as tiny whimpers of need escaped her lips.

Her need spurred him on.

Just when Luke thought he would surely explode from the years of pent-up and unrelieved physical and emotional yearning, he heard a footfall on the tiled entry.

He was faintly aware of Anne's gasp of surprise as his lips pulled away from hers.

Although his brain was fuzzy and his body was still wracked with desire, his years of training took over like a primal instinct. He stumbled to his feet and reached behind his back to pull his service revolver from its holster.

Bracing the grip with both hands, he swung the weapon toward the sound.

Mr. Farmer stood in the doorway, his thumbs tucked beneath his red suspenders, his lined and weathered face a mask of shock.

Sweat popped across Luke's forehead as he reholstered his gun. The crazy old fool, just walking in without knocking. He could have gotten himself killed.

With a halting gait, Mr. Farmer negotiated the two steps into the sunken living room. "I . . . uh, didn't mean to interrupt nothing. You . . . uh, forgot to get me that shovel. And trash bag."

"Oh, I'm sorry." Anne's breathy voice came from behind Luke. "I'll get them for you right now."

He turned, surprised to see that she, too, had risen to her feet. Although her comment had been addressed to the older man, she was staring at Luke in bewilderment, her eyes darting toward his gun.

Luke saw the dark mistrust in her eyes, yet, what could he say to ease her fears? He was operating undercover, carrying that gun with full legal authority. Yet, unless he revealed the truth of his assignment, what could he tell her?

He sighed and shrugged his shoulders. "You rest, Anne, I'll get that stuff. Is it in the garage?"

"I . . . uh, yes."

He ambled over to where the older man was waiting. "Okay, then, I'll help Mr. Farmer and—"

"Thanks, Luke," she interrupted, quickly crossing the room to stand behind them. "Now, if you'll both excuse me, I think I *will* take your advice and get some rest. This has been quite a day."

"Amen to that," Mr. Farmer concurred.

Luke watched Anne's face, watched as she shut him out. Obviously, he was being dismissed. She'd already patched up the tiny chink in her armor that had allowed him a brief glimpse of the real Anne. Not that he could blame her. She didn't need more violence and chaos in her life.

And violence and controlled chaos pretty accurately described his life, Luke thought. "Turning in early sounds like a good idea, although you should eat something first. Even a bowl of soup. Maybe you should plan on staying home tomorrow. Make sure you don't have a concussion."

"Maybe," she murmured noncommittally.

Luke paused at the door. "Should I call you later?"

Avoiding his eyes, Anne shook her head. "No, I'm planning on turning in early tonight."

Luke said nothing. He retrieved his hat from the hall table.

Mr. Farmer snapped a suspender and preceded Luke out the front door. "Young man, you sure are quick to pull out that firearm. Never seen a man draw so fast."

Luke had almost forgotten there were people who spent their entire lives without touching a weapon. Whereas he lay awake at night remembering the faces of the countless bloodied bodies he'd seen. Some he himself had slain.

He turned to tell Anne that he was sorry for bringing the ugliness of his world into hers. He hadn't meant to frighten her. But she'd already quietly closed the door behind them.

The sturdy snick of the bolt being slammed home as she double-locked her door echoed like a thunderclap in the still desert air.

Chapter Five

The next morning, the swelling on Anne's temple had gone down considerably, leaving only a faint bruise. She decided to ignore Luke's advice and open her bookstore. Maybe by drowning herself in work she could escape from the frightening and bewildering events of the past two days. Events that had kept her tossing and turning well into the night.

For a Friday, The Book Nook was unusually quiet. Normally, Anne would have welcomed the free time to catch up on her stock work and ordering. This morning, however, she found herself warily eyeing the lonely aisles, starting at every sound.

Her nerves were as taut as an electric fence. She misfiled invoices, lost her utility knife. She even botched her only sale, ringing it up as a charge instead of cash.

She was shelving a carton of new books when she stopped abruptly: she'd just put an entire stack of children's books on a shelf of romantic fiction. *Where's Waldo?* was now right beside a particularly spicy novel whose cover featured a dark-haired, brooding cowboy leaning against a split-rail fence. The cowboy whose shirt was opened to the navel, looked suspiciously like Luke McCullough.

A flash of heat ignited in her, kindling a warmth that crept up her cheeks as she remembered his kiss.

Oh, yes, that kiss.

If only he hadn't kissed her last night. Hadn't awakened that core of feeling that she'd thought long dead. If only she hadn't felt her heart coming to life like a butterfly emerging from its chrysalis. If only...

With a growl of frustration, she yanked the *Waldo* books off the shelf and toted them back to the children's section.

She was making way too much out of a simple kiss. Luke's lips on hers had only been the innocent capping off of a shared experience. A life-affirming ending to a life-threatening day.

Anne stacked the books in their proper place. Who was Luke McCullough anyhow? She had no idea why he was in Yuma in the first place. Or why he carried a gun.

Anne cocked her head as she was struck by a peculiar realization. The truth was, she couldn't recall Luke uttering a single word about himself. As though he had something to hide.

A queasiness roiled inside her. Had she been too trusting? Too accepting of his facile explanations? Several times yesterday, she'd had the sensation of being watched. More than once, Anne had felt a creeping along her spine as if some unseen person was observing her every move.

She couldn't recall having that feeling before Luke had shown up. Was he spying on her? Stalking her? But why?

Her restive thoughts were suddenly interrupted by a peculiar creaking sound at the front of the store. Had she been so distracted that a customer had entered without her hearing the bell over the door?

"Hello? Anybody there?"

Only a tension-laden silence responded to her call.

She listened intently for a few moments, but the worrisome sound wasn't repeated.

There was no one in the store.

Anne crushed the empty book carton, a frown of worry marring her normally composed expression. She felt like Alice after stepping through the looking glass. Nothing was as it seemed. Up was down. Day was night. Every person she encountered, every idea she formulated seemed the slightest bit off kilter.

She jumped, swallowing a tiny squeal as the bell over the shop door jangled.

Peeking around the corner, she saw a man, his back to her as he poked through a rack of books on tape.

A customer. Good. Nothing like a sale to buoy her spirits. In the summertime, paying customers were rare. The majority of Anne's income was earned in the winter, when the town was literally taken over by the ''snowbirds,'' those retirees who flocked to Yuma to escape bitter northern winters.

Blowing a strand of hair from her forehead, she wiped a speck of dust from the bodice of her seafoam green sundress and hurried to the front of the store.

The customer, a tall, very thin man wearing mirrored sunglasses atop his sharp, beaklike nose, had abandoned the cassette rack and was pacing just inside the door. His dark wool suit and somber silk tie immediately identified him as an out-of-towner.

While a Yuman might deign to wear a dark suit coat for marryings and buryings, no self-respecting desert dweller would don a wool suit in August. And if a wife absolutely forced a tie around the neck of her spouse, nine times out of ten, he would submit only to a bola string tie.

''Hi,'' Anne said, stepping behind the sales counter. ''Can I help you?''

The stranger cleared his throat and stepped toward her. His enormous Adam's apple bobbled as he spoke. ''Yes, maybe you can. I'm looking for the owner.''

"I'm the owner."

"Ah, yes, of course." He paused for a moment, as his eyes, hidden behind the mirrored sunglasses, scanned her face, as if committing it to memory.

Quelling a shiver of foreboding that was creeping up her spine, she forced a weak smile and glanced briefly at her own reflection in his sunglasses. "Is there something I can help you with?"

"Sorry if I was staring. You looked like someone I used to know. You haven't lived on the East Coast, have you, Ms...?"

"No. No, I haven't," Anne answered, the lie sticking in her throat. "I'm afraid I'm rather busy, so if you'd tell me how I can help you..."

"Oh, yes, of course you are." He looked pointedly around the empty store. "Name is Nevill. Dan Nevill." The stranger tilted his head, smiled perfunctorily and strode toward her, his right hand extended. With his bouncing Adam's apple, awkward long-legged gait and sharp nose, he reminded Anne of a stork.

The image was furthered by the way he swooped toward her, right hand extended, his too-large coat sleeve flapping as he quickly closed the gap between them. "I'm afraid I didn't catch your name."

"I'm Anne Farraday. How can I help you, Mr. Nevill?" She allowed him to envelop her hand in his bony fingers for a moment before pulling away, resisting an urge to wipe her palm on her dress. She leaned back, resting her hips against her desk. For some reason, the counter didn't seem to afford enough distance between them.

Anne shanghaied her professional smile back into place and asked, "If you're a book distributor, I'm afraid I order all of my stock through A&A Distributing, so—"

"No, no, I'm not trying to sell you anything. Quite the opposite, actually."

"I don't understand."

He pulled a dingy handkerchief from his jacket pocket and swabbed his face. "It's hotter than the hinges of hell outside. Don't know why anyone would want to live here. I understand that in the old days most of the folks that lived here were outlaws. At least they had a reason for staying in this hellhole."

Although Yuma was her home by chance rather than choice, Anne nevertheless felt a twinge of resentment at his comment. A lot of decent, hardworking people lived in this valley. Still, she didn't want to get into an argument with this man. Everyone was entitled to their opinion; and she wasn't the mayor, so it wasn't her duty to uphold Yuma's public image.

Standing quietly and offering him her most noncommittal smile, she waited for Nevill to continue.

"Well, to each his own, I always say." He patted his pockets, as though searching for a cigarette.

"Is there something I can help you find? Are you looking for a specific book?"

He pulled a hand out of his inside coat pocket and waggled a forefinger. "No, don't want any books. I must've left my business cards in my other jacket, but you see, I'm a lawyer. From Los Angeles?"

He spoke as if that should have meaning for her. If she didn't interrupt, Anne thought, surely he'd get to the point sooner or later.

Dan Nevill's Adam's apple bobbed several more times, then he spoke again. "I'm here on behalf of a client who wishes to make an offer to buy your store. Could I ask a few questions?"

She shook her head. "I'm afraid that would be point-less, Mr. Nevill. The Book Nook isn't for sale."

He smiled. A practiced, cheerless smile. "Come, come, Ms. Farraday. Everything is for sale—if the price is right."

His manner, and his darned sunglasses, were starting to annoy her. After mentally counting to ten, she forced a professional tone to her voice. "Not everything, Mr. Nevill." She spread her arms, encompassing the empty store. "Business isn't exactly booming, as you can see. Why would someone from Los Angeles want to take over a struggling bookstore in this 'hellhole,' I believe you called it?"

"I didn't mean to insult you, my dear." He pulled a small notebook out of his jacket pocket and flipped it open. "Now, how long have you owned this establishment? And is it a sole proprietorship, partnership or corporation?"

Anne's temper was quickly reaching the boiling point. Didn't this man understand English? "I believe I told you the Book Nook wasn't for sale."

Nevill cocked his long chin forward. "Are you serious? I mean, I thought that was a ploy to raise the price a bit. A common business negotiation practice, my dear."

Anne crossed her arms and glared. "I wasn't negotiat-ing, Mr. Nevill, I was serious. Now, if there's nothing else?"

He shook his head, finally removed the mirrored glasses and stuck them into his jacket pocket. Fixing a flat, muddy brown stare at Anne, he said, "My client was, perhaps, misinformed. We were told that the woman who owned this store was wanting to sell and move back East. Baltimore or Washington, D.C., someplace like that."

Swallowing a gasp at the mention of Baltimore, she mut-tered between tight lips, "No. That isn't me."

The lawyer stared at her, suspicion evident in his expres-sion. "I'm afraid I've come a very long way on what appears to be a wild-goose chase. But I can't imagine how my client could be wrong—''

The telephone shrilled.

Saved by the bell, Anne thought. "Excuse me, please," she said to Dan Nevill, then picked up the receiver. "Good morning, Book Nook, how may I help you? Oh, Mrs. Hernandez, how are you today?''

Deliberately turning away from the lawyer's questioning gaze, she cupped her hand around the receiver. Mrs. Hernandez was waiting for a new novel by her favorite mystery writer and phoned almost daily to see if it had arrived.

Looking over her shoulder, Anne saw the attorney had moved away and was scanning a selection of political thrillers. There was something in his body language that convinced her he was deliberately eavesdropping on her conversation.

Mrs. Hernandez had heard from her daughter that the novel she wanted was already in the bookstores in Phoenix.

A shadow in Anne's peripheral vision told her that her visitor had moved down the aisle, toward the cookbooks.

Mrs. Hernandez was a lonely woman, and her calls were frequently interminable. She was chatting on about her husband's refusal to do any housework, even though he'd recently retired. Then she went on to mention something about her cousin on her father's side.

Anne felt her mind drift away. Back to Luke. To that kiss. To the small dimple that dented his cheek when he grinned. She must have been daydreaming for quite some time, because she suddenly became aware that Mrs. Hernandez was speaking her name in a sharp tone.

"Anne? Are you listening to me? Should I call you back?''

"No, that's not necessary." Forcing her mind back to business, she reassured her anxious customer that she would phone the minute the book arrived. "Yes, I promise. Goodbye, Mrs. Hernandez."

Replacing the receiver, she glanced around for the attorney. "Mr. Nevill?"

No answer.

She came out from behind the counter and walked across the front of the store, peering down the aisles. As tall as Dan Nevill was, she should have easily been able to find him among the stacks.

"Mr. Nevill, are you still here?"

The air seemed to reverberate with a frightening emptiness. Anne's bookstore had become her second home, but today it felt as menacing as a Gothic mansion. It seemed to have absorbed the attorney into its walls.

After traversing each aisle of books, she went back to her cubbyhole office, then knocked on the rest-room door. The back exit to the alley was still locked. Yet, there was no sign of the lawyer.

The man had simply vanished.

How was that possible? How could he have walked out the front door without her noticing?

Because when Luke McCullough was on her mind, the world could crumble at her feet and she wouldn't know it.

A thousand questions whirled through her mind. A thousand fears. Was Nevill really an attorney? Or was he someone hired by Riczini to ferret out her location? Suddenly, William's "accidental death" loomed much larger.

Riczini had vowed to kill them both. Was he now, after two years, making good on that threat?

A kaleidoscope of patterns fell into place. She remembered those curious feelings of being watched. The rattlesnake. First Luke, then this man showing up. Was one of them a hired killer?

Was her imagination getting the best of her, or was she, too, scheduled for an "accidental" death?

TWO HOURS LATER, Anne had finally been able to put the lawyer's peculiar visit from her mind long enough to delve into her monthly accounts payable. This was the part of her job she liked the best: losing herself in the intricacy of paperwork. She loved numbers. Numbers were honest, finite, dependable. Numbers didn't change, cheat or lie. Two plus two always equaled four. Not at all like people, who never seemed to be equal to the sum of their parts.

William Gardner had been the product of a good family, educated, upwardly mobile. He should have been honest. He wasn't.

Luke McCullough was independent, courageous, seemingly altruistic. Did he, too, hide a dark secret?

The brass bell over the door jingled again.

Anne tossed her pencil on the desk and strode to the front of the store. A man in blue jeans and black cotton T-shirt was bent over, examining the magazines on the bottom rack.

"Good morning," she called.

The man stood up and turned around, his silvery-gray eyes glittering in the strong noon light.

"Luke!"

"Hi. I was in the neighborhood and thought I'd stop by. I wanted to see how you were feeling today. That bump on your noggin giving you fits?"

"No, I'm fine. Working like a packhorse. How about you?" There was a strange awkwardness between them, an awkwardness that hadn't been there before that kiss. It was as if they both knew their relationship was changing—they just weren't sure what direction it was taking.

She listened while he gently reprimanded her for opening the store, for not seeing a physician and for not answering her phone the night before. The truth was that she had turned off the ringer, afraid to take Luke's call while she was feeling so vulnerable. Afraid of her own response.

"Anne, are you listening?" Luke's voice was tinged with irritation.

Too late, she realized he'd stopped scolding her and was asking her out to dinner.

"Oh, I... uh, I don't know. I've let my paperwork slide and I really should—"

His shook his head, causing that stubborn lock of glossy black hair to dip over his forehead. "Please don't say no. It's very important that I talk to you soon. I'm... tied up tonight, but how about tomorrow? Please, Anne, I...I have something to tell you."

"That sounds ominous."

"Actually, I'm hoping what I have to say might ease your mind."

Ease her mind? As if a simple conversation could accomplish such a monumental task. Aloud, she said, "About what?"

"About me."

The room spun around for a moment, and the only sound was a hollow ringing in her ears. A peculiar fluttering low in her stomach rippled up, filling her with a soft, quivery sensation—like a covey of hummingbirds had just taken flight.

"Anne? Are you sure you're all right?"

"I... I'm sure."

"Good, you looked a little pale there for a second. I hope you get plenty of rest tonight." He tipped up her chin with his index finger. "And Anne?"

"Yes?"

"Be careful."

"Of what? Weird things only seem to happen to me when you're around, and you said you were busy tonight."

"I'm serious. That snake trick was probably a stupid prank like I told you, but sometimes pranksters carry their jokes too far."

Anne was having a hard time believing that the rattler in her mailbox was a practical joke, but Luke's optimistic attitude was contagious. Maybe she had been overreacting. Other than the snake, she'd had no true indication that anyone was stalking her. William's death was coincidental. It had to be.

Luke stroked her chin with the tip of his finger. "And remember what I said about getting some rest. You look like you need it."

"Thanks a lot."

"What's this—fishing for compliments? Give me a break, Anne Farraday. Anyone who looks as delicious as you do darn well knows it. Anyway, gorgeous, I'll see you tomorrow evening. Pick you up around six."

Before she had time to object, he winked and strode out the front door.

Held insensible by the faint, yet tangible, aura he'd left behind, she watched him amble down the dusty sidewalk. Her hands on automatic pilot, she rearranged a couple of magazines on the rack. Holding a glossy cover in her numb fingers, she thought about the date she'd just made. By default, perhaps, but a dinner date just the same.

THE PARADE of new men wasn't over, Anne discovered soon after returning home after work.

She stood in her driveway, thankful the day was over. Glancing up, she saw her next-door neighbor, Elaine Bittner, bending over, doing something to a scraggly hedge near her front door. Her hot-pink, tight shorts and cropped top were more suitable for a young girl than a forty-something widow, but Anne had to admire the woman's zest for life. Nothing ever seemed to get Elaine down. Besides, she had a very trim, very fit body.

Softly, Anne closed the car door. Normally, she enjoyed Elaine's good-natured gossip, but tonight all Anne wanted was peace and quiet.

She was too emotionally drained to even think about cooking dinner. She'd toss a salad, soak in the tub and, hopefully, get a full night of uninterrupted sleep. In fact, she'd gladly forgo the salad if some wonderful person would prepare a nice, luxuriating bath for her. With bubbles. Maybe a soothing glass of wine.

The image of Luke, with his jet-dark hair and crooked grin, jumped into her mind. Luke, offering her a chilled glass of zinfandel. Luke, blowing aside a cloud of soap bubbles that had settled on her—

Anne's unexpected and erotic fantasy was interrupted when Elaine turned from her shrubs. "Yoo-hoo, Anne! Come here."

Sensing that her relaxing evening was going to be delayed, Anne sighed and crossed to the small side yard that divided their properties.

She leaned against the plank fence and idly picked a dead blossom from a bougainvillea bush. "What's up, neighbor?"

Elaine peeled off her gardening gloves and strolled closer. She regarded Anne with a lifted eyebrow. "Boy, are you ever the popular one lately."

"Yeah, popular as the plague. Whichever of my admirers put that rattler in my mailbox was more interested in putting me under than taking me out."

Elaine's long fingers waved through the air, dismissing Anne's doleful observation. "You know perfectly well that hunk in the black Stetson was right. It was probably just a prank by a bunch of teenage boys. Kids have done worse in the name of fun. Hell, *I've* done worse. Besides, I wasn't referring to your mysterious snake handler. You had another visitor. Another *male* visitor.''

"Really?" Anne's eyebrows raised in surprise. She made a mental note to check and see if there had been a blue moon. Before yesterday, she hadn't had two male callers in the two years she'd lived here. Then she remembered Dan Nevill. "Oh, I know who it probably was. Some attorney showed up today wanting to buy the bookstore."

"Hmm," Elaine said thoughtfully. "He didn't look like a lawyer, but then, most people say I don't look much like a grieving widow, either."

Anne laughed. "More like the Merry Widow. But you're right, this Dan Nevill didn't look much like an attorney to me, either. Real tall, bony. Kind of looked like a dark stork."

Elaine slowly shook her head, a puzzled look in her vivid blue eyes. "I don't think we're talking about the same guy, kiddo. This one was tall, but I had an impression of sandy or reddish hair. And he sure wasn't storky. He was a big bruiser. Reminded me more of a middle linebacker."

Anne's eyebrows dipped in a frown. She couldn't think of a soul who would fit Elaine's description. Another stranger?

That odd sensation of disquiet crept up her spine again. She was about to question Elaine further when the older woman grabbed her arm.

"There he is! See, by those oleanders next to your front porch?"

Anne squinted her eyes against the sharp glare of the afternoon sun. At first, she saw only the softly waving oleander branches, laden with their lovely, but lethal, white blossoms. Then, from the shadows, a tall, stocky man emerged and stood on the porch. His face was shaded as he faced the two women.

When he made no move to approach them, Anne waved hesitantly and took a faltering step toward him.

"You're not going over there, are you?" Elaine whispered. "He could be an ax murderer, or something."

Anne stopped. Rolling her eyes, she scowled in mock chagrin. "Honestly, Elaine. Your sense of drama is giving me the willies."

Still, Elaine's offhand remark had given her pause.

Drawing a deep breath, she considered her options. She could go inside Elaine's house and phone the police. And tell them what? That a strange man—probably selling Fuller brushes—was camped on her doorstep? No, the only sensible thing to do was to go see what he wanted.

What harm could come to her in broad daylight?

She blinked away the memory of her near-fatal encounter almost exactly twenty-four hours ago. Okay, what were the odds of *two* similar incidents happening in broad daylight? Still, she could hear Luke's voice in her ear, warning her to be careful.

"Elaine, would you stay right here while I see what he wants?"

"Sure. No problem. You want me to come with you?"

"No. But . . . but just watch, okay?"

"Okeydoke."

Anne turned from her friend and crossed her tidy, if parched, front yard. The man who had obviously been waiting for her arrival made no attempt to meet her halfway. He stood, silent and looming, watching her approach.

When she reached the shelter of her arched porch, she halted, her foot on the first stair.

His face was still in shadows; and all she could see was the breadth of his chest, his meaty arms severely testing the short sleeves of his knit shirt and his massive legs, splayed like tree trunks. His body language was not the friendly demeanor of a door-to-door salesman. He looked like a confident Goliath waiting for David.

After a long pause while Anne gawked at his formidable bulk, he stepped into the light.

Elaine's description had been accurate. He was fair, freckled and had a country-boy face that was in absolute contrast to his body-builder physique. When he spoke, instead of the rumbling growl Anne was expecting, his voice was soft. Melodic. Sweet as a nightingale. "Sorry if I startled you, ma'am. You *are* Miz Farraday? Anne Farraday?"

Anne nodded.

The gargantuan stranger lurched forward. He stuck out a giant paw and smiled, a dazzling toothy grin that lit his homely features. "Name's Wally Spears. *Agent* Wally Spears. I guess you've heard about Mr. Gardner's death?"

Anne bobbed her head. "According to the papers, it was an accident. It *was* an accident, wasn't it?"

Agent Spears gnawed on his lower lip. "I haven't had access to the reports, ma'am. Matter of fact, I think that Mr. Gardner's death is still under investigation. But I'm here just in case."

"In case of what?"

"In case our old pal Riczini has an 'accident' in store for you. I'm here to kinda keep an eye on you."

Her eyes widened in astonishment. This . . . this hulk was the cavalry charging to her rescue? "Do...do you have any identification, Mr. Spears?"

"Call me Wally. Sure, I've got I.D., but—" he nodded to Elaine, who was intently watching them "—are you sure you want all your neighbors to know this is an official call?"

Anne wavered. No, she couldn't afford to have her neighbors know there was something "peculiar" about her.

Something that involved men with badges. At the same time, it seemed foolhardy to take Wally Spears into her home before she knew for certain that he was a government agent.

She looked up at the grizzly-like man with the kind blue eyes and made her decision. She couldn't go through life in a state of perpetual mistrust. And if they stood just inside the foyer with the door standing open, then Elaine could still hear her if she shouted for help.

"All right, Mr. Spears—Wally. I'm going to unlock the door and you step just out of sight and take out your identification. Deal?"

"Deal. Good thinking, Miz Farraday."

Anne unlocked the door and held it open wide. Spears lumbered across the porch and stepped inside. Holding her hand palm up, she gestured for Elaine to wait while she followed him indoors.

He had already pulled out a leather folder holding his badge and photo identification.

Anne took it from him and carefully examined the documents.

It *looked* very official. The badge number and the number on his I.D. card matched. But the truth was, if the darned thing was a fake, she had no way of knowing.

It was down to trust again.

How could she not trust this huge teddy bear?

Handing the folder back to the agent, she gave Elaine a thumbs-up signal and closed the door behind them. "How about some iced tea?"

"Sounds great."

"The kitchen's down this way." Breathing in a deep dose of courage, she turned her back on him and led the way down the hall.

An hour later, after polishing off an entire pitcher of iced tea and a plate of sandwiches, Wally Spears leaned back in his chair and patted his stomach.

"That oughta hold me a couple hours. Anyway, since we've got Riczini in custody again, you may not have anything to worry about."

Anne's head bobbed in agreement. "I hope you're right. So you really don't think William's death was connected with Riczini?"

He shook his massive head. "Of course, somebody in D.C. must think it's a possibility, otherwise I wouldn't be here. Anyway, for the next couple of days, wherever you look, you'll see my smiling face. So you can relax now, you hear? Agent Spears is near!"

She chuckled appreciatively. He was trying so hard to put her at her ease, to make her believe that she hadn't been forgotten by the government. And she did feel better, now that this big lug was on the scene.

But...but if Spears was the federal agent sent to protect her, then who was Luke McCullough? Deep in her heart, Anne had believed—had prayed—that Luke was her government-appointed guardian angel.

Maybe he'd tell her the truth tomorrow, on their date.

She squinched her eyes, shutting out the nagging thought that if he wasn't here to defend her, he could be here to assassinate her.

No! She wouldn't believe that. Couldn't believe it.

"Miz Farraday, you all right?" Wally's kind, homely face was creased with worry.

Anne reached across the table and patted his immense hand. "Just tired, but thanks for asking."

He pushed his chair back and got up. "Reckon you ought to get some sleep now. And, don't worry, I'll be right outside."

A quiver of apprehension shuddered through her. She'd thought he was going to move into her guest room. No one could get to her, she thought, if they had to go through this mountain first. "Why don't you just stay in the house?"

"Now don't you be worrying. I'll be comfortable in my car. Got a full thermos of coffee. A couple dozen doughnuts. I'll be fine."

"But wouldn't...I mean, I'd feel safer with you inside."

"If the bureau had assigned a team, one of us would be stationed inside the premises. But with just me, I need to be outside. That way, I can see if anybody drives up. Or walks up. Things I might miss if I was in the house with you."

Bowing to his expertise, she followed him around the house while he double-checked windows and doors. He poked in the closets, flashed a penlight into the attic. When he was finally satisfied that the house was secure, he made his way back to the front door.

"Be sure and put on the deadbolt behind me."

"I will. And, Wally?"

"Ma'am?"

"Thanks for being here."

He tipped an imaginary hat, winked and disappeared around the corner of the house.

By stepping to the edge of her porch, Anne could see him climbing into a nondescript late-model sedan parked across the street less than a half block away.

For the first time in days, she felt safe.

Chapter Six

Anne sat bolt upright in bed, listening for the sound that had awakened her. It was something different from the usual night noises.

This sound threatened her.

Beads of perspiration formed on her forehead as a cold shiver raced down her spine. She was hot and cold at the same time. Terrified, yet suffused with an icy calm.

Someone was in the house.

She didn't know why she was so certain, but somehow Anne knew. A prowler was in her home.

Leaning over to reach for the telephone, she stopped, her hand in midair. Was that a footstep?

Though she strained her ears for a full ten seconds, she heard nothing. Yet the sense of a malevolent human skulking in the darkness persisted. Someone was stalking her. She could feel his presence coming closer. And closer.

She snatched the bedside phone receiver, and with trembling fingers, punched out 911. Come on, ring, dammit. Why didn't the stupid number ring?

Maybe she'd misdialed.

Pressing the button to disconnect the call, she put the receiver to her ear and once again, more slowly, pressed the numbers. Nine. One. One.

The awful truth almost overwhelmed her—the phone line was dead.

She dropped the useless instrument back on the hook.

Screech!

Anne's heart leaped into her throat. That was the door to the guest bedroom. For weeks she'd been threatening to oil those hinges. The intruder was only two rooms away.

He was deliberately making his way down the hall. At any moment, he would be at her bedroom door. She was alone. Defenseless.

Gulping back the terror that was pounding in her chest, Anne sprang from the bed and dashed to the window.

With shaking fingers, she managed to unfasten the lock and push up the sheet of double-paned glass. She stuck her head through the opening but it was no use, her body would never fit.

For security, Anne had installed windows that would only open ten inches. Enough for ventilation but not enough to admit an intruder. The intruder had found another way in, but now she couldn't get out.

What in the name of heaven was she going to do?

A slithering sound right outside her door spurred her to action. Hoping to attract someone's attention, she leaned out the window to shout for help.

From its position on the side of her home, her bedroom window was directly across from where Wally had parked his car. Hope sprang in her heart.

"Agent Spears! Wally!"

Her voice drifted away like a shadow in the night. He couldn't hear her. The houses were on such large lots she wondered if anyone would hear her cries for help.

At that moment, she heard a muffled curse as her bedroom door burst open.

Acting purely on instinct, Anne dived for the bedside table. If she could turn on the lamp, its illumination might alert Wally that she was in trouble.

The intruder bumped into her bed and growled.

God, he was so close! She could almost smell him.

Squinting her eyes against the glare of light she knew would be blinding, Anne's fingers inched up the base of the heavy brass lamp.

Amidst a cacophony of noise—her own silent screams ricocheting through her brain, the burglar snarling, and the clamor of thoughts and images swirling through her mind—she finally found the button and flicked the lamp switch.

Nothing. The room remained bathed in inky blackness. For the first time, she noticed that the red numerals of her digital clock radio weren't glowing in the dark as they usually did. The power was off.

She was completely cut off from help.

A ragged breath only a few feet away told her the intruder had located her. She could sense, rather than see, his shape edging around the foot of the bed.

She grabbed the brass lamp, yanked the cord from the wall and clutched it to her chest. On legs wobbly with panic, she backed up, taking final refuge in the corner behind the bedside table.

He was on her side of the bed now. As he passed the window, the faint light of the quarter moon illuminated him for an instant.

He was hunched over, carrying something bright in his hand. His stance made it impossible for her to gauge his height, or even his weight. A dark, knitted cap was pulled low, hiding his features. His head-to-foot dark clothing camouflaged him. When he moved a step closer, his shape merely blended into the surrounding darkness.

Only the blurry pale oval of his face was visible as he inched closer. And yet closer.

He raised his hand and, for the first time, she was able to make out the shiny object in his fist. This man wasn't here to rob her. He meant to kill her! And he intended to make it look like an accident, for he carried a slender hypodermic needle. Its sharp point glittered in the moonlight.

Swallowing a scream, Anne gripped the brass lamp tighter. As the assassin lurched toward her, she swung out with all her might.

But the lamp shade softened the impact. The would-be executioner easily deflected the blow and knocked the lamp from her grasp.

The scream she had been valiantly trying to quell burst from her lungs as his viselike grip encircled her wrist.

Hammering with her fists, Anne fought her attacker. Kicking. Screaming. Pummeling. Striking blow after blow with her ineffectual fists. All in vain.

With a snarl of victory, the killer forced her onto the bed. The fingers of his left hand, like steel bars, pinned her flat against the mattress. With mindless force, his right hand raised the hypodermic needle.

Her eyes never leaving the deadly syringe, Anne used her last ounce of strength to push at that hand, but it was hopeless.

The assassin was much too strong.

If she had been capable of tears, she would have cried with the injustice. For after two years of hiding, this man was going to kill her in her own bed.

With a final wail of frustrated anguish, she felt a faint touch of the deadly needle on her flesh. In another instant, its sharp point would puncture her skin.

At that moment, a horrendous crashing boom exploded somewhere in the front of the house.

Her assailant froze, the point of the hypodermic needle hovering above her flesh.

Her heart thudded in her chest as strange, thrashing noises continued to reverberate from the other room. The man's fetid breath filled the air while his fingers held a death grip on her arm.

Then, her ears picked up the *thump-thump* of footsteps running down the hall. Agent Spears!

The intruder uttered a foul oath and released her.

A whisper of relief radiated through her body. But before she'd had time to take real comfort from his action, he grabbed the brass lamp and raised it over his head.

Anne cringed and stifled another scream. Somehow, she found the presence of mind to roll away, to the far side of the bed. Out of his reach.

From the corner of her eye, she saw him twist suddenly and aim the heavy metal base against her bedroom window.

Fragments of glass sprinkled down, showering the room like a cloudburst. Jagged shards glinted in the moonlight as they rained over her.

Intuitively, Anne threw up an arm to cover her face and rolled off the bed. She hit the floor with a bone-bruising thud. Acting out of pure, primal instinct, she curled into a ball, to make herself as small a target as possible, and cringed against the wall.

She thought briefly about running out the bedroom door, but knew it would be useless. Terror had overtaken her to the point that her legs wouldn't support her weight. Her only hope was to stay still, pray that he wouldn't find her in the dark.

She couldn't see her attacker, but waited like trapped prey for him to round the bed at any second.

But she wouldn't—couldn't—give up. Her life was all she had left and she'd be damned if she was going to make it easy for someone to take it from her.

She glimpsed movement in her peripheral vision and swiveled her head just in time to see another figure burst through the bedroom door. A beam of bright light skimmed across the walls as the newcomer scanned the area with a powerful flashlight.

"Anne! Where are you?"

The U.S. Cavalry's call to arms blasted by a bugle couldn't have been more welcome than the sound of Luke's voice.

"H-here, down here."

The flashlight's ray shifted abruptly, focusing its brilliant glare on her face.

"Anne! What's going on? Are you all right?"

In two powerful strides, Luke crossed the room and knelt beside her. He dropped the light onto the floor and pulled her into the protective circle of his arms. "Annie, honey, are you all right? Can you talk?"

Wrapping her arms around his neck, Anne clung to him like a frightened child. Oh, did this man feel good. So strong. So... so safe.

"Annie?" His voice murmured in her ear. "What is it, honey—what happened?"

"A...a man. In my room. He...he tried to kill me." She spoke calmly, but a tiny sob in her voice gave her away.

Luke reached for the flashlight, stood up and directed his beam around the room. The perp had broken the window and made his escape.

Half of him wanted to follow the perp, catch him and beat him to a bloody pulp with his own hands. But he knew he couldn't leave Anne alone in the dark.

The intruder would have to wait.

Reaching down, he slipped his arms around Anne's body and after shaking the covers to make sure there was no glass, he gently pulled her up onto the bed. Lowering himself down beside her, he drew her close. So close he could feel the unsteady thumping of her heart. Feel the tremors of fear coursing through her body.

For the second time in his life, Luke seriously wanted to kill someone. "It's okay, honey. He's gone. You're safe now."

His fingers brushed the threads of coppery hair from her eyes. Wiped away a trail of tears on her cheeks. "Hush, sweetie, you're going to be fine. I won't let anything happen to you. I promise."

Even as he said the words, Luke wondered how he was going to keep that commitment. He couldn't track down his leads, guard Anne night and day and get by on an hour or two of sleep. At least not for long.

But he knew he'd already let this latest lead on Scorpion grow cold. And he would deprive himself of sleep until he passed out. But protect Anne Farraday he would. Period.

With a groan, he held her tighter in his arms, wanting to pull her into his own body to keep her safe. When he'd been outside and heard her screams, his blood had pulsated through his veins as if his own life were in jeopardy.

He'd almost broken his neck stumbling through the dark trying to get to her, before he remembered the flashlight in his hand. He wasn't thinking straight.

It just went to show what could happen when you got personally involved with a civilian. He didn't want to think about the way this woman had infiltrated his mind. The way her gentle spirit had wriggled into his heart.

He'd long since given up any thoughts of a special woman in his life, so why did this one drive him half-mad with desire? And why now?

Giving himself a moment for his heart to settle back into a regular rhythm, he finally pulled back. He had to get himself under control. He wouldn't be worth a damn to Anne if he let himself become an emotional basket case.

This series of flubbed attempts on Anne's life bothered him. It didn't jibe with Scorpion's usual modus operandi. His hits were usually quick, clean and untraceable.

Had his informant been wrong? Had some auxiliary shooter been imported? Made sense in a way. Riczini wouldn't be expecting much trouble from Anne. Maybe he'd gotten cheap and sent one of his own gorillas to take care of her.

It didn't really matter, though, who was trying to kill her. The important thing was to get her under twenty-four-hour protection. Now.

Which brought up another major concern. By now, shouldn't the bureau have sent an agent to protect its last eyewitness against The Boss?

As soon as Anne was safe, Luke intended to make a few phone calls. And somebody better have some answers.

With a sigh, he pulled away from Anne, kissing her gently on the top of her head. "Come on, honey. We've got to assess the damage. Where're your lights?"

"I...I think he must have cut the power somehow. I tried to turn on a light to alert Wally—oh, my God! Where *is* Wally?"

"Who's Wally?"

"Wally Spears," she answered without thinking. "The agent the FBI sent to protect..." Her voice trailed off as she realized what she'd done. She'd broken the vow of silence that had kept her alive for the past two years.

Sitting here, alone in the dark with Luke, she'd felt so secure—so protected—that she'd let down her guard.

As if reading her thoughts, Luke's quiet voice soothed her fears. "Don't worry, Anne. I know all about your past."

"But... how? When? I mean—"

Outside, a cloud drifted across the moon, cutting the scant light altogether. A tiny shudder rippled through Anne, causing Luke to understand how much fear she was desperately trying to conceal. Running his hand along the sheet until he found hers, he laced their fingers together.

Part of her fear, he knew, was her own uncertainty about him.

The hell with departmental rules and procedures. For Anne's emotional well-being he was going to break his cover. He should have done it yesterday. She had to be going nuts wondering whether he was friend or foe.

He was going to tell Anne everything. After he got the power turned back on.

"I'll explain later," he said. "Right now, let's get some light on the subject. He probably just threw a circuit breaker. Where's your circuit box?"

"Outside the back door. To the left."

"You wait here. I'll go—"

"No! I'm coming with you." She swung off the bed and stood toe-to-toe with Luke.

"Do you have on any shoes?" he asked.

"No. Why?"

"Because there's broken glass everywhere. You'll be perfectly safe here. Just climb back up in the bed like a—"

"Like a good girl? In your dreams, Luke McCullough. I'm coming with you."

"Anne, believe me. You'll be a lot safer here. Take my gun and—"

"No. I'm coming with you."

Even though the room was as black as a coal miner's fingernails, Luke could still perceive the stubborn tilt to her jaw, the tensed posture of her shoulders and the rebellious gleam in her eyes.

Gritting his teeth, he asked again, "Are you sure you're not hurt?"

"No. Just a few bruises."

"Then, come on." Without warning, he ducked down, edging his shoulder against her waist. He stood up, bringing Anne into a fireman's hold. "Hang on and don't you dare complain," he muttered.

"But—"

"Not one word!"

Wrapping his left arm beneath her perfectly rounded bottom, he flicked on the flashlight and carried her back to the kitchen where he unceremoniously dumped her onto a chair.

His boots crunching on the broken glass that littered the kitchen floor, he disappeared outside.

A moment later, she blinked as the overhead fluorescent fixture flooded the room with brilliant light.

Anne rubbed her light-sensitive eyes and surveyed her usually spotless kitchen. It bore an impressive resemblance to a shot of an earthquake aftermath on the evening news.

Her patio door was shattered, its few remaining sections a mosaic of opaque fragments. The window over the sink was raised. A half moon of glass had been cut out just above the latch. The lacy curtains she'd paid a small fortune for were billowing out the open windows, their intricate lace pattern shredded from catching on the broken glass. One chair was overturned, and she couldn't imagine how the cannister of sugar had managed to find its way onto the tile floor. A tiny battalion of ants was already marching toward the white crystals.

Luke stepped back through the gaping patio door. "The power's all back on, but the bastard cut the phone lines."

She waved an arm, encompassing the wreckage of her kitchen. "How did he do so much damage without my hearing him?"

Luke ducked his head, looking slightly sheepish. "I'm afraid half this mess—maybe even most of it—is my doing."

"Yours?"

"I...uh, heard you screaming and uh...kind of smashed your patio door with that concrete planter you have outside. At least, you *used* to have a concrete planter. It kind of got smashed, too."

"And the sugar?"

"That thing—" he pointed to the overturned oak chair "—was right in front of the door. I tripped, my arm flew across the cupboards, things went flying and..."

"I see." She *had* left the chair in the middle of the floor before she went to bed. She'd been standing on it to brush a spider web out of the corner and forgotten to move it back.

"I could've been killed," Luke said defensively.

"I'm sorry. I'll try to be more careful. So if you broke the patio door, how did that man get in? Wally checked all the doors and windows before he—where *is* Agent Spears? He was parked right across the street."

"Looks like the assailant came in through the kitchen window. Trust me, I'll deal with your Agent Spears directly but, right now, we've got to get to a phone and get the police to put out an APB." With Anne's safety on the line, Luke could no longer afford to worry about the local authorities jeopardizing his mission.

Anne raised her bare feet up and tucked them beneath her on the chair. She tugged her thin cotton nightie over her knees and considered the implications of involving the local police. Yuma was a small town. A *very* small town in the summer. Not much excitement. The police would draw the media. The media would plaster her photograph in the newspaper, on the news.

Brushing a strand of hair off her face, she looked up at Luke. Evidently he had more experience in these matters, but it wasn't his life that would be dramatically altered. Again.

With a shake of her head, she said softly, "My contact in Washington told me to avoid the local authorities as much as possible. Not to stand out in any way."

He put a hand on her shoulder and squeezed. "I know it's scary, honey, but your cover is already blown. The best thing we can do now is throw out as big a net as possible and hope to snag this bastard."

Anne felt tears forming in her eyes. Her throat stung and she couldn't swallow. She hated to fall apart in front of Luke. But day after day, month after month, she'd been looking over her shoulder, living a life of isolation and fear. Now, he was asking her to disregard every rule her contact had given her, and step forward into the spotlight of public attention, become a closer target for Riczini's hit man.

Luke promised her that he'd protect her. And he *did* have this uncanny ability to show up exactly when she needed him. His perfectly timed rescues could no longer be chalked up to mere serendipity. It was obvious that, for whatever reasons, Luke had been secretly watching her for days.

"I want you to sit tight for just a minute," Luke said, interrupting her disturbing thoughts.

"Why? Where are you going?"

"First, I want to check out your bedroom. If we're real lucky, he might have left some clue—some scrap of evidence. Fibers from his clothing. A fingerprint on the windowsill—"

"He wore surgical gloves," Anne said suddenly. "I remember feeling them on my skin. When he tried to...to kill me."

What new manner of hell had Scorpion thought of this time, Luke wondered. A jolt of nausea shot through his gut when he thought of that monster wrapping gloved hands around Anne's fragile throat. Luke reached over and swept the tumbled mass of hair from around her neck. Her long, lovely throat was unbruised.

As if reading his mind, Anne shook her head. "He...he had a needle. A hypodermic. Oh, God, Luke, another second or two and he would have stuck that needle into me! What kind of madman is this?"

"The worst kind," he muttered. "Wait here. I'm going to check your room."

A few moments later, he stalked back into the kitchen and headed directly toward the busted sliding glass door.

"Now where are you going?" Anne called across the room. "Did you find anything in the bedroom?"

Luke ignored her second question and responded instead to her first. "I'm going to check on that so-called agent assigned to guard you. If that SOB is asleep, believe me, his next assignment will be—" He broke off at Anne's unexpected laugh. "What's so funny?"

"What kind of assignment could he get worse than surveillance duty in Yuma, Arizona, in August? I mean, it was only a hundred and ten in the shade today."

"Good point. Maybe the guy's already a screwup. Anyway, you stay here while I check."

This time Anne didn't argue, already feeling more secure now that the lights were back on. Luke picked up the flashlight, ruffled her hair and slipped out through the broken patio door.

When he was out of sight, Anne's common sense told her that she should run to Elaine's and telephone the authorities. They could force Luke to divulge his role in this nightmare. But deep in her fearful heart, she knew only one truth—Luke McCullough would never hurt her. Yes, he'd already saved her life twice, but that wasn't why Anne felt so compelled to trust this man.

It was the glimmers of pain that she occasionally glimpsed in his expressive pewter-gray eyes. It was the tender way he touched her, comforted her. It was . . . it was that kiss.

Luke was back in less than five minutes, his expression forbidding. ''No sign of him.''

''But his car was parked right across the street.''

He nodded. ''The car's still there. And it *is* a government-issue. No sign of the driver, though.''

''Maybe he went after the . . . the burglar.''

Luke made no comment on her inability to call her intruder what he was, a hired killer. ''Maybe you're right. Maybe Agent Spears is in hot pursuit,'' he said. The truth was, Luke thought grimly, Spears would surely have called for backup on his police radio before he set out on foot. The neighborhood should be crawling with cops.

''So what do we do now?'' Anne asked.

''Have you made up your mind? About calling in the local police? I can't canvass this neighborhood alone. Every moment we waste gives him more time to escape.''

Anne looked up at him. ''Will you stay with me until he's caught?''

Luke caught his breath. She couldn't know what she was asking. He had an assignment. An assignment that only peripherally included Anne Farraday. He wasn't designated as her guardian, although he wished he had been. He wouldn't have fallen asleep on the job as Agent Spears apparently had. Luke's directive had been, for three years now, to track down and bring Scorpion to justice. In whatever fashion he deemed appropriate.

But when he looked down into Anne's chocolate brown eyes, when he saw the trust in her gaze, Luke knew that apprehending Scorpion had long since ceased to be his mission. If he had to throw away fifteen years' service, Anne's safety was his primary concern this time. Every time.

With a soul-shaking jolt of comprehension, the knowledge struck Luke like an electrical current—he would protect this woman at all costs. Even with his own life.

His hand trembling, he brushed the sweet softness of her cheek, wondering at how easily she had enchanted him. His voice husky with newly awakened emotion, he whispered, "I'll stay with you as long as you want me, Anne."

She enveloped his large hand in her two smaller ones and held it firmly against her face.

Luke's heart was so swollen with unfamiliar tenderness that he feared it might burst. All right, he'd made a promise. Now he had to fulfill it. He couldn't do that by gazing at her beauty like a love-struck coyote howling at the moon. Right now, he had to get back on track. The best he could offer Anne was his expertise. He'd spent fifteen years tracking down murderers and thieves. This was the one gift he could give to Anne: he could free her from this cold-blooded assassin, this creature called Scorpion.

But, first, he had to start thinking like a special agent again.

Withdrawing his palm from the warmth of her cheek, he hooked a chair leg with his boot and sat down across from her. He reached in his hip pocket and pulled out his notebook and a stub of pencil. "Did you get a look at this creep?" he asked. "Can you describe him?"

Anne looked up, her eyes startled, confused at the sudden change in his demeanor. "Luke, I'm trusting you with my life. I need you to trust me. Please, tell me the truth. Why are you here?"

He took a deep breath and exhaled it slowly. Reaching into his shirt pocket, he took out a leather folder and flipped it open. He tossed the folder on the table. "Special Agent, FBI."

Relief poured over her like a warm bath on a winter night. Her instincts had been right all along. Luke was one of the good guys. An ally in this insane shadow game.

She traced the engraving on the gold badge with her forefinger. "Why didn't you tell me before? And, if you're from the FBI, was Agent Spears a phony? I don't understand."

Luke shook his head, rumpled strands of ebony hair falling over his forehead. "You weren't my assignment. I've been tracking a...a known criminal. I think he's been hired by Riczini to..."

He didn't finish but Anne knew the logical conclusion to his sentence: hired by Riczini to kill her. Trying to divorce herself from the terror that was creeping up her spine again, she asked, "So you were trailing him and stumbled on to me? Is that right?"

"Sort of. I had a tip that this criminal—only known to us as Scorpion—had been hired by Riczini to eliminate any witnesses."

"But why now? I mean, why not during the past two years?"

"Because he was recaptured a few weeks ago. Guess he got bored with South America, and decided to sneak back into the country. He flew to Mexico City, probably intending to drive north and cross the border at Matamoros or El Paso. Unfortunately for Riczini, the U.S. has a good rapport with the Mexican government, and they were happy to cooperate. The *federales* nabbed him at the airport. We ran the extradition papers through, and...voilà! Riczini's back in the good old U.S. of A. awaiting trial. In a maximum-security cell this time.''

"So he hired a killer to...to eliminate William? And me?"

Luke nodded. "Since Riczini's been out of commission the past couple of years, most of his little band of outlaws have split up. Gone to work for other crime syndicates. Struck out on their own. Whatever. But he's still got a few loyal soldiers. The bureau has had all of them under surveillance. As of last week, none of them had left Jersey. That's how Riczini was able to get past us on Gardner—by hiring outside muscle."

"This...this Scorpion?"

"Most likely. Anyway, I got the tip that Scorpion had come out to Yuma for a hit. That had me puzzled for a while. I mean, Scorpion is normally hired by some wise guy to eliminate one of his competition. Or a snitch in his own organization. This is the first that I've known of Scorpion being hired to...to take care of a civilian."

"Lucky me." Anne laughed mirthlessly.

"Problem is that Scorpion has always been like a shadow. No one has ever seen him. He's assigned his hits through a drop-box. The way I hear it, whoever wants his services wraps a certain amount of money in a shoebox, along with a piece of paper stating only the name and location of the intended victim, and has that box delivered—via messenger service—to a particular address in Switzerland. The money moves through three or four different couriers before it somehow makes its way to Scorpion. He keeps it varied enough that he's always one step ahead of us."

"So what do we do now?"

"Now, we hope that you saw enough that we can broadcast his description. Did you?—see him, I mean."

Anne shook her head. "No, not really. He was dressed in dark clothes. He was tall but not exceptionally so. Maybe five-ten or -eleven. Thin. But strong.'' Anne's eyes glazed as she recalled his steely grip holding her down, while that needle lowered closer. And closer.

"Not much," Luke said, sighing. What had he expected? That a civilian would notice something when neither the FBI nor Interpol had been able to pick up a concrete lead in over five years? He reached over and took Anne's hand. "Don't worry, honey. I won't let him near you again."

Her soft brown gaze was filled with faith. "I know."

"Where's your robe and slippers? We've got to get to a phone."

"In my closet, I can get them." She rose to her feet.

"No, remember there's glass everywhere. How am I supposed to protect you if you won't let me?"

Anne tossed her head, that hard glare of determination shining in her eyes. "You're supposed to protect me from that hired killer, not from life. I'll get dressed and be right back."

Stepping gingerly, she walked out of the kitchen.

Luke knew he was being a macho jerk. Overprotectiveness around women was one of his major flaws. Glenna had told him so time and again. And he knew that Anne was perfectly capable of avoiding the broken glass now that the lights were back on. It was just that he felt so helpless, so powerless to put Scorpion out of commission, that he was trying to make up for it by treating her like a china doll.

Anne was back, fully dressed, in less than five minutes. She'd donned a pair of well-worn jeans that hugged her in all the right places and a cotton top the same burnished gold as the highlights in her hair. She'd pulled her hair back into a ponytail, scrubbed her face until her cheeks shone and wasn't wearing a drop of makeup.

Luke thought he'd never seen such a softly beautiful woman in his life. Fresh. Natural. Full of fire and spirit. She was the embodiment of all the delightful wonders of the female gender. His hands itched to encircle her tiny waist, to pull her close, feel her womanly curves against him—

"Are you ready?" Handbag slung over her shoulder, Anne stood in front of him, a puzzled look in her eyes.

"Sure," he said, coming out of his reverie.

"The closest phone is next door," she said. "At Elaine's."

Luke glanced at his watch. "It's pretty late to yank someone out of bed. After two."

"She deserves it. She forgets her key at least once a week and wakes me up in the middle of the night for her spare. Honestly, I don't think I've ever known such a scatter-brained woman. Although she's very clever, you know. Last week, when I was opening a crate—"

"Anne—" he pressed his fingertips against her lips "—you're rambling."

"I know. I always do when I'm nervous."

Understanding her trepidation, he wrapped an arm around her shoulder. "I'll be with you every minute. Everything's going to work out, trust me."

She wished she could. But William Gardner and his lies and cheating had robbed her of the ability to trust anyone. Still, Luke *did* inspire confidence. He was strong, dependable and supremely competent in a crisis. And it wasn't as if she had any choice. She had to rely on him. "Okay, I'm ready."

"Atta girl. Now, remember, I'm not going to let you out of my sight until this mess is settled. Got it?"

Anne nodded bleakly. There was nothing to do but face the police and the press. Again. She didn't know which was worse, fighting off an armed intruder or facing the three-ring circus of publicity she knew was coming. Not that it mattered, she thought fatalistically. The die was cast.

Nevertheless, the dozen or so steps across the front yard felt like the thirteen stairs up the scaffolding to the hangman's noose.

Elaine's bell had barely stopped pealing when she swung open the door. "Anne! Is something wrong? Come in, sweetie."

She leaned forward and grasped the younger woman by the wrist, hauling her into the living room.

Luke followed, closing the door behind them. "We're sorry to disturb you at this hour, but Anne needs to use your telephone to report a burglary."

Elaine's eyes widened. "It's no bother. I just got home from a late date." Her husky voice lowered even more as she patted Anne's cheek. "You poor kid! What else is going to happen to you?"

"Nothing, I hope. Shall I use the phone in the kitchen?"

"No, use this one." She waved airily toward a flat, black designer telephone on a glass end table. "I'll go make a fresh pot of coffee. I'd be willing to bet that this is going to be a long night."

Not getting any takers on her bet, Elaine smoothed the hem of her black, long-sleeved turtleneck top over the slim-fitting hips of her matching slacks. "Make sure and ask for some cute cops. I just adore a man in uniform." She winked.

While Anne was on the telephone, Luke glanced around. He took in Elaine's sleek decor. Other than a crystal vase of fresh flowers, not a trinket littered a tabletop. The only picture adorning the walls was a free-form abstract in shades of rose and cream, apparently chosen to match the throw pillows on the sofa.

"They're on their way," Anne said flatly as she replaced the receiver.

"Come on, sit down and rest." He draped an arm across her shoulders and led her to the pristine cream-colored sofa. Sitting down next to her, he pulled her head onto his shoulder. "Everything's going to be all right. I promise."

Anne sighed. Some foolish part of her heart wanted to believe him. Believe that this slightly klutzy knight who'd come galloping to her rescue on a sleek black stallion could somehow make her life whole again.

And why not? He always showed up just when she needed him, as if they shared some kind of psychic connection. "Luke?"

"Mmm?"

"What *were* you doing at my house tonight?"

"I tried to phone you and—"

"Why? I mean, it must have been well after midnight and—"

"I guess I didn't realize the time. I was watching some movie on TV and must have dozed off. Anyway, when I woke up, I called you."

Anne smiled. "I'm glad you did."

"Me, too. When I didn't get an answer, I got worried. So I came on over. No one answered the front door, so I went around back to tap on your window."

"At midnight?"

"Time has no meaning to a knight seeking to rescue his ladylove." His husky voice belied the flippant response.

Just then, Elaine stepped back into the room carrying a tray laden with coffee fixings.

"Luke, could you bring the carafe in from the kitchen?"

"Sure." Although he would have preferred to stay cuddled against Anne's softness, he unwound himself from her sleepy embrace just as the doorbell rang.

"I'll get the door," Elaine called as Luke started in that direction. "You just bring the coffee."

"Yes, sir!" Luke saluted smartly and clicked his heels. Sometimes Anne's neighbor got on his nerves. As he went down the hall toward the kitchen, he looked over his shoulder and saw two uniformed patrolmen step into the living room.

Chapter Seven

An hour later, the two officers closed their notebooks and stood up. Anne had told them everything, omitting only the details of her entrance into the Witness Relocation Program and all information about her former identity. No sense taking a chance that information could leak to the press.

The senior policeman, Officer Diaz, studied Anne for a long moment. "Ms. Farraday, I think you've bought yourself a passel of trouble. We can dust the house for prints, but if this man is the pro you say he is, we won't find a thing. I can run a few extra patrols past your house at night, but he'll get wise to that in a hurry and just lay back until we pass."

"So, you're saying there's nothing I can do—just wait around for him to come kill me?"

"I know it sounds like that, and I'm sorry. Like I told you, we'll be turning this over to the detectives in the morning. Your friend here is with the FBI. I don't know what more we can do. I mean, we only have the vaguest description of a wiry, average-size man dressed in dark clothing. We can't circulate that among the motels. If we just had something to work with."

Luke turned to Anne. "I'm afraid the officer is right, honey." He sure wished he knew where Spears was now. "You haven't seen anybody hanging around lately? No unusual incidents, other than the one with the snake?"

She frowned thoughtfully. "I don't know if this counts for anything, but a man who said he was a lawyer came into The Book Nook today—yesterday, now. He said he had a client who wanted to buy my store."

"What time was this, ma'am?" Officer Almon asked.

"About ten-thirty. About two hours before you dropped by, Luke."

Officer Diaz clicked his ballpoint. "Do you recall his name? The name of his firm?"

Anne rubbed her forehead with her fingertips. "I don't think he mentioned his law firm. But his name was... Newton. Newman. Something like that. No—Nevill! That was it, Dan Nevill. Said he was from Los Angeles."

"Did he show you any identification," Luke asked. "And why did he think your store was on the market?"

"Oh, I think it was all a mistake. When I hung up the telephone, he was gone."

Luke arched an eyebrow at the two officers, a world of unspoken meaning in his glance. "Anne, did you get a look at this guy? Could you describe him?"

She nodded vigorously. "I'll say. He looked like a cross between a funeral director and a stork."

Elaine leaned forward. "That must be the guy you told me about. Tall. Skinny."

"Yes, that's right."

Luke reached over, and lightly held Anne's chin between his thumb and forefinger, drawing her attention back to him. "Think carefully, honey. Could he be the man who broke into your house tonight?"

Her eyebrows dipped in concentration. "Mmm...maybe. I *thought* he was quite a bit taller than the man who attacked me, but maybe not. It's hard to say, everything happened so fast!"

Officer Diaz pulled his notepad out again. "Maybe you'd better give us his description. If he's still in town, we'll find him. Then if he turns out to be who he says he is, no harm done."

After he finished pulling every tiny detail from Anne that she could recall, the two policemen left.

Elaine stood up, stifling a yawn. "I know this is a foolish idea, but since it's after three, I'd like to grab a few hours' sleep. Anne, you'd better stay here with me, in the spare room."

Before she could respond, Luke cut in, "Nice of you to offer, Elaine, but to tell you the truth, I was planning on putting her up at my place."

"Oh, but I have plenty of room."

"Under the circumstances, I think she'd be better off sleeping with me."

"Excuse me!" Anne jumped to her feet and glared at them, her fists resting on her hips. "I really don't appreciate being discussed like...like a piece of luggage being shuttled around. I'm perfectly capable of deciding where I'll sleep—and with whom!"

"I wouldn't touch that line with a ten-foot pole!" Elaine exclaimed.

"Don't look at me, " Luke muttered with a sheepish look in his eyes. "Seriously, though, you're absolutely right. I can be an overbearing jerk sometimes."

"And you know I'm a busybody," Elaine added. "So just tell us, where do you want to stay?"

"In my own bed. But I won't!" She added quickly when the two simultaneously began to argue. "Although it would be more convenient for me to stay here, maybe it's too convenient. I mean, this would be the first place the killer would look, if he's been watching me for a few days, and I'm sure he has. So I think I'll be safer with Luke."

Elaine's gaze raked Luke suggestively. "I wouldn't bet on it," she said, several layers of innuendo in her tone.

THEY STOPPED by Anne's house long enough for her to throw some things in an overnight bag. While she was packing, Luke tacked some old paneling he found in the garage over the broken windows and patio door.

"It's really more a psychological deterrent than anything else," he explained. "A dedicated burglar could get through that paneling faster than it took me to nail it up. But I guess it'll serve to keep any kids from wandering in."

As they turned out the lights and started back toward the living room, Anne looked around the little house she'd grown to love. It looked the way she felt—battered, bewildered and broken. She wondered if she'd ever feel safe in her little haven again.

She doubted it. Riczini had taken that bit of security from her. Just as he'd taken so much before.

This time, she wasn't going to turn tail and run. If her cover was truly blown, then so be it. She'd fight Riczini with every ounce of strength that remained in her body. She wasn't going to flee again. Wasn't going to let the government relocate her in Oshkosh, Wisconsin, or Deep Creek, Virginia.

If she couldn't go back to her old life in New Jersey, then she'd stay here in Arizona. Continue to build on the one she'd started.

Auggie Riczini better watch out. She was going to prove to that mobster that Anne Farraday, by any name, was a woman to be reckoned with.

Pulling her keys from her handbag, she turned to Luke. "Ready?"

He stepped out the front door and stood aside so she could lock it. "Willing and able."

"That remains to be seen."

Luke chuckled, happy to see that Anne had recovered from her ordeal enough to banter with him. Taking her by the elbow, he led her to his car. "That sounded like a challenge, Anne. Let me hasten to assure you, I'm up to a good challenge."

Five minutes later, he pulled into a circular driveway fronting a well-maintained ranch-style house. Pulling her bag from the back seat, he led the way up a flagstone path to the front door.

Anne waited while he unlocked the door, then stepped inside to disengage the security alarm.

"Come on, honey," Luke said. "I imagine you're dead on your feet. The spare bedroom's down here—right across the hall from me."

He carried her overnight case through a darkened living room, then snapped on a light, illuminating a hallway similar to her own with four wooden doors lining the white walls like evenly spaced freckles. Stopping before the first door on the left, he reached inside and turned on an overhead fixture.

The room was a little girl's fairyland. White four-poster bed frosted with a pink nylon canopy. A fluffy pink spread was topped by pale lavender pillows. The white walls were lined with Disney posters, most predominant was the Little Mermaid.

Anne dropped her purse on a shiny white bureau, littered with play-cosmetics and plastic jewelry. She nodded appreciatively and turned back to Luke. "I like your room. Did you decorate it yourself?"

He bit off a colorful retort and instead responded with a grin. "Actually, this room belongs to my namesake," he said, leaning against the door frame, his arms folded across his black T-shirt.

"Don't you think it's a little frilly for a boy? Not to mention pink."

"No, my namesake is a five-year-old female terrorist named Lucinda, also known as Lucy the Loud. Lucy is my goddaughter," he added to the unspoken question in her eyes.

"I didn't realize you had friends here. Although I shouldn't be so surprised. I don't know anything about you."

"My former partner, now retired on a service-related disability, moved here to be near his wife's family in El Centro. We've stayed in touch since he retired eighteen months ago. So when I found out I was coming out here on assignment, I called to see if they could put me up for a few days."

Anne looked around the empty room. "So where are they, your friend and his family?"

Luke laughed. "When Ernie found out he had a free house sitter and pet-watcher, in August, yet, he decided to head for cooler weather. Took the family up to the Sierra mountains for a couple of weeks."

"Smart fellow."

"Agreed. Anyway, I know it'll be like sleeping in cotton candy, but at least you'll be safe." He unfolded his arms and pointed to a small door in the corner of the room. "Private bath over there, nothing but the best for our Lucy. You'll probably find all the bubbles and bath toys you could ever want."

"Including a yellow rubber duckie?"

He leaned over and pressed his lips to the side of her head. A shiver ran down her spine as his warm breath ruffled the fine hair at her temple. She turned in his arms, nuzzling her lips against his neck.

Luke grasped her closely for a moment. He could stay like this, cuddling her in his embrace, all night. But all his carefully nurtured survival instincts were screaming red alert. This woman meant danger. For the better part of five years, Luke had managed to wrap his emotions up in a tiny package and shove them deep inside. But this small warm bundle of smoldering sensuality had found his hiding place. Little by little, she was tugging at the emotional strings he'd thought were so tightly bound.

Worse than the threat to his heart, Luke knew that if he lost his emotional detachment—lost his control—he could be jeopardizing Anne's life. That was a risk he wouldn't—couldn't—take.

Pulling away gently, he said, "Rubber duckie, huh? You'd better get some sleep. You're getting punchy. Good night, Anne. Try not to worry. Tomorrow we'll plot our strategy."

"Good night, Luke."

"Sleep tight, honey, and don't worry. You'll be safe here."

He started to close the door behind him when she stopped him. "Luke?"

"Yes, honey?"

"I . . . I just wanted to say thanks. For everything."

"No problem," he said with a wink.

He closed the door softly and a moment later, Anne heard the whisper of another door brushing against the thick carpeting.

INSIDE THE master bedroom across the hall, Luke pulled his T-shirt over his head and threw it across the room. His frustration level was rapidly approaching the red zone. He unzipped his jeans and pulled the rough denim down his legs, but removing the restricting material did little to relieve the tight pressure in his groin.

Didn't Anne know what she did to him when she was all soft and cuddly like that? He snarled in self-disgust. Mr. Control Freak who wasn't going to be affected by Anne's quick smile, her warm brown eyes.

He was better able to cope when those dark eyes were flashing with indignation, when she was sniping at him with that wicked little tongue.

Luke snorted. Who was he kidding? Whether she was sweet and demure, angry and snapping, or scared half to death, Anne's every mood made him want to sling her over his shoulder and haul her off to the nearest cave.

The only difference was that sometimes he wanted to haul her off to his cave to tame her, sometimes protect her and at other times, those hellish times, he just pure wanted to rip her clothes off and throw her down on the cave floor.

Right now, he wanted to make love to her until her red hair caught fire.

An hour later, Luke punched a fist into his pillow for the twentieth time and turned onto his other side. He didn't know who had told him that the desert temperatures dropped dramatically at night. He was as hot as the cobblestones along hell's main street and no amount of air-conditioning was going to cool him down.

The only antidote for his rather lusty affliction was sleeping peacefully right across the hall.

IT WAS ALMOST noon when Anne stepped into the kitchen, lured by the enticing aromas of frying bacon and freshly perked coffee. Luke was standing by the long, granite-topped counter breaking eggs into a glass bowl. Anne stopped in her tracks. Dear Lord, the man was so chipper he was whistling.

"Good evening!" he said cheerfully, "Glad to see you decided to get up. The sun will be going back down soon."

"We need to establish some ground rules here, Mc-Cullough. I hate cheery people before I've had my second cup of coffee. I especially hate cheery *whistling* people."

With a deft hand, he stirred milk into the eggs. "It's only early to you. I've already fed and groomed the horses, mucked out the stables—"

"I know, I know. And chopped a cord of wood, slopped the hogs and planted a field of hay."

Luke paused in his chores and waved a fork in the air. "You know, they say that people who are grumpy in the morning aren't getting enough—"

"L-uuke," she protested, "it's too early for sexual innuendo."

"I was referring to vitamins," he said innocently. "Why don't you have some coffee?"

Anne took a mug from a rack on the counter and poured herself a cup. Carrying it over to the table, she inhaled deeply and took a cautious sip. Mmm. Perfect.

She eyed her host with a new appreciation. Tall, dark, rakishly good-looking, reliable *and* he made coffee. What more could you want in a man?

Well, she could think of one more attribute, she thought, giving the well-filled seat of his jeans an appreciative look. *Now, stop that.* Hadn't she told herself no more fantasizing about Luke McCullough's silky touch on her body? No more tingly images of running her fingers through his shock of thick, dark hair. No more memories of his lips finding hers and—

"Hello, hello. Earth to Anne. Anybody home?"

"What?" she growled, embarrassed that her randy thoughts might have been reflected on her face.

"Are you thinking about sex again?"

She threw a teaspoon at him.

Ducking easily, he grinned. "Maybe you'd better have that second cup of coffee."

A few moments later, Luke set a heaping plate of crisp bacon and scrambled eggs in front of her, then lowered himself into a chair across the table. His own plate was impressively filled, as well.

"I don't eat breakfast," Anne muttered.

"Start. That's one of my ground rules. You need to be sharp and well nourished. As my grandmother used to say, *mangia, mangia*. Eat, eat."

Anne picked up a forkful of creamy scrambled eggs. "You're Italian? With a name like McCullough?"

"I did have two parents, you know. My mother, whose maiden name was Anna De Luca, by the way, was the first of her family born in the States. All the others were straight from the old country."

"Where were you raised?"

"Philadelphia. South Philly to be exact."

"We were practically neighbors. I'm from New Jersey."

He crunched a piece of bacon. "I know."

Anne came blasting back to earth. Of course he knew. He'd probably read a thick file telling everything about her. For a few moments she'd been able to forget why they were here together. Forget the terror that had been stalking her for the past few days. Forget that they weren't sharing a cozy breakfast as lovers.

"Anne? Are you all right?"

"I'm fine," she said, pushing back her plate. "Thanks for breakfast. It was delicious."

Luke frowned. "Did I say something wrong?"

"Of course not."

"Oh, it's one of those if-you-don't-know-what's-wrong-I'm-not-going-to-tell-you routines."

"No, really. Nothing's wrong. I just remembered, that's all."

Luke didn't have to ask what she'd suddenly recalled. It was written all over her ingenuous face. She was remembering the attack last night. First on Luke's agenda today was to get that syringe he'd found on her bedroom floor to the lab in Phoenix. Although no doubt the results would show a lethal, but virtually untraceable poison.

He had to admit one thing. Despite her soft, womanly exterior, this little lady was tough as shoe leather. The rattlesnake alone would have sent most civilians into shock. Not Anne. Then that brutal attack last night. Sure, she'd been shaken up a little, but this morning she was her old, feisty self.

He pushed his plate aside and leaned back in his chair. "Have you heard from the police this morning," Anne asked.

"Diaz phoned about an hour ago."

"Have they located Agent Spears?"

Luke's eyes darkened. "No. They gave his car a thorough going-over this morning. No sign of a struggle. Whatever happened to him, didn't happen in his car."

"I just don't understand it," Anne murmured. "He told me that he was going to stick like glue to me until this mess was over. If this horror story ever ends, that is."

"It'll end," he assured her. He only hoped they were both still alive when it did.

Suddenly restless, anxious to do *something*, Anne drummed out a tattoo on the tabletop with her fingertips. "Last night, you said we'd plan our strategy this morning. So let's get a game plan together. What's on your agenda and what can I do?''

Luke carried their empty plates to the sink and poured fresh coffee into their mugs. Dropping back into the chair across the table, he stared at her for a long minute.

"Anne, you've taken a lot the past couple days and come through like a trooper."

"Uh-oh. I sense more wonderful news," she said with more than a hint of sarcasm.

Luke's black eyebrows dipped in a worried frown. "Not really news. More like an idea . . . something that's been nibbling at me all night. This might be painful for you, but I have to talk with you about it."

Taking another sip of coffee to give herself time to assimilate his ominous words, Anne finally leaned back in her chair. "Let me have it."

"It's about Gardner's death."

"If you're going to tell me that it probably was murder, I've already figured that out."

Luke ran a fingertip along the rim of his mug. "No, it's not that. Not exactly. As I understand it, Gardner's body was never recovered?"

Anne grimaced. "That's right."

"And Gardner comes from a fairly wealthy background?"

"Exceedingly. He didn't have to work nights at the cafeteria to get through Harvard. But what's the point?"

Luke combed his hair with his fingertips. "This is just a theory, you understand."

"Just spit it out."

"Okay, try this scenario on for size. Anne, suppose your old boyfriend *didn't* die in that explosion. What if he set up some kind of phony accident so that his death would make headlines?"

Picking up Luke's train of thought, she continued, "And William could go away somewhere and live quite nicely on Daddy's millions—without having to look over his shoulder all the time."

"Exactly."

Anne considered the possibility. That was precisely the type of diabolical scheme William would devise. "It's a theory certainly worth exploring."

Luke nodded, excitement shining in his eyes. "Let me add some thickener to that plot. Suppose that instead of staging this so-called accident to get Riczini off his tail, Gardner planned this whole thing with The Boss's approval."

"I don't quite follow you. Why should Riczini let William off scot-free?"

Luke stood up and began pacing the kitchen. "This is all supposition, of course, but remember, Riczini has been out of the country for two years. His organization has fallen apart. I imagine his money is running low, and legal fees aren't cheap for lawyers like the ones he hires."

Anne's quick mind sped ahead. "So if William got Daddy-Dearest to donate a sizable sum to the August Riczini Scholarship Fund—"

"That's right! The Boss would be killing two birds with one stone, so to speak. William wouldn't be able to testify at his trial, because, theoretically, he'd be dead. And, second, there'd be some badly needed cash flowing into the Riczini coffers."

Luke pulled out a chair and straddled it across from Anne once again. "But here comes the tricky part. The part that worries me. You're still a fly in Riczini's ointment."

"We already knew that—whether or not William's really dead."

"Yeah. But remember how I've been saying that Scorpion had to have an accomplice?"

Anne paled as Luke's meaning became clear. "You think that William's here. That he's helping Scorpion to kill me?"

Luke looked away from the sudden agony in her deep brown eyes. "I'm saying it's a possibility."

For a long moment, neither of them spoke. Then Anne's voice, soft and fragile, broke the silence. "Last night—the man who was in my room. I...I didn't mention it earlier because it was only an impression, but...but I felt like there was something familiar about him."

Luke's eyes narrowed. "Could it have been Gardner?"

She looked up at him, her wan face blank, her eyes glimmering with unspoken pain. "It was nothing I could put a finger on, but I felt as if I knew my attacker. Everything was so fast—so sudden. But that man last night was about the same build as William."

Suddenly, Luke couldn't stand to look at the anguish in her eyes any longer. That jerk she'd been engaged to had already destroyed her life. It would be worse, much worse if she believed that a man she'd once loved was now trying to kill her.

Reaching across the table, he took her trembling hand in his. "Okay. We've decided that Gardner's being alive and on the scene is a possibility. Not a probability. The odds are that he's actually fish bait in the Atlantic Ocean."

Anne gulped as an acrid wave of bile rose in her throat at Luke's graphic description.

"If he did make an unholy alliance with The Boss, I still wouldn't want to be in his shoes," Luke offered. "Revenge is a powerful motivator, and Gardner was responsible for Riczini's going down in the first place."

"And me. I called the authorities. I talked William into turning state's evidence."

The living-room clock chimed and Luke glanced at his watch. "Good grief, it's already one o'clock! The whole day's going to be shot if we don't get a move on pretty soon."

"So, what's the game plan?" she asked.

"Well, I've got a few more people to call. Maybe I can get a line on Scorpion's movements."

"What am I going to do?" If he thought he was going to leave her home crocheting doilies, he had another thought coming. Anne was prepared to explain her point of view, in very firm terms, when he surprised her with his next suggestion.

"You said you could handle a gun. I'm going to give you one and station you back at your house for a few hours."

"Why?"

"To wait for the repairmen. I've contacted the phone company, and they're sending someone out to fix your phone lines. I've already called a glazier to replace the windows and patio door and I've also called a locksmith to come out and install deadbolts. I think iron grilles on the windows and patio door would be a good idea, as well."

"I'm not going to live like a convict behind bars."

"Then you'll stay here with me."

"I'll stay where I please."

"Anne, why are you so hostile all of a sudden? You know I'm only trying to help you."

She chewed on her lower lip. "I feel so darned helpless, Luke. If there was just something constructive I could do to help myself."

"There is. Don't you have a contact point in Washington? Someone to call in case of an emergency?"

"Yes, they gave me an emergency phone number."

"Then I want you to place that call. They should know what's going on. I've already reported Spears as missing to the bureau, but you should let the witness protection boys know he's disappeared. Give them his description and find out if he was really the person they dispatched to keep an eye on you. In all likelihood, the bureau has already started the ball rolling based on my phone call. But I'm in a totally different section from the men you've dealt with; and protecting you until this current threat is over is really within someone else's purview. I imagine they'll send out another agent, probably two. One to check into Spears's disappearance and one to watch over you.''

Just what she needed, Anne thought, two more strange men to show up. She already had enough strangers in her life. First Luke, then Dan Nevill, then Wally Spears.

They all had credible stories, but one of them might have tried to kill her. If only she could just put a face to this blank horror.

Anne looked across the table at Luke's guileless face. By saying he was from a different section, he'd complicated any possibility of her checking his identity. Was he truly an agent? Or a very clever, very careful hit man? Like the notorious Scorpion. No! She refused to believe that he could be anything other than the gentle protector he'd already proven himself to be.

She wouldn't even want to live if Luke turned out to be the hit man. Anne had accepted a lot in her life, but she simply refused to cast Luke in that role. He would never betray her. Never.

Chapter Eight

By late afternoon, the last pane of glass had been replaced, and Elaine was helping Anne sweep up the debris. Wiping a strand of platinum hair from her eyes, Elaine stuffed the broom into the closet and plopped down into a kitchen chair.

"Whew! I'm not used to all this manual labor."

Anne opened the refrigerator door. "How about a soda?"

"Sounds divine. Diet if you have it."

"Ice?"

"Nah, just give me the can if it's cold." Elaine reached for the can, then pushed it back. "You didn't open it. I have to watch my fingernails, you know." She waved her incredibly long hot-pink fingertips.

Anne chuckled and popped open the two cans, then took a seat across from her friend. "You had bright red nails yesterday. What do you do, change the polish hourly?"

"Depends on what I'm wearing," Elaine said defensively. "You know, honey, it wouldn't hurt you to pamper yourself a little. Get a manicure. And you should wear your hair down—men love long gorgeous hair like yours. Especially now that you've got Luke McHunk hanging around drooling over your shoulder."

Anne lifted her can to her lips and took a long draft of cola. "There is absolutely nothing between Luke and me," she said archly.

"Yeah, and if you buy that line, I've got this snowplow I'll sell you."

Anne laughed, imagining anyone owning a snowplow in this blazing western Arizona climate.

"You can laugh all you want," Elaine continued, "but I've got eyes. I saw how he was looking at you, all protective and menacing. Like a male wolf at breeding time."

"That's ridiculous," Anne protested. "We just got thrown together in the middle of an investigation he was on and . . . and he feels an obligation to protect me."

"Baloney. That guy's got it bad and so do you. Trust me—I know about men."

Anne took another sip and ran a fingertip around the rim of the can. "I've been thinking—"

"That's dangerous. I make it a point never to think."

"Be serious a minute, Elaine. You know, last night you heard me tell the police about my past. Yet you didn't act shocked or even surprised."

Elaine emptied her soda and stood up. "Honey, nothing surprises me anymore. I gotta get going."

"No, wait a minute."

With a frown, Elaine sat back down. "I hope this doesn't mean that we're going to be swapping secrets, or something. I've never been much good at girl talk."

Anne reached across the table and took the older woman's hand. "Elaine, all I know about you is that you're a widow and apparently left well off. Tell me about yourself, how you came to Yuma. You have to admit this is a strange place to move to—by choice."

"Are you kidding me? Listen, honey, my husband *did* leave me well off. I guess I didn't tell you he was a lot older than me. And that's why I moved here—I like older men and this town is crawling with them in the winter.''

"But where did you move from? Do you have any children?''

"What—are you writing a book? Oh, wonderful, here's Mr. Gorgeous in the flesh.'' Elaine pointed as Luke appeared on the patio, inspecting the workmanship of the glazier and locksmith.

Anne got up and unlocked the door for him. "Did you find out anything?''

Luke shook his head. "Not a thing. Seems our quarry, Scorpion, has completely dropped out of sight. Oh, hi, Elaine, didn't see you sitting there. Got another soda, Anne?''

"Sure.'' She had just handed him a can when the telephone rang. Anne picked up the receiver. "Hello? Oh, Mr. Farmer, how are you doing?''

She felt a jolt of guilt, suddenly remembering she'd told the old gentleman she was going to invite him over during the weekend. That conversation seemed so long ago. But how was he to know that her entire life was crumbling around her ears? Actually, maybe an impromptu barbecue wouldn't be a bad idea. Mr. Farmer, Luke, Elaine. It would certainly help take her mind off her troubles for a time. Besides, there was safety in numbers.

"Mr. Farmer, I was just thinking... Luke and Elaine are here right now, why don't you come over and we'll cook out on the grill?''

His voice, suddenly frail and quavery, answered. "No. I'm not feeling too well. The main reason I called, Miz Farraday, I need to talk to you.''

"Well, why don't you come over?''

"No! Somebody might see me. Can you keep a secret? It's very important.''

A feeling of dread swept over her. Whatever the elderly man wanted to confide in her, Anne instinctively knew that it was something she wouldn't welcome. She turned away from two pairs of questioning eyes and looked out the patio door, watching the tranquil turquoise water in the pool. Taking a deep breath, she said quietly, "Yes, of course I can. What is it?"

"I don't want to tell you over the phone. Just that it has to do with the trouble at your house last night. I don't rightly know what to think or who to trust. So I'd be beholden if you didn't mention this to anybody."

"All right."

"Good. I feel better already. Can you come over soon's your company leaves?"

Anne's breath quickened. Could Mr. Farmer's information have something to do with Luke? "Yes, that will be fine."

"And Miz Farraday?"

"Yes?"

"I, uh, don't rightly know if what I've got to tell means anything. I mean, there could be a logical explanation."

"I understand."

"Just don't say a word to anybody until we talk. Okay?"

"Certainly. Thanks for calling."

Anne slowly replaced the receiver and turned around. Luke and Elaine were watching her with curiosity.

Luke spoke first. "What was that all about? You look like you've just seen a ghost."

"Oh, nothing important."

"It was that old man from down the street, wasn't it? Mr. Farmer?" Elaine asked.

"Yes. He was just calling to see if I was all right. I guess he saw the police car here last night."

"At four o'clock in the morning?" Elaine snorted. "What was the old busybody doing up at that hour?"

Anne shrugged and sat down again at the table. "It doesn't really matter. You know, I'm getting kind of tired. I think I'd like to take a little nap."

Elaine jumped up and tossed their empty containers into the recycling bin. "Well *I* have a hot date tonight, so I need to go get beautiful. Are you leaving, Luke?"

"In a minute."

She patted Anne's shoulder. "Well, for pity's sake, let the poor girl get some rest. She looks like she didn't get a wink of sleep last night, you naughty boy."

To Anne's complete amazement, a flush of bright red crept up Luke's neck. And to think she was half suspecting him of being her attacker. It was laughable. Luke was special. Warm, honest, caring. He was…Luke. Whatever Mr. Farmer saw, or thought he saw, certainly had nothing to do with Luke.

"Oh, my, is this man a modern wonder," Elaine gushed. "Sexy as hell and doesn't know it. Amazing."

"Goodbye, Elaine," Anne said pointedly.

"Oh. Guess I wore out my welcome, huh, kiddo? I don't have to have the door slam on my rear. Bye, guys."

With a final pat at her perfectly coiffed platinum hair, she whirled out of the room. A moment later, they heard the front door shut behind her.

Luke was the first to break the silence. "Whew, a little of that woman goes a long way."

Anne laughed. "She doesn't mean anything by it. It's just her way."

Luke caught his breath as her rich laughter filled the air. He'd never heard anything quite like it. Anne's laughter was like a happy song. Bright. Tinkly. Filling the space between them with a lighthearted melody. This woman should laugh more often. She deserved days brimming with laughter…and nights overflowing with love. Someday she would be free from this hell, and she'd share her wonderful gift of laughter with some lucky man. A pain shot through his gut as Luke realized that he wouldn't be the man to share her times of joy. He'd used up his quota of happy.

He reached across the table and tilted her chin with his forefinger. "You should laugh more often, Anne."

"I, uh, what do you mean?"

"I mean you're too serious. Too sad." He wanted to pick her up and whisk her away to a paradise where there was no fear. Where there was no past, only a future.

His fingertip trailed up, tracing the shape of her mouth, touching the tiny spot at the corner where sometimes the tiniest dimple appeared. He wanted to pull her into his arms, taste her mouth, feel her softness curl into him.

But he had sworn to protect her, he couldn't allow himself to lose his equilibrium.

Pulling back, he cleared his throat. "So, did you get through to Washington?"

"Yes. The description I gave them of Wally Spears matches the agent who was sent out here. What could have happened to him?"

He looked at her for a long, hard moment. God, all this worry and fear were starting to tell on her. Oh, she was still a knockout, but there were pale blue circles under her eyes. Worry and fear had etched tiny lines between her eyes. And it wasn't only fear for herself—he could see her concern for Spears mirrored in her soulful eyes.

Luke frowned. To his way of thinking, only one thing could cause a good agent to desert his post. Although the Yuma Police forensics team hadn't found any traces of blood in the unmarked car, Luke didn't think it likely they'd see Agent Spears alive again.

Not wanting to give Anne anything else to worry about, he changed the subject. "Are you coming back over to my place tonight?"

Again, Anne surprised him with that inner core of forged steel. Facing him directly, she searched his face for the truth. "You think Wally Spears is dead, don't you?"

After only a moment's hesitation, he nodded. "I can't think of any other explanation for his disappearance."

She thrust her chin forward, only the slight quiver of her bottom lip betraying the depth of her emotions. "We can't give up hope. He was—he *is*—a nice man. And there seems to be a real shortage of nice men lately. Present company excluded," she added rapidly.

Luke didn't want to offer her false hope, so he said nothing. For all her determination, all her true courage, Anne was still an innocent in his world. He only hoped she could keep some of that innocence . . . and her life.

Instead, he picked up the thread of his earlier question. "Are you going to come back with me? I really don't want to leave you alone until this is over."

She sighed, the dark sadness returning to cloud her eyes. "*If* it's ever over. But I can't hide out in your shadow forever, Luke. I'll have to open The Book Nook on Monday. I should have opened today—Saturday is my busiest day."

"I know, but until we get this creep in custody, I just don't want to take any chances." He didn't want to remind her that William had been "safely" out on the open sea when he was killed. *If* he was killed. Scorpion wouldn't hesitate to put a few sticks of dynamite in the bookshelves if he thought that was his only option. Luke wanted to thoroughly comb that bookstore before she reopened it. There was something fishy about that "lawyer" showing up the other day.

He looked up at Anne. She was drawn, agitated. Maybe it *would* be best if she stayed in her own home. She'd be more comfortable with her own things, feel more in control. It wouldn't take him long to give the horses fresh water and hay. He could throw his own gear together and be back within an hour.

The idea of spending another night with Anne—knowing she was only a heartbeat away—rekindled that fire in his loins. The one that was threatening to break into a full-scale conflagration.

Quickly outlining his plan, he stood up and walked around to stand behind her chair. "I'm going to check all the locks on the windows, then go get my stuff. I should be back within an hour."

Anne looked at the clock and tilted back her head to gaze at Luke, her eyes wide with innocence. "I seem to recall a certain man inviting me out to dinner tonight."

Damn! Now that Scorpion had declared himself, so to speak, Luke was leery of taking Anne out in public. Scorpion could take one quick shot and disappear in the crowd. He was an expert at taking full advantage of the panic that always ensued whenever there was a public shooting.

Luke leaned over and kissed the smooth skin of her forehead. "A dinner I promised you, and a dinner you shall have! For you, my special lady, Chef Luke shall prepare his world-famous—or is it infamous?—fettuccine Alfredo. With hot, crunchy parmesan garlic bread and a robust Chianti that will knock your knickers off."

"Never mind my knickers, just feed me."

"Spoken like a true gourmand. All right, I'll have to stop at the grocery store, so add another forty-five minutes to my E.T.A." He glanced at his wristwatch. "Shall we dine at eight? On the patio?"

"Sounds good. Shall we dress?"

He leaned over until his mouth was close to her ear, his right arm encircling her body just below her breasts. With an evil leer in his voice, he whispered, "Dress? And spoil the mood I hope to create? I should say not! Haven't I ever told you about the old Italian custom that says a first dinner should be shared in the buff?"

"In that case, maybe we'd better not dine on the patio." Anne pushed his hand away and rose to her feet.

"You're right. How about a more ... intimate atmosphere. Say ... your bedroom?"

"Another old Italian custom?"

"*Sí, signorina.*"

Anne crossed her arms and frowned. "Haven't I ever told you about the old Irish custom that says a fair maiden should drop-kick a wolf who makes lewd suggestions?"

Holding his palm over his heart, a wounded expression on his face, he said earnestly, "You can't blame a guy for trying. After all, it's in my blood."

Putting her hand behind his back, she gave him a gentle push toward the door. "Okay, Romeo, be on your way."

"Ah, Romeo, one of the other great Italian lovers. There was also Lothario and Luigi the Baker. I come from a long line of great Italian lovers."

"I think the Irish part kind of offsets the Latin-lover part, doesn't it?"

He stopped in the doorway, clutching the frame to keep her from forcibly ejecting him. "Oh, no! The Irish adds mysticism, poetry."

"And blarney."

"You are a hard woman to seduce, Anne Farraday."

"Next time, let me know when you're trying to seduce me and I'll pay more attention."

He clutched his chest with all the theatrical fervor of an opera star. "You wound me, fair maiden. To the quick."

She laughed, thoroughly enjoying his boyish sense of fun. William had never been sure enough of himself to be silly or playful. "Take your wounded 'quick' and go fetch my dinner."

After Luke had finally left, blowing extravagant kisses to her as he backed out the door, Anne took a quick shower and changed into a navy-blue cotton jumpsuit. As she wrenched the zipper up, she had the irreverent thought that if nothing else, this tight jumpsuit should keep the randy Mr. McCullough out of her knickers!

Winding her hair into a loose, swirly topknot, she grabbed her house keys and stepped into a pair of serviceable blue canvas deck shoes.

Mr. Farmer had hinted that someone might be watching her house. Maybe by sneaking through Elaine's backyard, she could make it to Mr. Farmer's unseen.

Double-checking to see that all the locks were secured, she put her house keys into her pocket and slipped out the patio door. No lights were on at Elaine's. Apparently, she'd already left for her date. Anne stopped by the small gate that divided their properties, listening for any unusual sounds. Where *did* Elaine go on all these hot dates, she wondered. Yuma wasn't known for its nightlife. In fact, she'd once heard a visitor proclaim that he'd "done" the entire town in less than an hour.

When she heard no odd noises, Anne opened the gate and slid through. Elaine's house, in fact, the entire neighborhood, was as still as a crypt in an abandoned churchyard.

Noiselessly, she crossed Elaine's patio and made her way to the side gate on the far side of her neighbor's house. Dusk was deepening in the sky and a spectacular burnt-orange desert sunset was just fading on the horizon. Anne realized that she'd grown to love these summer nights, when the air cooled down and the sky was emblazoned with splashes of vivid color.

Once she reached the front yard, Anne hid behind a large cypress tree and stared up and down the empty street. Only Agent Spears's empty car stood like a silent sentinel, watching her movements.

Keeping close to the oleander hedge that lined her side of the street, she quickly traversed the short distance to Mr. Farmer's small frame house.

Like Elaine's, his home was also cloaked in darkness. Usually, she could see the flickering light from his television reflected in the living-room window. For the first time since The Trouble, Anne forgot her own worries, her own concerns, long enough to think about her elderly neighbor's lonely existence. Why had she never stopped to chat with him? Would it have killed her to spend a few moments listening to his war stories?

If this mess ever ended—no, *when* this mess was over, she vowed she'd make time for him. And for other new friends. She was still alive, and she was going to enjoy life again.

Straightening her shoulders, she marched up Mr. Farmer's front walk and pounded on his door.

She waited a few moments and tried again. Still no answer.

Maybe he was around back, enjoying the dazzling sunset—where any sensible person would be, if they weren't hiding from hired killers. She sighed, imagining for a moment that she was one of the "real" people who led normal lives, cooking on the grill while the kids played tag in the quiet streets.

She'd never know the simple pleasure of that kind of life, so she may as well stop dwelling on it.

Anne followed a path of concrete stepping stones around to Mr. Farmer's rear patio. The old wooden porch swing was empty.

Again, she felt that pang of guilt. Was this how he passed time, sitting in his swing, recalling the old days? How horrible to be alone.

But he was no more alone than she was. And when Luke left, she'd be even lonelier.

Stifling that unbidden reminder, she crossed the sandstone patio and knocked at the sliding glass door. "Mr. Farmer, are you there? It's Anne Farraday."

The house resonated with silence.

Pressing her face against the glass, she looked into the dim dining room. She could make out the old walnut dining set that was probably an antique now. Mr. Farmer had bought it for his wife as a wedding present. Even through the gloom, she could see the glossy shine on its surface. Mr. Farmer was a fastidious housekeeper. It was as if by keeping his wife's treasures sparkling, he could keep her memory alive.

Anne could see nothing out of place, no sign of the old man except...except something white was lying on the floor in the living room. His worn leather recliner was blocking her vision but it looked like a shirtsleeve. He must have dropped it when he was doing his laundry.

As her eyes adjusted to the poor light, she concentrated on that shirtsleeve. Something wasn't quite right. It was as though...as though his arm was still—

"Mr. Farmer!" Anne pulled her house keys from her pocket and used them to rap sharply on the glass door.

The old man didn't stir.

Using her hand to shade her eyes from the sun's last rays, she pressed her nose against the sliding glass door. Panic welled in her throat as her eyes saw and her mind finally digested the horrible sight.

The back of Mr. Farmer's white shirt was soaked in blood.

Chapter Nine

Scorpion leaned back in the shadows of an ancient cotton-wood tree and watched the commotion in front of the old man's house. A team of paramedics wheeled out Nosy Farmer on a stretcher, a white sheet covering him up to the neck. Intravenous bottles clanked above his head as they rushed him to the waiting ambulance. Obviously, the old man was clinging to life.

Still, the situation could be salvaged. Things might be a little stickier now. The timetable would have to be advanced.

Slipping deeper into the shadows, the assassin disappeared into the fading twilight. Anne Farraday's time was short now. Very short.

WHEN LUKE TURNED ON TO Anne's street, his heart nearly stopped. The small cul de sac was lit up like a carnival midway. Red, blue and amber lights were flashing; and the sidewalk was lined with spectators.

A cold chill raced up his spine as he pulled the pickup into her driveway. His mind screamed with the thought that during his absence, Scorpion had gotten to Anne.

There were so many emergency vehicles, squad cars, ambulances, a full-size fire engine, that it was impossible to locate the center of the commotion. Luke jumped from the truck and raced up Anne's sidewalk.

Only after pounding on her locked door for a full minute did the truth start to penetrate his fear-numbed mind. The police, paramedics and firemen weren't at Anne's. The house was dark and empty.

Luke ran back out into the center of the street in time to see emergency technicians hauling a gurney from the back of Mr. Farmer's house. Hardly aware of his movements, Luke covered the short distance between the two homes in a few long strides.

His breath was harsh, stinging in his chest when he spotted Officer Diaz and his partner, Almon, waving bystanders aside so the ambulance could depart. Luke ran up to Diaz and grabbed his arm. "Anne! What's happened to Anne? Tell me, man."

With a calm motion, the patrolman pulled Luke's hand from his sleeve and took him by the elbow, guiding him to the relative quiet of the sidewalk. "Easy, McCullough. Nothing's happened to your girlfriend. It's the old man."

"Farmer?"

"Yeah. Ms. Farraday's right over there."

Luke swiveled his head, following the arc of Diaz's pointing finger. Anne was huddled beneath a cottonwood tree, her arms crossed, hugging herself. Her face was pale, she looked frightened. Worried. But unharmed.

Luke felt like a condemned man who was granted amnesty at the eleventh hour. Anne was safe.

Taking a deep breath of fresh, calming air, he trotted across the yard to join her. "Anne! What's happened?"

He drew her close, and she dropped her head on his shoulder. "It...it's Mr. Farmer. I found him on the living-room floor. He wasn't moving. There was blood everywhere."

"Are you all right?"

"Y-yes. I ran home and called for help. Mr. Farmer's doors were all locked, and I didn't know what else to do."

"You did exactly the right thing, Anne. There's nothing more anyone could do."

"I wish I knew what happened. I tried to talk to the police, but they were too busy to answer my questions."

"Why don't you go home and I'll see what I can find out."

She shook her head. "No, I'll wait here."

Luke grasped her lightly by the shoulders. "Look, you've had a hell of a shock—and it's certainly not your first in these past few days. You should sit down before you collapse. Besides, Diaz and Almon might talk to me more readily if I'm alone. Fraternal ties. All that cop bonding."

Anne managed a reluctant smile. "Maybe you're right. But you'll let me know right away?"

"Of course. You stay in the house until I come back. Understand?"

Anne hesitated. She didn't want to leave poor Mr. Farmer. What had happened to the old man? An accident? Had he fallen, perhaps hit his head on a sharp corner of the wooden table she found him lying near? But she knew that couldn't explain all that blood.

No, Mr. Farmer's misfortune was undoubtedly related to the information he'd been so eager to impart to her. Privately.

Much as she didn't want to believe it, another innocent person had been ensnared in this nightmare.

"Anne?" Luke's voice broke through. Speaking softly, he gave her a gentle shove. "Please, go back to the house."

She nodded and walked away.

After the ambulance pulled out, blue lights flashing and siren screaming, Luke crossed the street and spoke quietly with the police. Officers Diaz and Almon had filed a report with headquarters after the break-in at Anne's house and Agent Spears's eerie disappearance. Someone had had the good sense to check out Luke's story. As a result, the entire Yuma police force was ready and willing to assist Luke in any way he needed.

According to their preliminary investigation, it appeared the octogenarian had been struck from behind with a blunt, wooden instrument. Wood fragments had been imbedded in his wound. Sounded to Luke as though somebody had thumped the old man a hell of a blow with a baseball bat. Still one of the most effective weapons for close-range assaults.

Officer Diaz was the first to give voice to Luke's concern. "Do you think there's any connection between the attack on Ms. Farraday and the one on Mr. Farmer?"

Leveling a steady gaze at the patrolman, Luke answered, "How many random attacks do you normally average on the same street within a twenty-four-hour period?"

"None," Diaz mumbled. "This is a quiet part of town. We don't get two calls a year out this way."

"Yeah, and those are usually to pull somebody's kitty off the roof," Officer Almon added.

"How's the motel search going for our so-called attorney Nevill?" Luke asked.

"I talked with the detectives this morning," Diaz replied. "So far, they haven't turned up a thing."

Luke raised a skeptical eyebrow. "Nothing? How many motels do you have in this town?"

Almon shrugged. "Three dozen, maybe."

"And the closest town is over sixty miles away. Do you really think he would have stayed in El Centro if his business was here?"

Almon, clearly not an innovative thinker, shrugged again. "Maybe the guy really was a big-shot lawyer from L.A. Maybe he went back to California after he talked to Ms. Farraday."

Diaz snorted and elbowed his partner good-naturedly. "Sure, and maybe my wife's gonna cut up her credit cards. No, that guy's still in town holed up in one of the trailer parks or somewhere. Unless—"

He broke off, a startled look on his face as he stared over Luke's left shoulder.

Turning slowly, Luke gazed into the misty darkness. Although twilight had completely fallen, he could make out the perfect pale oval of Anne's face as she stepped from the shadow of an old cottonwood tree.

In a few steps he covered the distance between them and roughly grasped her shoulders, lightly shaking her. "Anne, I told you to go home. Why didn't you listen to me?"

He couldn't see her eyes in the darkness but he could feel her tense beneath his touch.

Tugging away from him, she said softly, but with steely determination, "This is my life, Luke. I have a right to know what dangers I'm facing. This madman—this Scorpion—is trying to murder *me*. Not you."

He stood, bewildered, as she walked with stiff shoulders to the squad car where the two officers were watching the interplay with obvious interest.

Luke shoved his hands through his hair. The woman was right. He was an overbearing, obnoxious jackass. Even if she was kind enough not to say it. And she was right on another count, the more informed she was, the better prepared she'd be to protect herself.

With a helpless flap of his hands against his thighs, he joined the others.

Anne spoke first. "Officer Diaz, I think you were about to make a point."

He shrugged. "Not really. All I was saying was that this guy—your lawyer friend—seems to have melted into the woodwork. We've checked every motel and flophouse within a fifty-mile radius. This perp's just flat disappeared."

"Unless," Anne said, her soft voice somehow holding more power than the heavy masculine tones, "unless he has a confederate helping him to hide out."

The three men exchanged surprised glances. Luke growled beneath his breath. Anne's observation was something they should have thought of earlier. It also fit with his private theory that Gardner might be alive and well. But Anne had to be the one to put it together. She was one hell of a woman. Beauty, courage and brains.

"Good point," Luke said. "That would explain a lot. The bad news is, that if Scorpion's hiding out in a private residence, we don't have a prayer of finding him."

"So we'll have to flush him out," Anne said nonchalantly. "Set a trap. Use me as bait."

Diaz shook his dark head. "That's too dangerous."

Luke quickly agreed.

"I'm not going to just sit around and let this creep pick his time and place to kill me!"

Resisting an urge to wrap a protective arm around her, a gesture he was sure she wouldn't appreciate at the moment, Luke had to admit that she had a valid argument. If he were Scorpion's quarry, he'd damn sure feel the same way. But he wasn't going to allow anyone to take unnecessary chances with Anne's life. No matter how much she protested. "Later, if we have to, we can talk about some kind of a trap. Right now, I think we should examine the possibility of Scorpion's having a partner."

"Have you had any indications that your killer might not be working alone?" Diaz asked.

"No," Luke admitted. "And it's certainly not his modus operandi. Still, it would explain why you haven't been able to find him."

Officer Almon rolled his eyes and tipped his hat back with his thumb. "Jeez, now you're trying to tell us that a *team* of hired guns are after that lady? Give me a break, McCullough. This shyster, Nevill—if he *is* your gunman, probably found some barfly to shack up with. We can't check out every gin joint in town, you know."

Luke hated to admit it, but the officer had a good point. In fact, it was almost routine with some hired killers to find a willing "girlfriend" the moment they came into a new town. But nothing in Scorpion's dossier led them to believe that he'd established this pattern. Still, in a town this small, maybe he'd altered his normal routine for this hit.

He hoped so. It was daunting enough trying to track down Scorpion, let alone worrying about *two* thugs lurking out there waiting for a chance to kill Anne.

Anne's quiet voice broke into his thoughts. "Poor Mr. Farmer."

She sounded so guilt-ridden, Luke could resist no longer. Slipping an arm around her slender waist, he pulled her to his side. "There's no real proof that the attack on Mr. Farmer was connected to you."

"There's something I didn't tell you." Her voice had dropped to a near whisper. All three men drew closer to catch her next words. "He called me this afternoon."

"What did he want?"

"He wanted me to come to his house this evening. He said he had something important to tell me. About the assault on me last night."

Luke exploded. "For crying out loud! Why didn't you tell me this sooner?"

For a long moment, she didn't answer. When she did, her voice was unexpectedly strong. Direct. "Because he asked me not to. He told me not to trust anyone."

Officer Diaz broke the awkward silence that followed Anne's announcement. "But you didn't find out what he wanted?"

"No. He was on the floor...covered in blood...when I arrived. Looks like he knew something pretty important."

No one seemed to know what to say. The only sound was the scratch of Officer Diaz's pen as he scrawled a notation in his notebook. "I guess that's all we'll need for tonight, then. Unless you have any more surprises for us, Ms. Farraday?"

"No."

In silent accord, Luke and Anne left the officers to complete their investigation and walked toward her house. When they reached the tall, gangly ocotillo cactus beneath the streetlight by her driveway, he stopped and cupped her chin, forcing her to face him. "Anne, there's something we have to get clear. Did you think I told you to stay indoors just because I like the sound of my own voice? Because I like to give orders? No, Anne, I had my reasons and—"

She reared her head back, pulling free. "Which do you think was more likely—that Scorpion was going to take a shot at me in full view of half of the sheriff's department or that knowing everyone was busy outside, he'd be waiting inside?"

Shoving his fists onto his jeaned hips, Luke returned her glare. This was one stubborn woman. And he hated it when she was right. "Did you even lock the door?"

"I never unlocked it."

"Oh." They faced off for another ten seconds until Luke broke the gridlock. "Then I guess I'm being a horse's rump again."

"If the saddle fits..."

He sighed deeply and led the way to the house. Taking the key from her outstretched hand, he unlocked the door. When they were inside, he flipped on the foyer light and bolted the door behind them.

Holding her tenderly by the shoulders, he pulled her close and murmured into her hair. "I'm sorry, Anne. I shouldn't have yelled at you earlier. I... I just got scared when I saw you standing there all alone in the darkness."

"Luke, you can't put me in a steel vault to keep me safe."

"I realize that. But you're going to have to trust me more. This is my business and I'm damned good at it."

She nodded against his chest. "I know that."

He breathed deeply, relief slowly coursing through him. He *had* been scared.

He pulled her closer, as if he could shield her from harm with his body. "Listen, if we keep you fairly confined, then we don't have to constantly check the bushes, your car, your store. If the killer thinks you aren't going to be leaving the house, then we've really narrowed his range of opportunities."

Anne considered his logic, and found it made sense. She nodded her acquiescence. "Okay, I'll stick close to the house. For now."

"Good. Right now I want you to stand right here while I check out the house. Got it?"

"Yes, Luke."

Not quite certain about the sincerity of her sudden capitulation, he nevertheless reluctantly released her and carefully searched the house. When he returned, she was still standing on the exact spot where he'd left her.

He didn't know whether she was actually trying to obey with his order or whether she was gently mocking him. He decided not to ask.

Right now, she was tired and compliant. He had a feeling, a bad feeling, that her innate independence would burst forth when she'd rested. To his amazement, he found that he missed the ornery Anne.

"Okay, Anne, all clear. Come on into the kitchen and I'll fix us some coffee."

While Luke filled the drip pot and measured out the grounds, Anne perched on the edge of a kitchen chair, nibbling on a fingernail. "Luke?"

"Yeah, honey?"

"About Mr. Farmer. Do you think he'll be all right?"

Luke flipped the switch on the coffeemaker and crossed the room to stand behind her. He placed his hands on her shoulders and rubbed gently, as if in doing so he could ease away her troubles. "The paramedics said he was in pretty bad shape, honey, so I don't know. I just don't know."

A single tear traced down her cheek. "I just hate the thought of that sweet old man alone over there, lying on the floor. Maybe in pain."

"I don't think he suffered much, honey. I'm pretty sure that he lost consciousness right away." Luke pressed his lips into the springtime freshness of her hair. He wanted to reassure her, promise her that everything was going to be fine, but, right now, Luke didn't feel very confident. The only thing he knew for sure was that he would protect her with his life.

He only hoped that it didn't come to that.

Pouring two mugs of coffee, he set one in front of her and lifted the other to his lips. "How about if I fix us that dinner now?"

She smiled sadly. "Thanks, but I don't have much of an appetite at the moment. I think I'd like to go to the hospital and see how Mr. Farmer is doing. He doesn't have any relatives nearby. Only a son in Colorado. I guess I should try to reach him."

Luke stood up. "Good idea. Go wash your face and make the phone call while I put the groceries away. Then I'll drive you there."

Anne's somber mood lasted all the way to the hospital where they were told by a rotund Nurse Oliver that the patient was in emergency surgery. Anne gave the soft-spoken nurse what scant personal information she knew about Mr. Farmer. The nurse then directed them to the neurosurgical waiting room and told them that someone would let them know when the operation was over.

"But you folks should probably wait at home," Nurse Oliver clucked like a fretting mother hen. "We'll call you."

"No, thanks, we'll wait here," Anne insisted.

"But it might be hours, honey."

"That's all right."

The heavyset nurse leaned over and patted Anne's hand. "There are a couple of pretty lumpy couches in there, but you're welcome to curl up and take a nap. Just let me know if you'd like some pillows and blankets."

"Thank you. You're very kind." Anne turned away and started in the direction of the waiting room.

"Do you have a cafeteria?" Luke asked.

Nurse Oliver glanced at the wall clock over her head. "I think the grill's already closed but you can get cold sandwiches and coffee. Take that elevator down to level one and turn left."

"Thanks." Draping an arm around Anne's shoulders, he led her to the waiting room. She seemed to take comfort from the warmth of his body.

Inside the brightly lit waiting room, she curled up in the corner of an old, overstuffed sofa and stared off into space.

He wished he had a magical kiss, like the knights and princes in fairy tales, so that he could touch his lips to hers and kiss away all of her problems. At a sudden aching in his hand, Luke looked down. His fist was clenched in helpless rage, the knuckles white with tension.

Realizing he had to maintain his professional detachment, at least to a certain extent, he forced a cheeriness he didn't feel into his voice. "How's about a nice cup of coffee and maybe a yummy hospital sandwich?"

Anne smiled wanly. "Sounds wonderful. Maybe if we're lucky, they'll have some gelatin. Hospitals are big on gelatin."

He sighed dramatically, relieved that her innate sense of humor had returned. "Oh, the demands you make on me, you wench. Sure, today you're satisfied with a bowl of gelatin, but tomorrow you'll want chateaubriand—in Paris!"

"Good idea." She smiled. "It's a date."

Luke didn't want to leave her alone, not even long enough to pick up sandwiches and coffee, but she'd only nibbled at her breakfast and hadn't eaten anything since then. Reaching over to tuck an errant curl behind her ear, he asked, "Will you be okay until I get back?"

She groaned theatrically, resting the back of her hand across her eyes. "I'll count the seconds until your return, but I'll survive."

"Smart ass, woman." He leered at her rounded hip, jutting up so temptingly. "Actually, you have a singularly lovely ass, if you'll forgive the vulgarity."

"I don't. Forgive you, that is. That's a disgusting phrase."

The thoughts that were flitting through his mind regarding Anne's perfectly shaped posterior were anything but disgusting to his way of thinking, but Luke decided this might not be the appropriate time to push it. She'd already thrown a spoon at him this morning, and the only thing nearby was a heavy-looking table lamp. He decided not to risk it.

"I think I'd better go to the cafeteria before I really get into trouble," he said.

"Good idea, McCullough."

He strode out the door, whistling. At least his suggestive teasing had helped bring Anne out of her bleak mood. He only wished he could clear his mind of the provocative images their banter had evoked. Images of Anne lying naked and silky in his arms. Images that were driving his blood pressure up into the danger zone. *Concentrate on the gelatin, McCullough,* he admonished himself sternly.

But there were some very interesting possibilities in a tub full of gelatin.

SHORTLY AFTER midnight, a weary-looking doctor stepped into the waiting room, still dressed in his green surgical scrub suit. "I'm Dr. Laszlo. Are you folks Edwin Farmer's family?"

Anne, who had fallen asleep with her head snuggled against Luke's chest, sat up. "Not family. Just friends."

"I really should be talking with his next of kin."

Luke reached in his pocket and flipped open his identification folder. "This man's injury *is* official business, Doctor. Anything you could tell us would be helpful."

Dr. Laszlo hesitated a moment, then said quietly, "He's hanging on to life by a thread. We won't know anything further until—and if—he regains consciousness."

"When do you estimate that might happen?"

The doctor shrugged. "Not for two or three days at the earliest. He had a pretty severe skull fracture, so it's routine to keep the patient in a drug-induced coma for a period of time after the surgery. Helps keep the swelling in the brain under control.''

Luke stood up and stretched. ''You'll keep us informed? It's urgent that I speak with Mr. Farmer as soon as possible.''

Dr. Laszlo nodded. ''Leave your name and phone number with Nurse Oliver.'' He patted Anne's arm and rose to his feet. ''We'll do our best, Ms. Farraday. He's a tough old buzzard.''

''Thank you, Doctor,'' she murmured. ''I appreciate all your help.''

''If there's nothing else I can do for you folks, guess I'll try to catch some shut-eye.''

''There's just one more thing,'' Luke said. ''I'm going to ask the local police to arrange for a guard outside his room. In the meantime, I'd like you to restrict the people having access to his room to the bare minimum.''

The doctor regarded Luke for a long moment. ''Do you seriously think there'll be another attempt on that man's life?''

''It's certainly a possibility.''

''I'll do what I can, then. Good night, folks.''

''Good night, Doctor.''

Luke turned to Anne. ''Now that we can have some peace about Mr. Farmer, what say we get you home and in bed, Ms. Farraday?''

''Is that another proposition, Mr. McCullough?'' She looked up at him, her eyes wide in feigned innocence. Her hair was mussed and her face flushed from sleep. She looked adorable.

''Don't tempt a starving man, Anne. He might take you up on it.''

Anne was still quiet, but not so morose, on the short ride back to her home. He couldn't imagine what she was going through. She cared about her neighbor and was hurting because he was.

As a special agent, Luke had always stayed outside the periphery of emotion. "Maintaining an objective viewpoint" he'd called it. Only once before had he been personally involved. That was when he became involved with Glenna. Glenna, whose throaty, sexy laugh had gotten past his hard shell of indifference, causing him to momentarily let his guard down. Glenna, who'd paid for his lapse with her life.

Not this time, Luke vowed silently as he parked the car. No matter how much his need for Anne tore at his gut, no matter how much his lips yearned to taste hers, no matter what—he wouldn't lose his objectivity again. Wouldn't let Anne down.

Cautioning her to stay in the car while he checked out the house, Luke inspected the premises, finally satisfying himself that no one had entered during their absence.

Standing in the entry, he motioned her out of the car.

Anne slipped out the door and into the house while Luke stood guard, his hand on the gun holstered against his waist. Maybe he was being overprotective, but he wasn't taking anymore chances. This attack on the old man proved to Luke that Scorpion was getting desperate. The assassin had made some mistakes. Luke sensed that Scorpion was rapidly losing control of the situation. Unfortunately, there was no way to forecast what irrational steps an out-of-control killer might take.

After he'd double-locked the front door and checked the remaining points of entry into the house, Luke walked Anne down the hall to her bedroom. He turned on the bedside light and made a production of checking the closet and beneath the bed, hoping his overt actions would make her feel more secure.

She needed a decent night's sleep. She stood beside the bed, staring longingly at the fluffy pillows.

"Have you got a spare blanket and pillow?"

Anne looked up. "Oh, in the hall closet. Where are you going to sleep? I...I don't have a bed in the guest room, only a desk and..." Her voice trailed off, as if she no longer had the energy even to speak.

"Don't worry about me. I'll bunk on the couch."

"Oh, that's so uncomfortable."

"I'll be fine."

He leaned over and brushed his lips against the fading bruise on her temple. "Get some sleep. Things will look better in the morning."

She smiled. "Where have I heard those words before?"

He grinned in response. "And was I right? Didn't everything seem better this morning? It's only the nights that are giving us trouble." In more ways than one, he thought.

"You're an incurable optimist, Luke McCullough."

"Just trust me."

She laughed mirthlessly. "I haven't heard that line since high school. And it didn't inspire trust then, either."

He walked away from the bed, pausing in the doorway. "You're a hard woman to please, Anne Farraday. Now get some sleep before I think of another—infinitely more interesting—way to pass the night."

Anne followed, placing her palm on the inside of the door frame. Leaning around the edge, she whispered to Luke's retreating back. "One of these days, I'm going to take you up on one of your lecherous offers."

"I'll make it worth your while. Trust me."

Luke disappeared into the living room, and she slowly closed the bedroom door.

Anne went into the small bathroom off her bedroom and scrubbed her face and teeth. She pulled her favorite oversize nightshirt from the drawer, put it on, and climbed into bed, expecting to fall asleep before her head touched the pillow.

Instead, she discovered that suddenly she was wide-awake.

Luke was right. She *was* exhausted, yet her mind was like a carousel, spinning round and round. The events of the past few days were like the horses on that carousel, parading past her time and again.

Outside, a cool breeze kicked up and the spindly branches of a palo verde tree scratched against the side of the house.

Was Scorpion out there, even now, waiting for her to drop into slumber?

In the distance, the grumble of thunder echoing across the silent desert was followed by a blinding flash of lightning. The electrical storms so common during the summer had always been one of the best parts of desert living, in Anne's opinion. But tonight, the familiar roar of thunder sent a crackle of fear coursing through her body. The lightning made her jump, reminding her of the brief flash of Luke's gun after he shot the rattlesnake.

Would nothing ever be the same again?

As the storm crept closer, she found herself growing more restless. As though danger were creeping toward her on those jagged currents of electricity.

She glanced at the glowing red numerals on the clock by her bed. Almost one-thirty. Would she ever sleep at night again? Ever feel safe in her own bed?

Yes. The answer came quickly, without hesitation. One person made her feel secure, cosseted. One person could give her the comfort she so desperately needed. The same person she didn't dare take to her bed, for she instinctively knew that if she ever gave herself to Luke, she would lose her heart forever.

A loud clap of thunder jolted her upright.

Almost automatically, as if she were hypnotized and programmed to follow a specific path, she rose slowly from the bed and padded down the hall to the living room. Standing in the arched entryway, she listened to the quiet, even sound of his breathing. She knew he was awake. She knew he was aware of her standing there...wanting him.

"Luke," she whispered.

"Don't do this, Anne." His husky voice was like a caress in the darkness.

"Please, I'm afraid."

"I'm right here, you're perfectly safe."

There was a long hesitation before she spoke again. For a moment, Luke thought she'd returned to her room. "I know I'm safe right now. That's not what I'm afraid of."

He didn't want to ask, but some force stronger than his own will compelled the question. "Then what are you afraid of?"

"I...I'm afraid of never feeling loved again. I'm afraid of spending the rest of my life alone. Untouched. Never even...even knowing what I'd missed. Missing you."

She sensed him stirring on the sofa, then, without a sound, he was standing in front of her.

"You don't know what you're doing. I can't."

"Why? Don't you want me?"

A deep shuddering groan escaped his lips as he pulled her to him. As if in a trance, he raised his fingers to her face, caressed her cheek, then trailed slowly, tantalizingly down her throat. "Want you? I want you like my lungs want air. But more importantly, I want you alive. Safe."

Her voice was soft, a silken promise in the darkness. "I'll always be safe with you. You promised."

He slid his hand to the back of her neck, burrowing it in her thick, auburn tresses. With a force drawn from raw need, his lips sought hers.

Anne sighed, a shimmer of ecstasy circling in the pit of her stomach. So, this is what a kiss was all about. This was the kind of kiss that poets suffered for, that men stormed off to war for and that women waited a lifetime for.

She wrapped her arms around his waist, shivering when she touched his bare flesh. He was clad only in his briefs, and the slight prickle of hair on his legs teased her thighs. The hard, tense planes of his back felt like the finest marble beneath her touch.

His lips pulled away, but her hands moved up his back, delving into his glossy black hair. She drew his mouth back to hers.

His lips were lush, sensual. Incredibly soft against hers. Luke encircled her in his embrace and began kissing her more deeply. Each thrust of his tongue seduced her with its provocative seeking. The taste of him filled her mouth with an aromatic bouquet like a perfectly aged wine. She was drunk, giddy with the feel of him. The sense of him.

His probing continued, finding and filling the hidden valleys of her mouth. Anne's breath lurched painfully in her chest. Her senses reeled crazily, out of control. Anne was hypnotized, a slave to the sweet taste of his mouth.

"Oh, Anne, no, we can't...I can't." Yet even as he spoke, his arms were sliding beneath her hips, pulling her up into his arms.

Her hands crept up his back, holding him close, crushing her aching breasts against his chest. For a moment, she thought her heart had actually taken flight, but it was only Luke, effortlessly carrying her down the hall. Into the bedroom.

As if she were a precious ornament made of fragile spun glass, he tenderly lowered her to the bed. His teasing, taunting mouth brushed the proud nubs of her nipples. She whimpered with desire and laced her fingers behind his neck, urging him to her.

A loud crack of thunder, immediately followed by a jagged flash of white-hot light filled the room. Anne felt as charged as that storm. Her need was every bit as strong as that clap of thunder, as powerful and frightening as that jolt of lightning. "Oh, Luke, hold me. Take me."

"Shh, Anne, darling. We . . . we can't do this. Not now." His breath was hot against her neck.

Anne didn't know where her wanton need came from. Never before had she experienced this almost animal lusting, this horribly desperate need to make the world go away. Just for tonight.

"Luke, don't talk. Please, just . . . just be with me tonight. I won't ask for anything tomorrow. But I need you so desperately tonight."

"Oh, God, Anne. I'm only a man. This isn't the right time. I promised myself that—"

She cupped his face between her hands and stared up into his silvery eyes. He wanted her, it was evident in the fire burning in his gaze. She couldn't be wrong. And if she was, she'd live with that tomorrow. If she even had a tomorrow.

Slowly, deliberately, she pulled his head down until his lips were only a heartbeat from hers. "Don't leave me tonight, Luke. I'm begging you."

Pulling free from her grasp, he plunged his hands into the tumbled mass of her curls. With startling ferocity, he lowered his head and captured her mouth with his.

After a long, breathless moment, Luke drew back and stared into her eyes. "Anne, I made a promise to myself. That I wouldn't give in to my selfish need until you were safe. But, God help us, we've gone too far to stop now. I've never wanted—no, never *had* to have a woman like I have to have—"

He broke off suddenly, burying his lips in the downy softness of her coppery hair. "Dear, sweet Anne, I've wanted you, ached for the feel of you for so long . . ."

"I know," she murmured. "I told myself I couldn't get involved, and I understand that we may only have this night. But . . . but Luke, let's make it worthwhile."

He lifted his head until his black-fringed eyes, hooded with passion, were looking deep into hers. "Then let's not waste another moment."

Never in his life had he experienced this sense of perfect compatibility. A woman whose body demanded satisfaction with no less urgency than his own. Tomorrow be damned, he had to have her tonight.

At last, when their passion was finally spent, he fell forward, raining gentle kisses on her face. "Oh, dear Lord, Anne. What have we done? What have *I* done? I caught you at a weak moment. When you were so vulnerable. I never meant to take advantage of that—"

"Shh, Luke."

Wriggling until they were resting side by side, she cradled his head against her shoulder, his warm breath only inches from her still-sensitive breast, and ran her fingertips through his thick hair. "Luke, I'm not sure who took advantage of whom. All I know is that we can't think about what we should've done. But if I have to die tomorrow, then I thank you for tonight."

In a sleepy voice, he whispered against the hollow of her throat. "You're a remarkable woman, Anne Farraday. You deserve a stronger man."

"Go to sleep." She lay quietly in the moonlight, feeling the residual pulsing between her thighs, listening to the even rhythm of Luke's breath.

A stronger man? She doubted if one existed. If she'd scoured the earth, looked through every tiny town and large city, Luke McCullough would be the man she would have chosen as her soul mate.

That she'd found him out here in this desert wilderness was almost miraculous. It was also so utterly sad.

Because now that she'd found her perfect man, the one fate had set aside just for her, Anne knew that before long she'd have to let him go.

Chapter Ten

The sun was already high in the sky when Anne awakened. Its shimmering rays were peeking between the slats of the venetian blinds, one bright beam falling maddeningly across her eyes.

Giving in to the languorous warmth, she stretched, feeling like an overfed cat who's been luxuriating for hours in the sun. Mmm, she couldn't recall the last time she'd awakened feeling so invigorated. So deliciously alive.

Then she heard the shower running at full blast in her bathroom. A male voice, a rather off-key baritone, was warbling a barely recognizable version of "Oh, What A Beautiful Morning."

The night before and her unexpected, inexcusable and unbelievably wanton behavior, came rushing back with the force of a raging waterfall. A blush of embarrassment, beet-red and bone-deep, started in her toes and crept up her body until her entire being was suffused with a crimson glow.

Had she gone completely insane?

Luring him into her bedroom? Worse, begging him to make love to her.

Suddenly aware that the shower had stopped, Anne bounded out of bed, startled to find herself totally naked. She never slept in the nude.

At that moment, the connecting door to the bathroom opened and Luke strolled into the bedroom. He stopped in the doorway, tall, tan and totally nude except for a thick white towel draped carelessly across his shoulders. "Good morning! Sleep well?"

Anne yanked the sheet off the bed, clumsily covering herself, and stormed past him into the bathroom.

Through the closed door, the silken murmur of his voice taunted her. "Actually, I thought we were pretty good last night. Certainly nothing to go into hiding over. I figure I at least deserve a 'Hello, Luke. Goodbye, Luke. Thanks for the memories.'"

"Oh, shut up," she muttered through the closed door.

"Is this your usual just-woke-up-foul-mood or a special one based on last night?"

"I'm warning you, McCullough. Go away."

There was a moment's silence before he spoke. The teasing tone was gone, his voice was soft, serious. "Okay, coffee's ready whenever you are. But before you come out—just shut up and let me finish," he said when she tried to interrupt. "It's my turn now. If you're embarrassed or upset about what happened between us last night, I've a good mind to turn you over my knee and paddle that luscious rear of yours. Granted, our timing wasn't the best, but what we found last night was very real. Very special. And I won't have you cheapen it by being embarrassed. Understand?"

He didn't wait for her answer, but plunged on. "Now get your clothes on because breakfast will be ready in five minutes. Or don't get dressed." He raised a dark brow suggestively. "We can just eat breakfast in bed, if that's what you want."

"But I don't eat—"

"Don't give me that garbage about not eating breakfast. You're turning into skin and bones. And I like your curves."

Anne leaned against the bathroom door listening to what was the longest speech she'd ever heard Luke make. He sounded so sincere that she found herself recalling their turbulent lovemaking in a different light.

She had been wild. Abandoned. Every fiber of her being had quivered with a tempestuous fire. And it had been good. Very good.

And why not? They were simply two people reaching out to each other during a time of tremendous stress. Like lovers in a war zone. He was right. There was no need to feel ashamed of her needs. No need to be embarrassed because she'd practically dragged him to her bed.

But if she had a brain in her head, she couldn't allow a repeat performance.

Because Anne had awakened to another more shattering reality. She was falling in love with Luke McCullough. Every bossy, virile inch of him. She wanted to clutch that long-legged, infuriating, incredibly sexy man to her breast and run for the nearest deserted island. But, deep in her heart, she knew that could never be.

If they weren't both killed before Scorpion was caught, Luke would soon be leaving for another assignment. She'd be given another new identity and relocated. When all this was over, they'd never see each other again.

She turned the shower on high and stepped beneath the prickly blast. Never see Luke again. The words kept thundering through her mind. A pain slashed through her heart as strong and powerful as a physical blow. She'd heard the old phrase that it was better to have loved and lost than never to have loved at all. She wasn't at all sure about that. Right now, she'd give everything she possessed if she could will herself not to fall in love with Luke McCullough. Not to have to endure the certain pain she knew was waiting for her when they parted.

Anne turned off the hot water and stood under the spray until it turned icy cold, until her chattering teeth forced her mind from its melancholy thoughts. There'd be time enough to think about her loneliness when Luke was gone. All the time in the world.

LUKE WAS JUST dishing up the scrambled eggs when she stepped into the kitchen. He glanced over his shoulder and smiled broadly. What a knockout! A sparkling ray of sunshine in her cotton slacks and matching top of soft buttercup yellow. Her thick red hair was pulled back in a ponytail, emphasizing the hollows beneath her cheekbones and her full, pouty lips. Lips that still looked slightly swollen from his kisses. She looked good enough to eat. Luke bit the side of his mouth hard enough to push away the tempting image.

He didn't know what the future held for them but today he had to concentrate on protecting her. Things were coming to a head. He could feel it in his bones. Smell it in the electric air.

Pouring a steaming mug of coffee, he placed it in front of her and lightly kissed the top of her head. "Good morning, sunshine."

"Hi."

"Hmm, still cheerful I see. Well, eat up because I have several things to talk to you about."

Anne looked up quizzically. "Why? What's happening?"

Luke topped off his own mug and returned to the table. He turned the wooden chair around and straddled it, facing Anne. "I made a few phone calls this morning."

Anne's forkful of egg stopped in midair. "And?"

"First, I phoned the hospital. Mr. Farmer's still in a coma, but he's holding his own."

She nodded and bit into her eggs. "That's really a good sign, isn't it?"

"Yeah, the doc said it was very good. Next, I called Washington. After a lot of procedural rigmarole, I found out that they're dispatching an entire team of agents. They should be here sometime late this afternoon. The bureau doesn't take kindly to one of their agents . . . going missing."

Anne swallowed a mouthful of soothing coffee to give herself time to compose her thoughts. "A team you say? That means that you'll . . . be free again. To pursue your own investigation."

"That's right. But I'll be able to do it without worrying about you. A full team will mean twenty-four-hour, live-in surveillance. One agent inside. At least one outside. Actually, they'll probably use two men after . . . after Spears. No one will get within a hundred yards of you."

She looked at the wall clock over the stove. Almost ten. "So, what do we do for the next six hours or so?"

Stay alive. To Anne, he said, "I think Scorpion's going to make his move within the next twenty-four hours. I'm going to move all my gear out of Ernie's house. It's easier to keep one place secure than two. You stay here—with my gun, and keep this place locked up as tight as Fort Knox."

"What about the horses? I don't have the facilities to keep them."

Luke bit off a chunk of buttered toast and nodded. "I know, I've already thought about that. There's a rancher who boards horses over in the foothills of the Kofa Mountains, about an hour from here. I'll get the horse trailer hitched up, and we'll take them over there as soon as I get back."

"Is that safe—to go driving all over the countryside?"

He carried his empty plate over to the sink. "Safe as any-place, I'd guess. I filled the truck, checked the oil, all that stuff yesterday. We'll take a full canteen of water, just in case. But in some ways, if *we* control the environment, it's better to keep moving."

Anne stood up, carrying her own plate to the sink. "What you're saying is that it's better to be a moving target than a sitting duck?"

He chuckled. A nice laugh, but one without humor. "Nicely put. Anyway, here's my gun. Keep it within reach."

Giving him a mocking salute, she said, "Aye-aye, Skipper."

He kissed her lightly on the cheek. "I love a woman who understands her place in life."

Punching him on the shoulder, she took him by the arm and led him firmly out of the kitchen. "You'd better get a move on, McCullough, before I'm forced to hurt you."

Luke stepped out onto the small front porch and looked up and down the street. The rustic western setting looked as peaceful as a scene on a postcard. "Okay, Annie, I'll be back in an hour or so. Stay out of trouble, will ya?"

Placing the palm of her hand firmly in the small of his back, she *helped* him on his way.

Stepping back inside, she double-bolted the front door and checked the other doors and windows. Her sweet little adobe had turned into a veritable fortress. It was hard to believe that only a week ago, she'd stood on the front porch every morning and watched the glorious Arizona sunrise.

A quiet dread stole over her. Soon, very soon, it would all be over. Would she still be alive when the sun rose tomorrow?

She couldn't think about tomorrow or Scorpion, or even Luke's departure. One thing at a time. One moment at a time.

Anne went back to finish the kitchen cleanup while she waited for Luke. She tossed a couple of apples and fresh granola bars into her handbag. They might want a nibble later. She rinsed off their few dishes and stared out the window into the backyard. The pool looked so peaceful, so inviting. And so *green!*

Things had been so hectic these past few days that she'd forgotten to put chemicals in the pool. By afternoon, it would be full of algae.

She slid Luke's 9-mm automatic into her waistband and unbolted the patio door. The pool supplies were kept in the small shed at the rear of the yard. It would only take her five minutes—tops—to get the chlorine and pour some into the pool.

Luke's voice whispered in her head. *Stay in the house.*

He was probably right, but he wouldn't be the one scrubbing yucky yellow algae off the pool walls. Besides, the entire backyard was fenced in chain link. She could see someone coming from any direction. There were no tall buildings around, so unless Scorpion was on Elaine's roof, Anne would be safe from sniper fire.

And *no one* would be hiding in that utility shed. No one except a few spiders and field mice. It was already approaching one hundred degrees outdoors. The shed had practically no ventilation so the temperature inside would be at least twenty or thirty degrees higher.

Taking a deep breath, she slid open the door and stepped out onto the patio.

Holding her shoulders back and exuding a confident air that she didn't really feel, Anne marched around the pool. By the time she reached the shed, she was starting to feel more secure. She no longer had that eerie sense of unseen eyes following her every move.

Pausing to stick the key into the padlock, a faint, peculiar odor wafted past. She had no idea what it could be. The sickly sweet scent was coming from inside the shed.

A frown creasing her forehead, she unhasped the lock and swung open the door.

The nauseating odor, a hundred times stronger now, almost overwhelmed her. Every instinct in her body screamed at her to slam the door and run back into the house. Get away. Far away.

But she stood rooted in place.

For her eyes had adjusted to the dim light inside the small shed, and she was struck by a horror she'd never imagined.

Agent Spears's body was lying in a rumpled pile at her feet.

A coldness washed through Anne as if she'd been trapped in a snowstorm. The blazing Arizona heat melted away. She was frozen into an emotionless chunk of ice. Anne didn't think she'd ever feel anything again.

LUKE WAS STRUCK with an overpowering sense of *déjà vu* when he pulled Ernie's rig into Anne's cul de sac. Wasn't it just last night when this very street had been lined with flashing lights?

Strange, though, that today he didn't feel that sense of panic. Or crippling fear. This time he was numb.

Something bad, something unspeakable had happened.

He climbed out of the truck and walked toward Anne's house. A dozen or so uniformed officials were milling around. Just as Luke reached her yard, two men in white jackets wheeled a gurney from the back of the house.

This time, however, no pale, grizzled old man was beneath a shroud of white sheets. This time the gurney was holding a firmly zipped black rubber body bag.

Bile rose in Luke's throat. His mouth watered, and he knew he was going to be sick. He stopped in his tracks as sweat beads popped up on his forehead. He bent over, gulping air.

Dear God, not Anne. Please, not Anne.

He felt a firm hand on his shoulder. From somewhere in his fog, Luke heard the now-familiar, slightly accented voice of Officer Diaz. "It's not her, McCullough. Do you hear me? Anne Farraday is safe. She's inside."

Luke lifted watery eyes. Not Anne?

Without waiting for another word, he darted into the house.

Anne was sitting on the sofa. Pale, ghastly pale. Trembling. But alive.

Luke fell to his knees beside her and took her small, cold hands in his. "What...what happened, honey?"

Like a small, lost child, she lifted wary eyes. "Agent Spears, Luke. I found him. In the shed. The smell, Luke. It was the most awful thing I've..."

Luke nodded. He wasn't surprised to discover that Spears was dead; they'd suspected that all along. He wanted to get the details. Wanted to shake Anne until she turned blue for ignoring his warning and going outdoors. Most of all, he wanted to take her in his arms and crush her so tightly that she became a part of him.

He did none of those things. Anne would be all right. Some protective force in her body had shut down all feeling. Later, she'd feel sick, outraged and saddened. But right now, it was kinder to leave her to her numb emptiness. He decided to go in search of the homicide detective in charge of the crime scene.

Spears had been killed with a single gunshot wound to the head. The body had decomposed badly because of the extreme heat, so they hadn't yet determined where he was shot or when. The homicide detective promised to keep Luke informed of all developments.

Ten minutes later, Luke rejoined Anne, where she still sat unmoving on the sofa.

"Annie? Come on, honey, the detective said we can get out of here."

"We can't just go off and leave him. Alone."

Luke knew who she was talking about. He also knew she was suffering from shock. He had to get her away from the scene of so much horror. "There's nothing we can do for Wally Spears now. Come on, honey."

The ice in her veins melted suddenly, and she was awash in a warm flow of grief. Anne gulped, trying not to give in to the tears that were forming in her throat. Agent Spears had been such a big teddy bear of a man. So kind. "Did he have a family?"

He nodded again. "A wife and twin boys. Five years old."

"Oh, Luke!"

"For what it's worth, honey, it was the life he chose. It's a decision we've all made."

"What about his wife?" she railed, angry at Luke's apparent indifference, angry at the injustice. Just damned angry. "Did his wife choose to lose her husband? To be widowed with two small children? It's just so unfair!"

Luke's hand covered hers. "There are no easy answers, honey. Life's unfair. You ought to know that as well as anybody."

Anne leaned back against the cushions. Part of her wanted to run back into bed, pull the covers over her eyes and hide until someone chased the bogeyman away. But some other part of her, some stronger, angrier part, needed to do something.

It was all her fault. She had to accept that and learn to live with it because somehow she was responsible for everything. For Mr. Farmer's injury. For Agent Spears's death. Hell, the way she felt right now, she was responsible for the original sin.

Rising to her feet, she took Luke's hand. "Let's get those horses out to the boarding ranch. Before they die, too."

LUKE KEPT his eye on the oversize sideview mirror as they sped along Interstate Eight. Another pickup truck, shiny black, had been two cars behind them for the last couple of miles.

He couldn't get a good look at it because the trailer they were towing blocked his vision, but Luke had noticed a black pickup come around the corner behind them shortly after leaving Anne's place. He was probably being overly cautious; in this part of the country, every other vehicle was a pickup of some kind. Still, it made him edgy. Pulling this double horse trailer, Luke was forced to stay in the slow lane. Out here on the open highway, most drivers sped along at least five or ten miles an hour above the legal limit.

But that black pickup was poking along at about the same rate as Luke.

He patted the comforting weight of his gun in the shoulder holster.

When he saw the sign for their turnoff, Luke put on his turn signal. Letting up on the gas, he headed for the exit ramp, keeping an eye on the black pickup. As he eased off the interstate onto the state highway, he glanced out the window. The black pickup didn't take the exit.

Luke continued to guard their rear as they drove, slower now, along the two-lane road that stretched to the foothills. Consulting the scribbled directions he'd taken from the rancher over the phone, Luke started watching for the next cutoff.

A few moments later, he spied the dusty, bullet-pocked sign. According to the rancher, they were only about ten miles away at this point. And there was still no sign of the black pickup, or anyone else for that matter, following them.

Braking slowly, he turned left and they continued their journey along a gravel-strewn dirt road. Although the heat was stifling, a brisk breeze wafting through the open windows of the truck eased their discomfort.

Glancing at the sideview mirror for the dozenth time, he was relieved to see only emptiness behind them. At least out in this desolate wilderness, it would be difficult for someone to follow them without being detected.

Anne had barely spoken since they'd left the city. Determined to get her mind off the terrifying events of the past few days, he started whistling—just because he knew it would annoy her.

Although she glanced his way, she ignored his off-key efforts. Clearing his throat, he launched into his repertoire of bawdy songs and limericks. He was greatly relieved when Anne turned around and stared at him. He knew she was coming out of shock when she laughed aloud when he badly missed a particularly high note.

"My good woman, the customary response to a recital like this is applause, not derision."

"Customary?" Anne scoffed. "Don't tell me that you've had the nerve to sing for other captive audiences."

Luke grinned. "Why, I'll have you know that once in this little bar in Sicily, a table of sailors paid me big bucks to entertain them." He slowed down to swerve around a deep rut and immediately broke into another bawdy song.

Anne stuck her fingers in her ears. "Please. Mercy."

Luke glanced in the mirror. So far, so good.

As a precaution, he scanned the truck's instrument panel. It was easy to overheat driving through the desert. Oil pressure, normal. Temperature, normal. Gasoline, empty.

Luke's eyes popped. No way this tank could be empty. Before they left Anne's house, he hadn't driven more then twenty miles since his last fill-up. Reaching over the steering wheel, he thumped the fuel gauge with his fingertip.

"Something wrong?"

He frowned. "I sure hope not."

Anne instantly caught his implication. If they ran out of gas, they'd be stranded out here in the open. She leaned out the window and stared intently into the passenger sideview mirror. Only miles of sandy, cactus-littered countryside. Yet, she felt those prickles of fear begin. If they were being followed, their pursuer was keeping his distance.

They made another mile or so before the truck started choking and coughing.

"Damn!" He eased the truck over to the edge of the dusty road.

"Well, at least your temper's working." Anne twisted in the seat. "Now, what are we going to do?"

No doubt about it. Anne had regained her equilibrium. Along with her smart-alecky, wisecracking sense of humor. Which was usually at his expense, he noted. Rubbing his hand across his sweaty forehead, he said, "We're only seven or eight miles from the boarding ranch."

"We can't walk that distance in this heat!"

Luke forced a smile. "You're forgetting, angel, that we are currently toting two, able-bodied horses. Let's give them some water and saddle up."

Anne frowned. "You picked a hell of a day for a horseback ride."

"Unless you have a better idea."

She shrugged.

Luke looked out the window, focusing on the hot afternoon sun still burning overhead. Anne was right, they'd have to take it very slowly or this heat would kill those horses. He only hoped the blazing sun was the only enemy waiting for them.

But they didn't have many choices left. "No sense wasting time," he said. "Now that we've stopped, it won't take long for those animals to get overheated in that trailer. I guess I'd better get them into the open air."

He yanked his Stetson off a hook behind him, opened the door and stepped down onto the sandy ground. Reaching above the visor, he pulled out a map and spread it open on the seat he'd just vacated.

"Ah-hah, I *was* right."

"About what?" she asked, watching his finger trace a thin gray line on the map.

"This is the old Pima Trail. There's supposed to be a natural spring up here. According to my handy-dandy little hiking guide." He patted his shirt pocket. "This used to be a neutral zone among the Indian tribes, because there was always water at the spring. There's a small trail leading from behind that spring. If we take that route instead of staying on this road, we'll cut out a couple of miles."

Anne shot him a sharp look. "Not to mention that it would be more difficult for him to follow us if we get off the main road." If anyone could call this rutted cow path a main road, she thought, grumpy at the idea of having to ride in the scorching sun. And morbidly curious about the suddenly empty gas tank.

He nodded. "I was kind of thinking along those lines. *If* he's back there. I haven't seen so much as a tumbleweed moving since we left the interstate. But we can't be too careful."

Anne slipped on her sunglasses and leaned forward, peering through the dusty windshield. "How on earth will you find some old hidden spring out there?"

"Easy. I bet I can point it out from here."

"Oh, please, Mr. Modesty, do enlighten me."

"Hmph, didn't you know I was a Boy Scout? See that line of cottonwoods over there?"

Her skeptical gaze followed the direction he was pointing. "Yeah, so?"

"So those roots have to be near a source of water. And I'm willing to bet it's our spring. Any takers?"

"Not me, *kemo sabe*." She brushed a loose strand of hair back into the elastic that held her slightly wilted ponytail. "I would never argue with an Italian-Irish, former Boy Scout, *nouveau* Indian tracker. Not me."

"Bah. Where's your sporting blood?" Pulling his Stetson low onto his forehead, he stalked off. He reappeared a few seconds later carrying a tin bucket. Whistling as if he hadn't a care in the world, he strolled confidently toward the stand of cottonwood trees.

Anne leaned back against the hot vinyl seat watching the enticing sway of his tight rear in his jeans as he walked away from her. Her pulse jumped erratically. Luke McCullough was turning out to be a man of many enticements.

Fun. Good-natured—usually. An adventurous yet sensitive lover. Steady. Strong. Protective.

Protective. With a bittersweet smile curving her lips, she closed her eyes. For a while there, she'd completely forgotten why they were riding out on the desert. Forgotten that they were running from a man who wanted to kill her.

She'd let her imagination take control, letting her believe that Luke was with her only because he wanted to be. Not because he'd sworn to protect her.

With a sigh, Anne opened the passenger door and dropped to the ground. The craggy peak in front of them rose like a majestic eagle, spreading its rocky wings across the horizon. The high desert was a study in contrasts, she thought, looking at the soaring mountain. She turned around and stared down into the valley, at the sprawling metropolitan area. Other than the whistling sand blowing against the sagebrush, only a ghostly stillness wafted through the air.

Yet she couldn't ignore those prickles on the back of her neck. Scorpion wasn't far away. She could feel his evil presence.

Luke came strutting back from the cottonwood grove and set his bucket on the ground. Water sloshed over the edge.

Without so much as an "I told you so," he went back around behind the truck and led out the two animals by their reins. "I brought water pouches for the horses, we'll bring them with us. I never like to run short of water in the desert."

He nosed the tin bucket over to Bounty while he rubbed Ladybug's muzzle. "I think that trail in the guidebook starts right over there." He pointed to a rocky outcropping just to the left of the cottonwoods.

"Lead on, McCullough."

Taking the bucket from the greedy stallion, he waited patiently while Ladybug drank her fill. "You want to grab the canteens and backpacks out of the truck while I saddle the horses?"

"Sure."

She pulled their gear from the truck bed and slung the canteens around the saddle horns. She looped the leather straps of her shoulder bag around Ladybug's saddle horn and waited for Luke to finish saddling Bounty. While he cinched the girths, she wiped a bead of perspiration from her forehead and looked down into the valley below. Yuma and all the trouble looked like a fuzzy, muted dream below them. Even the narrow black ribbon of Interstate Eight seemed so far away. She could see the truck trails and side roads shunting off the freeway. Only an occasional vehicle stirred up a dust cloud.

Most people had sense enough to stay out of this heat. She resented that she and Luke were forced into it.

"All finished," he said, pulling off his black Stetson and wiping his forehead with a forearm. "Damn, it's hot. I don't know how those farmers stand it." He nodded toward a field patchworked with shades of green several miles away. "Must take a hell of a lot of water to irrigate this soil."

"At least you have a hat," she observed. "I forgot to bring one."

Luke frowned. "You have to cover your head or you'll get sunstroke." He opened the truck door, pulled the seat forward and rummaged behind the seat. "Here," he said, bringing out a battered straw hat. "This isn't real fashionable but it'll work."

Anne took the badly stained hat and plopped it on her head. "Perfect. I don't suppose you have a gallon of fresh iced tea behind that seat, do you?"

"Nope. You'll have to settle for lukewarm water." He handed her a canteen and she took a long drink.

After Luke took a swig, he slung the canteen strap back around the saddle horn. Tossing one of the backpacks to Anne, he donned the other, heavier one. "Ready?"

"Ready as I'll ever be."

"Okay, a few pointers. Don't just walk up to a strange horse and try to mount her. Talk to her for a minute—"

"But I know—"

"Will you just listen for a minute? How do you expect to spend a couple of hours on horseback without getting a few pointers?"

"Pointers! It seems to me, Mr. Hotshot Cowboy, that the first time we met you were having more than a little difficulty with your own horse. Now you want to give me pointers?"

"That was different."

"Oh, really?"

With legs splayed in frustration, he curled his fists on his hips. "You just might be the most bullheaded woman I've ever known. I'm trying to tell you the basics to make your ride a little easier."

"Maybe I don't *need* your basics! Maybe I—"

He cut in. "Just listen, okay? You said you'd follow my instructions."

Anne eyes sparked with fire. "Yes, any instructions that pertain to my safety. I didn't say that I was accepting you as my lord and master for life!"

"Are you saying I'm bossy?"

"I'm saying Genghis Khan was bossy. You're impossible!"

"And I suppose you're an expert equestrian?"

"I might be, but you wouldn't know." She tossed her ponytail in indignation.

"Oh, I'd know, Anne."

"Is that so?"

"Yes. But don't listen to me. Just go ahead and do it your way."

"Fine. I will."

"Fine." He glared one last time and stomped over to Bounty, lifting his foot into the stirrup.

Muttering beneath her breath, she approached the chestnut mare. Softening the tone of her voice, she spoke gently. "Hi, Ladybug, we're going to be friends. Aren't we?"

Ladybug nickered softly.

"See? She likes me," Anne said confidently, then raised her foot into the stirrup. Hoisting herself easily into the saddle, she flicked the reins and and expertly led Ladybug over to the trail.

Luke watched in consternation, then burst into laughter. Anne *was* an expert horsewoman. She rode that horse as though she were born in the saddle. Anyone else would have chewed his rear for an hour for being such an arrogant jerk. She had a more subtle, infinitely more effective, approach. She'd let him make a darn fool of himself and then watched him wallow in what remained of his inflated ego.

His grin broadened. She was really something.

"Aren't you coming, Luke?" Her voice snapped him out of his introspective moment.

He looked up. She was high astride Ladybug, tapping her finger on the saddle horn.

"Yes, Anne," he said with exaggerated meekness.

He turned to take one last look at the horizon behind them. Off in the distance, a dust cloud rose and hovered. A car? Or just a dust storm?

Clicking his tongue, he urged his mount toward Anne. If that *was* Scorpion stalking them, they only had about a five-mile lead. It would take the assassin a mere few minutes to catch up with them.

The quicker they got to some cover, the happier he would be.

Chapter Eleven

Anne kept a light but firm hand on the reins and talked gently to her mount as they threaded along the boulder-strewn path.

She pushed back her straw hat and wiped a sheen of perspiration from her forehead. The blistering afternoon sun beat down on her, lulling her into drowsiness as they plodded along the dusty, twisting trail.

Out of the corner of her eye, she saw Luke turning in his saddle every few moments, scanning the empty landscape. Anne didn't have to look. The prickling up her spine and neck had stopped. If Scorpion was following them, he was keeping his distance.

After a while, they came to a small clearing. To break the monotony, they picked up the pace, accelerating to a slow trot. It was too hot to push the animals, though, so after a few moments, they slowed to a walk again.

They rode along in companionable silence for some time. When Luke glanced at his watch, he was startled to see that they'd been riding for an hour. It was time to give the animals a rest and water. Anne could use the rest, too. Although she hadn't complained, he'd noticed her head bobbing occasionally. Poor kid, she must be emotionally and physically exhausted.

"Let's head over to that stand of boulders at the foot of the mountain," he said. "We can sit in the shade while we rest the horses."

"Sounds good," she replied. With a gentle click of her tongue, she guided Ladybug toward the rocks.

Once they dismounted, Luke took their canteens and poured a small amount from each into two tin pie plates that he'd packed beneath the bedrolls. He tethered the animals to a large mesquite bush and pulled the saddles from their backs.

"That won't hold them, will it?" Anne asked, eyeing the careless loop of the reins.

"They'll be fine. If they really decided to take off, that wouldn't stop them, but unless something spooks them, they'll be happy to stand right there. It'll be easier to undo if we need to make a fast getaway. If you...uh...need some privacy, you might want to take a walk." He pointed to a chest-high stand of mesquite bushes a few yards away. She took his cue and walked in the direction he'd indicated.

When she returned, the animals were still lapping their water, and Luke was ambling back from the opposite direction. Plucking their canteens from the saddles, he carried them over to the rocks.

Finding a shaded alcove, he peeled off his backpack and dropped it on the ground. One large boulder, smooth and flat, was wedged amongst the others at a slight angle.

"Looks like an extra-firm double bed," he said, indicating the sloping rock with a tip of his head.

"Keep your mind out of the bedroom, McCullough. It's too hot."

"Never too hot, my dear. We'll just have to find our own way of cooling off." Catching Anne's wrist in his hand, he pulled her down beside him.

"Tired?" he asked, handing her a canteen.

"A little." She sipped at the warm water, then pulled off her own backpack and tossed it onto the ground. Wiping her lips, she said, "It's so glorious out here. Sometimes, for a few minutes, I can hold on to the pretense that we're just out on a leisurely horseback ride."

"Me, too. You're fun to be with, Anne."

"Luke?"

"Hmm?"

"Do you think he's back there? Stalking us."

He raised onto one elbow and looked down into the valley. Their own truck was out of sight, separated from their view by the arc of the foothills. Off in the distance, however, they could see the flickering ribbon of the interstate and the tiny threads leading from it that he knew were the few side roads.

Except for an occasional jackrabbit, nothing moved.

He shook his head. "I don't think so. I was worried for a while, but that pickup I saw wasn't pulling a horse trailer. He'd be on foot. In this heat. No. We're safe for a while. Only a fool would try to catch up with us right now."

A fool, or a madman. And Scorpion was neither. He was a cold-blooded, ruthless killer, but he wasn't foolhardy.

She poured a little water onto a hanky and mopped her face. "Want some?"

"Nah." He thumbed his Stetson to the back of his head. "Better save it. I don't want to run low."

Anne recapped the canteen.

They leaned back against the warm rock, legs stretched out in front of them. It was a lazy kind of afternoon. A few flies buzzed around their heads, but nothing else stirred.

"Luke?"

"Mmm?"

"Where did a boy from South Philly learn to ride a horse?"

"Probably the same place a girl from Jersey learned to ride," he teased. "Actually, my father's older brother has a ranch in Wyoming. One summer when I was about eight, my mother had to have an operation. Dad knew she'd need some time to recuperate, so he farmed out us kids. I was lucky. My dad scraped up enough money for my airfare and I was shipped off to Uncle Seamus's ranch."

"Weren't you scared? I mean going so far away from home."

"At first. But after I saw the ranch—well, it was love at first sight. I had never even imagined a place where you didn't hear the sound of cars honking. Or neighbors fighting. Where as far as you could see, there was nothing but land and sky."

"So your uncle taught you to ride that summer?"

"And a lot more. The Irish are a thrifty breed, you know. Old Uncle Seamus didn't abide anybody not working for their keep, so he treated me like one of the hands."

"At eight years old?"

Luke laughed, his face worry-free as he relived the warm memory. "I loved it. Boys like discipline, you know. Why else would we line up to join the marines?"

"I guess I never thought about it like that."

"Anyway, Uncle Seamus worked my little buns off that summer. But I never complained. Not once. I knew I was doing okay when after about a month he took me into town and bought me my first cowboy boots."

"I think that's the least he should've done. Taking advantage of a little boy like that."

He shook his head. "No, he didn't take advantage of me. He taught me the value of hard, honest work. Taught me how to pick out the constellations in the night sky. Taught me that in some parts of the world, a man's word is still his most valuable possession. Uncle Seamus is a grouchy old cowboy, but I sure love him. Anyway, I must've done something right because the next summer he paid my airfare. And every summer after that until I graduated from high school.''

''Do you ever see him anymore?''

Luke shrugged. ''Not as often as I'd like. It's hard. You know, I only have so much vacation time, and the holidays, but if I don't go home, it upsets my mom. So I try to sneak a trip to Wyoming whenever I can. You ever been up to Wyoming?''

''No. When the government helped me relocate, they sent me on a circuitous route that took me everywhere but through Wyoming, I think.''

''How did they work it?''

''First, I flew from Jersey to Detroit. Then to Chicago. Changed planes again and flew to Denver. Then to San Diego. And finally, by bus, to Yuma. And each ticket had a different name on it. Once I got off the bus here, an agent was waiting. He drove me to my house and gave me all my new identification credentials. Other than a few details, that was pretty much it.''

Luke glanced at his watch. ''It's almost three o'clock. You ready to saddle up?''

Actually Anne wanted to stay right where she was... forever.

''Oh, not yet! Once we drop off the horses, and hitch a ride back to the city, the FBI will be camped on my doorstep. I'm not ready to face all the questions. All the moving around again. Please, Luke, just another hour?''

He sighed and pulled her closer to him, until her head was leaning on his shoulder. ''Okay, honey, one more hour. But you shouldn't be so uptight about it. I'll be there every step of the way.''

''Except when you're chasing Scorpion.''

He heard the accusation in her voice and hated the truth in it. "Yeah."

There didn't seem to be anything else to say, so they sat quietly, lost in their own thoughts.

"Are you through being mad at me?" Luke's hand snaked across the rock and clasped hers.

"I wasn't really mad, just...irritated. But then, I seem to be easily annoyed these days."

"You certainly have had the provocation. I haven't helped much, being my usual overbearing self."

Her fingernail lightly scratched his palm. "Oh, you're not so bad. Sometimes."

Silence stretched out between them. A lazy, catlike silence as warm and seductive as a lover's smile.

With a deceptive carelessness, he turned over onto his side. Tracing her mouth with the tips of his fingers, he smiled gently. "Last night was incredible. The way you came to me. I felt ten feet tall and capable of slaying a dragon with my bare hands."

Anne turned her head, but not before he spied a pink flush creeping up her cheeks.

With his fingertip on her chin, he tilted her head back until her gaze met his. "Don't be embarrassed. You were wonderful. Refreshing. I hate those coy games couples feel compelled to play. Don't apologize for being a real woman. A highly desirable, sensuous woman. You...you made me feel like a..."

"Like a sex object?"

"Yeah!" He grinned. "You women have had the market cornered on that for way too long. On behalf of my male counterparts, I demand to be your token sex object."

"You're hired." She reached up and ran her finger along his firm jawline. She loved the faint black stubble that seemed to reappear five minutes after he shaved.

Luke's thick, black lashes flickered as he closed his eyes, bringing his lips to hers. He slipped his tongue into her mouth, delving into the sweetness. Slowly. Savoring it. His pace matched perfectly the languorous mood of the sun-filled afternoon.

Anne stretched, kittenlike, and wrapped her arms around his neck, her fingers tangling in the crisp hair at his nape.

The long, deliberate, incredibly tantalizing kiss started a warm spiraling in her stomach, which gradually spun outward like a slow-moving tornado.

How could one kiss be so potent? So filled with delicious promise?

All day she'd told herself she shouldn't be falling in love with Luke. It would be madness. Why was she setting herself up for the pain, the broken heart that was sure to follow?

But even while she'd been busy denying it, she'd been falling deeper and deeper into the dangerous well of love. It was too late. No matter how shaky her future, while she had Luke here with her, she was going to throw her normal reticence away. Hurl caution aside. Live for this moment.

For this man.

Moving her hands slowly, she thrilled to the width of his shoulders, the lean muscle of his back that tapered down to his narrow waist. His sexy hips.

The wild hunger she'd felt last night had shifted. Not eased, just evolved into a hunger of her soul as well as her body. Only with Luke had she experienced a sense of total completeness the first time they'd made love. They'd enjoyed an emotional as well as physical release.

Now she wanted to explore those feelings, slow down the cadence, luxuriate in the sensations of their bodies. She would pretend that time was their plaything, that they had forever.

"Anne?" His voice whispered in her ear, then he gently nipped her lobe.

"Mmm..."

"Aren't you... hot in all those clothes?"

She smiled lazily. Yes, she was *very* hot.

The blazing heat, added to the inferno building inside her body, was taking its toll. She was melting, inside as well as out. Her very core was dissolving into a hot, burbling mixture of love and old-fashioned lust. Her hands shook as she helped Luke tug off her cotton top, then tried to pull his blue T-shirt out of his jeans. She wanted to get all of these clothes out of her way, so she could feel the delicious texture of his skin next to hers and drown in the sensation of becoming part of him.

Luke's magical hands easily stripped away the rest of their clothing; and he lay back, his beautiful body exposed. Proud.

Leaning over him, Anne slowly rubbed the sensitive tips of her breasts against his chest, teasing him, taunting him with her hardened nipples. Her breasts tingled as she luxuriated in the tickling curls covering his heated flesh. Too soon, she had to stop. Her knees were weak, wobbly with the weight of her desire. She had to cling to him as he left a trail of kisses along the side of her throat, nipping lightly at the hollow of her neck.

"Oh, Anne, I can't get enough of you. I want to make the world go away. I want to consume you."

Anne understood only too well. Every time she looked at him, her blood pressure raced out of control. "Take me, Luke. Now."

He groaned, overcome by the fullness of her response. "My pleasure."

He lowered her down onto the cool, smooth rock, then eased down beside her.

He was going to take it slow this time, he told himself. He had an hour. One precious hour to embark on a diligent exploration of her delicious curves and hollows. Luke wanted to know everything about her. What made her shiver with pleasure, what caused her to gasp with delight, what set her nerves to trembling. What he could do to take her to heights she'd never felt before. He would make her truly his.

Last night's fiery union had been explosive. Sensational. But this time, he wanted it to be fuller. Richer. A perfect joining of spirit and body.

Anne writhed beneath his touch, losing herself to his beguiling fingers. His mouth was everywhere: on her lips, her breast, toying and teasing the sensitive skin below her navel. He seemed to know her better than she knew herself, his touch setting off new and dizzying sensations. She felt that first, itchy hunger quiver within her as he finally claimed her.

Despite his intention to keep their pace slow, the fires blazed out of control, melting and fusing them in an inferno of incredible passion.

"Luke, my sweet, sweet darling." She called out his name as her body lifted, reached to capture him.

As if they were two bodies with one soul, his need was sparked by her hunger and he held her close, thrusting them into the shattering explosion of oneness. With her legs wrapped tightly around his waist, his hands beneath her, urging her against him, they drifted slowly back, settling at last into the peace of total fulfillment, still locked in each other's arms.

Anne was only dimly aware of Luke's withdrawal. He turned, pulling her into the safety of his embrace. The shattering climax of their lovemaking had left her so delectably weary that she could do no more than snuggle closer to his splendid, now-familiar body.

She'd never known a man's lovemaking could be like this. Never dreamed anyone could make her feel so totally loved. So complete.

The heat, their pent-up anxiety and all the frustrations and fears of the past few days were taking their toll. Within minutes, Anne was dozing. Luke smiled softly. She looked like a redheaded angel when she was asleep. It was a sight he wouldn't tire of in a thousand lifetimes.

Gently disengaging himself from her, he slipped his clothing back on, wishing he could join her in her carefree slumber. But he had to stay alert, be prepared for any contingency.

If only they were a normal couple, living normal lives, without the threat of an unseen executioner following their every move.

In a few minutes, they'd have to go back and face reality again. But for now, he wanted to believe that he and Anne were stranded on a desert island. They had only each other. The sun was theirs. The magnificence of the day belonged only to them.

With a sigh, he closed his eyes. A moment later, he was gently snoring beside her.

The sun was sinking low in the sky when Luke awoke, suddenly alert.

"Anne? Better wake up, honey. We've overslept."

"Mmm... Another hour," she begged, sleepily wiping her eyes.

"I wish we could but if we don't get a move on it'll be dark before we get to the ranch."

She sat up and stretched. "I suppose this means I have to put my clothes back on?"

Luke looked at her, frank appreciation in his eyes. "Nope. You can ride back to the stables like Lady Godiva if you want to. 'Course, I might have to shoot most of the ranch hands. But if you want that on your conscience..."

"Oh, all right, since you put it that way. I guess I have to keep the women from becoming widows." Without a twinge of modesty, she stood up and slipped into her panties and bra. Looking up at the fading sunlight, she hurriedly donned the rest of her clothes. "My gosh, we did oversleep. Those poor horses must be ready for the barn and dinner. Actually, so am I."

"Ready for the barn?"

"No, dinner. Feed me." She picked up her backpack and slipped her arms through the straps.

Luke grinned up at her. "You do require a fair amount of tending, woman."

"Get up, lazybones. You still owe me a fettuccine dinner."

With a toss of her head, she walked back out into the clearing, heading for the horses.

Before Luke had time to rise to his feet, the quiet afternoon air was shattered by the deafening crack of rifle fire.

Chapter Twelve

Anne felt something sting her cheek. Something fast and furious zipped past her face. Instinctively, she threw herself to the ground as another burst of gunfire blazed in quick succession.

Covering her head with her arms, she scurried into the shadow of a tumbleweed and waited for the next bullet.

The air rang with an ominous silence.

As if from far away, she heard Luke's voice calling her name. She shifted her arm slightly and opened an eye. His white, anxious face was peering at her from behind the nearest boulder. He held his service revolver in his hand, his quick alert eyes were scanning the surrounding wilderness.

"Anne! Are you all right?"

"I . . . I think so," she managed to answer from between chattering teeth.

"Stay still. Don't move."

He didn't need to repeat that order. Her limbs were trembling as if they were filled with cold soup instead of bone and muscle.

"Did you see where the shots came from?" Luke asked.

"N-no."

"Well, don't move a muscle. Maybe he'll make a mistake and show himself."

For several long, tension-filled moments, she lay still. Waiting. Waiting for her stalker to make another attempt on her life.

Only the scream of a red-tailed hawk prowling overhead disturbed the silence.

"Doesn't look like he's going to show. Just stay where you are, honey. I'll get you out of there." Luke disappeared behind the boulder. A few seconds later, his head peeped back around. "Now lie perfectly flat. I'm going to try something."

She watched as his hand appeared around the curved granite. He held a long stick with his black Stetson wobbling on the end. Slowly, he reached out until the tip of the hat emerged from behind the rock.

"Thwang!"

Another shot rang out.

Luke dropped the hat and swung his revolver in an arc, following the horizon.

"Did you see him?" she asked.

Luke nodded, never taking his eyes off the desert floor below them. "Yeah. At least I caught a bright flash. Probably the sunlight glinting off his rifle barrel."

From the corner of her eye, Anne saw the horses moving restlessly. Bounty reared slightly, and the frightened mare raised her head and whinnied in response. Anne held her breath. If the horses took off, she and Luke would be stranded. Easy prey for a killer with a long-range rifle.

A long, relieved sigh escaped her lips when Bounty settled down and Ladybug nuzzled close to him.

Then, suddenly, the air exploded again, quickly followed by a horrendous staccato rhythm as Luke returned the fire.

"Did . . . did you get him?" she asked breathlessly.

"No. He's out of my range, but I think I scared the hell out of him."

Luke thrust his revolver into his waistband and pulled a
pair of small, folding binoculars from his backpack. He
scanned the horizon as far as he could and still remain sheltered by the rocks. "There!" He pointed behind her. "Some
kind of vehicle—looks like an off-road bike—is about a mile
down the path. He must have hiked in on foot. That's why
we didn't hear him."

Anne nodded. She had her own worries. The horses were
moving around again. Bounty had jerked his reins free from
the bush and was backing away, toward the trail leading
down the hillside. The mare tossed her head, tugging at the
reins as she tried to follow him.

Not wanting to impart her mounting panic to Luke, she
willed herself to speak calmly. "What are we going to do,
Luke? We can't stay here all night."

"I've got an idea. I want you to start crawling toward me.
I'm pretty sure he can't see you or he wouldn't have stopped
shooting. But I'll cover you just in case."

"Wh-what good will that do?"

"If we can circle around to the other side of the horses
without his seeing us—we might have a chance to escape
through these boulders."

"We have to hurry. I think the horses are about to take
off."

"I'm surprised they haven't already," Luke responded, a
grim edge in his voice.

Anne closed her eyes, took deep invigorating breaths and
slowly counted to ten. When at last she felt her nerves settle
down, she asked, "Are you sure he can't see me?"

"I've got him spotted behind some shrubs in that arroyo
below. I'm sure he can't see you unless you stand up."

Her heart beating wildly, Anne forced her mind to concentrate on soothing images, meadows of wildflowers, starlit
nights. Anything to blank out the terror that was threaten-

ing to consume her. Taking a final deep breath of courage, she started scrabbling toward Luke and the rocks. Luke and safety. Luke.

With every movement, she waited for the gunshot. Waited for the blinding pain of a bullet ripping through her flesh.

Never had she been so frightened. She'd hyperventilated until her lungs felt as if they would burst. Not even when Scorpion had broken into her bedroom and come after her with that hypodermic syringe had she been so afraid. At least then she was able to see her enemy—even if he was just a dark shadow. Now she was crawling for her life from an unseen, yet very lethal threat.

Anne felt the dampness of perspiration rolling down her forehead, trickling past the corner of her eye. Funny, she felt cold. Clammy. Yet she was sweating.

She looked up. She was only about twenty feet from Luke's worried, beloved face.

"Anne! You're bleeding! How badly are you hurt?"

Reaching up, she dabbed at the damp smear she'd thought was perspiration. Her fingertip found a small nick on her cheekbone. "I'm okay," she hastened to assure him. "I must've been hit by a flying bit of rock or gravel." *Or a ricochet,* she thought, remembering with a shudder the way the bullets had whizzed back and forth over her head.

But she didn't stop moving.

An inch at a time. Then a foot. Always, ever closer to Luke. Ever closer to safety.

She bit her lip as a cactus needle pierced her thigh. Fought down a cough as sand clogged her throat. Her eyes. Her nose. She held her breath to avoid inhaling more dust.

"Come on, honey, you can do it." His deep, husky voice encouraged her, gave her strength when she felt her own ebb.

At last, the shadow of the boulder fell across her and she jumped to her feet and lunged for Luke. He leaned for-

ward, into the line of fire, to grab her and push her down
behind him, safe in the covering shelter of the rocks.

The ambusher's rifle cracked again—hitting Luke's gun
and knocking it from his grasp.

Luke watched, helpless, as his weapon flew across the
clearing and landed, teetering on the edge of a drop-off.

At that moment, the horses bolted, their thundering
hooves kicking up dirt and pebbles as they raced down the
narrow trail. Bounty's rear hoof flicked against the grip of
Luke's revolver as they galloped past.

As the dust settled, Luke felt his spirits falling like his revolver—a hundred feet to the desert floor below.

For a moment, he was plunged into a feeling of total
hopelessness. Desolation. He felt paralyzed with helplessness.

He'd let Anne down. Again.

He should have been looking behind them, watching for
Scorpion. Oh, when they first left Yuma he'd kept a steady
eye on the rear-view mirror, wary of anyone tailing them.
But as the miles passed, he'd obviously been too easily sat-
isfied that they'd eluded the gunman. Just as obviously,
Luke had been wrong.

Then he'd allowed his need for Anne to take command.
While he'd been making love to her, their pursuer had taken
advantage of Luke's distraction.

Now all he had left to protect her with were his wits. And
protect her he must.

Blowing a strand of hair out of his eyes, he picked up his
battered hat and plunked it onto his head. Using precious
seconds to regain his self-control, he finally turned to Anne.

She was scrunched down in the corner, her arms locked
around her knees. He expected to see a look of wide-eyed
terror, but her huge brown eyes were gazing at him with absolute trust.

A strange, almost foreign feeling folded over him like a golden cloak.

Ever since Glenna's death, his self-confidence had been eroding like a sandy beach during a tidal wave. But he did know one thing—he was a darn good agent. Placing modesty aside, he was one of the finest agents in his branch. Maybe in the entire bureau.

Since he'd come to Arizona and immediately fallen prey to Anne's charms, he'd allowed his attraction for her—his fear for her safety—to stifle his natural abilities.

No more. If he couldn't outwit some thug who made his living killing innocent women, then it was time to turn in his badge. Scorpion might be ruthless, canny. But the fiend was no more ruthless than Luke could be. Especially with Anne's life on the line.

Kneeling beside her, he took her face between his palms. "I want you to listen to me very carefully, Anne Farraday."

"Yes, Luke."

"Up until now, I've pretty much mucked things up. I've been so worried about you—been so much on the defensive—that I haven't made any offensive preparations. But I want you to know that if I have to pull that monster's arms and legs off with my teeth, he won't get to you. You have to believe me. Trust me. Please."

Her voice was as soft and reassuring as spring rain on the desert. "I do trust you, Luke."

"Good." He gulped, almost choking on the overwhelming love that was curling through his chest. He might not be the man to provide this woman with the happiness and peace she deserved, but he'd do his best to keep her alive so she could find it.

But first he had to find a way to get them back to civilization.

He stood up. "We've still got about an hour before night falls. I think if we can climb higher up this mountain, he won't be able to find us. Then, about daybreak, we can circle around behind his vehicle. Either hot-wire it or remove the distributor cap and disable it."

"What about the horses? Maybe we could find them."

He shook his head. "I doubt it. They're probably headed back to the spring where we parked the truck. Although they may help us in another way."

"How?"

"If they wander onto the highway, someone is bound to call the authorities. We'll have to keep a sharp eye out. They might send a search party."

"Let's hope so."

He reached down and grabbed her hand, helping her to her feet. "At any rate, I'd say we'd better get out of Dodge City here. The longer we stand around, the closer Scorpion could be."

In reply, Anne grabbed her own backpack and strapped it on. "Let's go then."

Luke took a step back and gazed up the mountainside to better familiarize himself with their surroundings. They were completely exposed on the cliff face so he decided to take the more circuitous route through the nooks and crevices until they were well out of Scorpion's sight.

It was going to be a steep, treacherous climb in places and he hoped Anne was up to it. She'd taken a lot of abuse these past few days. Fortunately, she'd been in good physical shape before this ordeal began. *Very* good physical shape, he thought, remembering with a shudder of desire the way her breasts curved so perfectly into his palms.

He better quit thinking about her sumptuous body and get them out of there.

Taking her hand, he decided to try following the base of the mountain. Keep them moving away from where he'd last seen Scorpion—at least until Luke could find an easier path up the mountain.

But there was no other path. And after only about ten minutes, the trail took a sharp, upward turn.

He stopped to allow her to catch her breath. He'd been setting an arduous pace, but she hadn't uttered a word of complaint. His own leg muscles were burning with exertion, even though he followed the bureau's stringent exercise regimen. Anne must be half-dead from exhaustion.

The sun had dropped behind the mountain, and only its faint orange and ochre glow was offering any light. In another half hour, the path would be too dangerous to climb without light.

He had a powerful flash in his pack, but knew it could also serve to point out their progress to their stalker.

Then, somewhere below them, a twig snapped sharply.

The air was hushed for a moment, silent with apprehension. Then the sound of small creatures darting for safety rustled in the night air.

Scorpion was coming after them.

They had no place to go but up. With only a few moments of light remaining, he hesitated to climb higher. But they had no choice. To stay where they were was to invite certain death.

Anne nodded and, without a word between them, they continued their ascent.

Clumsy with fatigue and trepidation, they inched up the mountain. Once, Luke glanced back and caught sight of Anne's pinched, white face. He snarled and bit his lip until a drop of blood pooled at the corner of his mouth. He couldn't stand that this was happening to her. If he could trade his life for hers, he'd rush down to meet Scorpion right now. But that was a fantasy he couldn't afford to indulge. He had to concentrate on keeping up their spirits and putting more distance between them and Scorpion. Forcing a confident smile onto his lips, he winked at her and continued climbing.

Even in the dim light, Anne recognized the emotions flitting across Luke's face. She knew he was frightened. Oh, not for himself, but for her well-being. She wondered briefly why she wasn't swamped with fright. Why she felt this peculiar calmness every time she looked up and saw Luke in front of her.

She knew why. Luke's intellect and unmatched physical strength were evident in every inch of his incredibly masculine body—from the brawn of his powerful legs to the masterful muscles rippling beneath his sweat-dampened shirt. She saw untold courage in the tilt of his head and valor in the shining cast of his gray eyes.

Her heart filled with pride. Anne knew there was no one on this earth she would rather be with—would trust more—in this situation. Her cold, rational, logical self recognized and understood the danger they were in. But her soft, bursting heart assured her Luke would keep her safe.

When he stopped for a rest, she leaned against his shoulder for a moment's respite. He reached around and patted her shoulder. "We'll make it, sweet," he whispered.

And she believed him.

At least until she heard the crackling sound of brush breaking somewhere below them. Needles of fear pierced her flesh like a thousand pinpricks. The man who was trying so desperately to kill her was rapidly gaining on them. Anne could almost feel his hot, rancid breath on her neck.

"Come on, let's go." His urgent whisper spurred her on as once again, they began their ascent.

Anne grabbed his waistband for support. Soon she wouldn't be able to see him, but she had to know he was there. As long as he was with her, Anne knew her strength wouldn't fail.

She almost stumbled when Luke stopped without warning.

"What is it?" she whispered. "What's wrong?"

Anne could no longer make out his features in the dim light, but she could feel his frustration shimmering in the air between them.

Blowing out his breath in a deep sigh, he said, "I think we've reached some kind of path, but it's too dark to see. Sometimes these mountain ledges break off suddenly. I don't want to risk going farther."

"What . . . what do we do? We can't just sit here and wait for him to come find us."

"I want you to sit down. Better yet, lie down on your stomach."

"Right here?"

"Yes." There was a soft rustle as she lowered to the ground. Then Luke stretched out beside her.

She was confused. She'd never had any wilderness survival training, but she knew the desert's temperatures dropped dramatically at night. They needed to find shelter. "We can't sleep here—out in the open, can we?"

"No. But I want to use my flashlight for a minute, take a survey of the topography. That light will be like a beacon for our friend, Scorpion. So the lower we are to the ground, the less of a target we'll be."

"Makes sense." Her voice sounded calm, accepting. Even to her own ears. Inside, barely hidden by her composed facade, Anne's nerves felt like thin strands of frayed string. Much more pressure—one more assault on her spirit—and she might snap in two.

Luke fumbled through his knapsack for the flashlight. The rattle of stones falling behind them reminded him that Scorpion was gaining ground.

Luke breathed deeply, forcing himself to stay in control. *Keep your cool, McCullough.* He had to keep telling himself he could outwit this madman. For Anne's sake, he *had* to.

When his fingertips finally grasped the flashlight, he trained it first on the ground in front of them. They were on a plateau carved into the mountainside, a flat semicircle about thirty feet across. The surface was perfectly smooth, as if it had been blasted out with dynamite.

He lifted the flash, focusing its beam directly in front of them.

Suddenly, he frowned. Something didn't look right. Not at all.

He rose to a low crouch and duck-walked forward. After a few moments, he stopped and swiveled his beam around the small clearing. A few shrubs ringed the semicircle. He flashed the light up the side of the mountain. Other than a few ominous-looking dark patches, there was no cover. No shelter.

"What is it?" Anne's hushed voice called out.

"Shh. Sound travels far at night," he cautioned. Twisting on his heels, he scooted back to where she lay waiting.

"What is it? What did you see?"

He sucked in his upper lip and ran a weary hand through his hair. How could he tell her? She'd been so very brave for so long.

It broke Luke's heart to have to give Anne more bad news.

Of the four possible directions—there was no good choice. On the left side, the rocky face of the mountain rose like a jagged, vertical monolith.

Off the path to their right was a sharp drop-off, the crumbling, uncharted side of the mountain.

The killer was following directly behind them.

And in front of them where he'd just scouted was the worst news of all. The little plateau ended abruptly in a sheer cliff. If they had just gone a few steps farther, they would have been plunged hundreds of feet down the mountainside.

They were boxed in. Trapped.

Looking into her sweet face, he wondered how the hell he could tell her that they'd reached the end of the trail.

Chapter Thirteen

Judging by the crashing noises in the brush, it sounded as if their pursuer was only seconds behind them. Panic wouldn't help them, Anne knew, but she had to fight to keep its choking, grasping tentacles from taking hold. What were they going to do?

There was no escape. They had no weapons, other than their hands. Could they somehow take Scorpion by surprise and overpower him?

Following the beam of Luke's flashlight, she looked for a heavy rock to use as a weapon.

Now even the weather was turning into their enemy. The wind was kicking up, producing an eerie moaning in the emptiness. For the first time, Anne noticed the mist creeping up the mountain. And the cold. She shivered. Earlier, their exertion had fueled their body heat, but now, with every passing moment, the chill deepened within their bones.

Another strong gust whirled across the plateau, blowing sand and pebbles into her eyes. Anne stifled a scream as a huge tumbleweed blew into her face. They needed to find shelter. Soon. Very soon.

Kicking the scratchy tumbleweed aside, she wrapped her arms around her face while she continued her search for a large enough stone to use as a weapon.

Then, the cloud cover overhead shifted and the full moon emerged, casting the entire area in a silvery glow.

Luke looked up, flicked off his flashlight and continued investigating the sparse shrubbery surrounding the mountain's base. He nosed behind larger bushes and boulders, obviously searching for a hiding place.

Suddenly, Anne's voice hissed out of the near darkness. "Luke! Quick. Come here."

Abandoning his search, he blinked rapidly, trying to wash the sand from his eyes. He hoped she'd found a miracle—he was out of them. Once Luke could see clearly, he rushed across the clearing to where she was bending over near a jumble of weeds and brush. Her teeth were chattering with cold.

"What? Did you find something," he whispered.

Even with the wind muffling their voices, they had no way of knowing how far sounds were traveling.

Pulling aside the spiny leaves of an overgrown yucca, he shone his light into a dark crevice cut into the rocky mountainside. About four feet in height, the crevice was wider at the bottom, forming a triangular-shaped cave. The opening was just about wide enough for the two of them to fit inside.

Using hand gestures and occasional whispers, they decided that tiny cavern was their only hope. They could gather dead branches and scrub to conceal the opening. It *might* work in the darkness. Unless some wild animal or a den of rattlers had had the idea first.

A loud clatter of rocks falling shattered the quiet.

Scorpion! He couldn't be more than a hundred yards behind them.

Placing one palm firmly in the small of her back, and the other on top of her head to keep her from banging into the rock face, Luke shoved, and Anne stumbled into the miniscule cavern.

Holding her hands over her mouth to stifle the moan of apprehension she felt rumbling in her chest, she watched helplessly as Luke hurriedly returned to the clearing.

Grabbing the huge tumbleweed that had blown into her face, he rushed up the trail, in the direction from which they had just come. Toward Scorpion.

Using the tumbleweed like a broom, he swept away traces of their footprints. *Hurry, Luke, hurry,* she called silently. Any moment now and the man who was intent on stalking them till their death would be upon them.

Luke worked quickly, scuffing the earth to the entrance of the tiny cave, then scooted in beside her. Together, they pushed the crackly branches of the tumbleweed in among the yucca leaves, covering the cave opening.

Inside, the cavern was higher and deeper than it looked from the outside. Although the space easily accommodated both of them, Anne found herself squeezing closer to Luke. The breadth of his body was reassuring, and she drew strength from him. He wrapped an arm around her and brushed her face lightly with his lips. Suddenly, she began to believe it was possible that Scorpion wouldn't find them.

After a few moments of huddling together, Luke leaned forward and carefully parted a slot in the yucca leaves. Anne bent her head close to his. By peeking through the branches, they could see the clearing.

The full moon spotlighted the area almost as if it were a stage in an avant-garde theater and they were the only audience. The atmosphere was hushed, yet alive, sparking with tension. Even the wind had suppressed its howl, as if it, too, were waiting for the curtain to rise and the principal players to take their places.

The clouds shifted overhead, and slowly, ever so slowly, the arena before them darkened until only a tiny gleam of light beamed down onto the plateau. At that moment, the shuffling sound of heavy footsteps sounded just offstage. Anne held her breath and clasped Luke's arm in a viselike grip.

As their eyes adjusted to the semidarkness, the clouds shifted again and the clearing was plunged into blackness.

Then, with all the drama of a seasoned thespian, the villain staggered into the center of the clearing.

Materializing like a ghostly apparition, the tall, lean torso slowly became discernible in the night. Anne narrowed her eyes, trying to identify her pursuer. There was something familiar about him, but specterlike, he kept blending with the shadows and she couldn't get a clear image. For a moment, she had been certain he was the lawyer, Dan Nevill, but now she wasn't so sure. He seemed shorter. Stockier.

William? It was possible, but . . . impossible to tell in the darkness.

His rifle was clearly visible in his left hand. In his other hand, he was holding something smaller. Another gun? Then, Anne heard a sound—*snick!*—followed by a piercing white light. She blinked and covered her eyes with her hand. The light moved away, and she realized he'd turned on a heavy-duty flashlight and was carefully searching the area.

The shifting beam made his movements easy to follow as he paced back and forth, scanning the small clearing. They could make out his body bending, as he peered over the mountainside, perhaps looking for a ledge where they could be hiding.

Then he moved back to the center of the clearing, and swore darkly. After standing motionless a full minute, he turned, then began walking slowly toward their makeshift hideout. Shining the powerful torch directly into their faces.

Anne shoved a knuckle into her mouth and bit down. Hard. Luke gently disengaged himself and leaned in front of her, holding his own flashlight like a bludgeon.

Scorpion stepped closer. And closer still. The tips of his scuffed hiking boots were less than a yard away. Anne was sure the killer would hear her heart thumping in her chest. Hear her breath coming in short spurts. Smell her fear.

Then, miraculously, he moved away.

His probing light focused above them, up the mountain.

Anne exhaled with a deep sigh and she realized that she had been holding her breath. She wanted to scoot back next to Luke, to absorb some of his strength and courage. But she was afraid to move a muscle, worried she might dislodge a pebble or somehow make a sound that would bring Scorpion back.

Maybe, she thought, if they kept very still, he would turn away and go back down the mountain. Give up.

But her hopes were short-lived. Scorpion set his flashlight on the ground and began picking up bits of rubble. Sticks. Broken branches. After a time, he dumped his armful of trash into the center of the clearing and bent down.

She heard a tiny rasping sound, then the unmistakable odor of sulphur wafted into the cave as Scorpion lit a match. His small pile of rubble caught like kindling; and soon, a small fire was burning.

Scorpion looked around, then walked to the edge of the clearing and grabbed loose, dead branches and added them to his blaze. Crossing the clearing once again, he stopped in front of their cave and started to pull on the tumbleweed hiding the opening.

Reaching forward, Luke held the tumbleweed firmly in place. Scorpion yanked once. Twice. Then cursed and stalked away.

When he reappeared, he dropped down on the other side of the camp fire.

A horrible premonition swept over her and Anne turned to face Luke only to see her fears confirmed in the grim expression on his face. Scorpion was going to spend the night right there. In the middle of the clearing.

Twenty feet away from them.

When morning came, surely he'd find their hiding place. They only had until dawn to figure out how to escape.

Then, the lonely mournful sound of the wind returned, echoing Anne's feeling of isolation. At every juncture, fate had thumbed its nose at them. But Scorpion hadn't won. At least not yet. This...executioner...this galling, heartless monster was relentless.

But so was she. With Luke by her side, they would somehow beat him. She'd been through too much, given up too much to quit now.

Somehow, during the night, they'd come up with a plan. Find some way to defeat Scorpion. He wasn't going to win this time. At least, not without one hell of a fight.

Luke tugged at her arm. Anne turned her head, and in the flickering glow of Scorpion's firelight, she saw Luke pointing to the rear of their small cave.

Puzzled, she twisted around.

In a dark, shadowy recess, concealed by Luke's body, was another—smaller—opening going deep into the side of the mountain. Using a crude sign language, Luke instructed her to hold his flashlight over his shoulder and shine it into the hole, while he searched.

Frightened that Scorpion might see the light or hear them moving around, she shook her head.

Placing her chin between his thumb and forefinger, he bobbed her head up and down. Yes, he was telling her.

She took the flashlight from his hand.

With gentle fingers he touched her cheek and turned away, wriggling into the opening. Slithering on his belly like a huge viper, he disappeared into the passage. A second later he backed out and signaled for her to give him the flashlight, then he crawled once again into the mouth of the other cavern.

Anne was alone. The seconds loomed like minutes while Luke was gone. She squinched her eyes shut, straining to hear any sound, any movement that would tell her he was nearby.

Finally, a lifetime later, his head poked out of the opening and he motioned with his fingers for her to follow him. A sick feeling clutched at her stomach. She hated dark, tight spaces. She didn't want to crawl down that narrow passage to... to what?

What did it matter? If they stayed where they were, by morning Scorpion would find them and they'd surely be killed. Maybe there was another way out of this cavern. Maybe there was a concealed passage that would take them out to the other side of the mountain. Things like that were always happening in movies. But Anne didn't have to remind herself that if the recent events of her life were put in a film, it would be a horror movie. And she'd be cast as the luckless victim.

Luke nudged her knee with his finger and motioned with his hand while silently mouthing his command. "Come on. Hurry."

She didn't have to be a lip-reader to understand him.

Anne drew a deep breath and expelled it in a long fatalistic whoosh. Oh, the hell with it!

Quickly, before she chickened out, she flopped over onto her stomach and closed her eyes. Hands in front of her, clutching at Luke's pant legs, she crawled behind him down a seemingly endless passage.

Finally, he stopped and sat up. Anne opened her eyes to total and absolute blackness. She gasped, her fear tangible, quivering in the air.

Luke pulled her next to him and whispered in her ear. "Shh. It's okay. Watch."

Twisting until the breadth of his back was covering the cave opening, he switched on the flash.

They were sitting in a cavernous enclosure the size of a small bedroom. Not quite tall enough for them to stand, the space still had a much higher ceiling than the little cubbyhole they'd just vacated. They could crawl or sit up quite comfortably in here.

As Anne looked around, her short-lived hope faded. The alcove, though deep, didn't offer a tunnel to the other side of the mountain. The walls were solid granite and there was no apparent exit. Still, it was dry and flat. It was a little warmer here, affording a bit more protection from the bitter cold that Anne knew would come later in the night.

Besides, she thought, closely checking the rim of the cozy chamber, there were no wild creatures unwilling to share their accommodations, and there was room for them to stretch out. *And* it was farther away from Scorpion.

Far enough away so that she and Luke could talk softly without danger of being overheard. All in all, their temporary abode was quite suitable.

Except it *was* noisier than the first cave. There must have been an imperceptible crack in the walls because the wind's shrieking was much louder here. Maybe a storm was brewing outside and Scorpion would get blown off the plateau. She could only hope.

Luke took her arm again and pointed toward the far wall. Following his lead, they crawled to the opposite side and peeled off their backpacks. The burden on her shoulders eased as if she'd been carrying a sack of bricks all day. Rotating her arms, she worked out the kinks in her shoulder blades, the knots in her neck.

"Here, let me do that." Luke's whisper sounded like a gunshot. It seemed hours since she'd heard his voice. It was as warm and bolstering as warm honey on homemade biscuits.

Biscuits. Honey. With a start, Anne realized she was hungry. Starving.

Yanking her purse strap off her shoulder, she rummaged around and brought out the granola bars and two large, shiny red apples.

A virtual feast.

Luke grinned his appreciation. "You never cease to amaze me, Annie Farraday," he whispered, biting into the sweet, juicy pulp.

It was getting colder now, bitingly cold. Her breath puffed with each bite. Luke huddled closer. Anne scooted next to him, laying her cheek against his shoulder, savoring the warmth of his body. Neither of them spoke while they polished off their apples.

Later, when they'd finished the granola bars, they leaned back to rest, finally replete.

To save the batteries, Luke had turned off the flashlight and they were alone in the absolute darkness. Curling up against him, she asked, "Luke, there's no way out of here. We have to figure out a game plan."

"Got any suggestions?"

Wordlessly, she shook her head.

Luke's sigh of frustration filled the air between them. "I don't know what we're going to do. *Yet.* But now that we're at least temporarily safe and finally got some food in our stomachs, we need some rest. But don't worry, honey, we'll figure something out. It'll take more than that fiend's got to stop a team like us.''

A team. How sweet those words sounded. How... permanent somehow. But how could she even think about permanence when their future was only secured, at best, for a few more hours?

A strong, howling wind dropped the temperature another few degrees in their temporary dwelling and she cuddled closer, absorbing the warmth of his body. Offering hers.

''Come here,'' he murmured, pulling her onto his lap.

He wrapped his arms around her and rested his chin on the top of her head. ''Better?''

''Mmm. Much.''

Curling against him, Anne thought again about how much she'd grown to depend on this man, how much she...she *loved* this man. This quiet, strong man about whom she knew so little.

''Luke?''

''Hmm?''

''Have you...have you ever been married?''

He sighed heavily and was silent for so long she thought he might not answer. Finally, a deep sadness in his voice, he said, ''No. Almost was once but didn't quite make it to the altar.''

''Why?''

Again that long, penetrating silence.

''That's all right, we don't have to talk about it. I didn't mean to pry,'' Anne said.

''No. You're not. Prying, I mean. It's just that I've buried all those feelings for so long that it's hard to bring them out in the open. But maybe it's time.''

She waited, sensing that he was gathering his thoughts, dealing with his own emotions before he shared them with her. At last, he started talking. "It was about five years ago. There had been several mob-related hits in Las Vegas, and the tourist bureau was getting nervous. Anyway, they appealed to the FBI, and I was assigned to track down this rather productive shooter. While I was working, I met a cocktail waitress named Glenna Glaser."

"What did she look like?" Anne couldn't resist asking.

"Blond. Buxom. Exactly the kind of woman you imagine when you think of Vegas."

"Oh." Anne's hand involuntarily dropped to her own adequate but not outstanding bosom.

As if reading her thoughts, Luke laughed grimly. "It was *not* her breasts I was attracted to. Anyway, during the course of the investigation, Glenna and I became . . . involved. She was the first woman I'd ever really cared about."

Anne said nothing, listening while Luke struggled with what was obviously a very painful past.

After a few moments, he picked up the thread of his story. "I fell hard. I should have taken myself off the case because I'd lost my concentration. But I didn't realize it at the time."

Anne heard the bitter disappointment in his voice. After all these years, he still blamed himself for whatever happened. That guilt must have taken a terrible toll on his confidence.

"One night in my hotel room . . . after we'd made love, I fell asleep."

Forcing a quiet, soothing tone into her voice, she asked, "And?"

Luke shrugged helplessly. Anne could almost see his guilt, weighted on his shoulders like a pair of anvils. He didn't speak again for almost five minutes. When he did, his voice was heavy, wracked by long years of merciless guilt. It was obvious from his tone of self-disgust that although others might forgive him, he couldn't forgive himself.

"Anyway, I must have been getting too close to the hit man, and he decided to give me a warning. One I wouldn't misunderstand. Near as we were able to reconstruct, someone came to the room that night. Without waking me up, Glenna must have opened the door and... The hit man used a knife. He was fast and silent. I slept through it all and found her body in the living room when I woke up an hour later."

Anne didn't know what to say. What to do. She had no words that would ease his pain. How he must have relived every moment. How horrid these past few days must have been for him.

She recalled the last night, when she'd lured him into her bed. If Scorpion had managed somehow to get to her last night, Anne knew she would have had to bear an equal share of the responsibility.

Twisting in his arms, Anne reached up and touched his mouth with her fingertips. She caressed the strong, beloved planes of his face, and stroked the lids of his mesmerizing gray eyes. "I'm so sorry," was all she could say.

"Close your eyes, honey. We'd better try to grab a couple hours' sleep while we can."

"Luke, I'm not afraid. Somehow, together, we'll get out of this. Alive."

Luke felt her unguarded love reach up and envelop him in its sweet cloud. How had he—they—allowed this to happen? There was no future. None. Why were they both so willing—no eager, to put themselves through the kind of hell he knew would ultimately claim them?

If—and that was a huge if—they survived this night, got off this mountain alive, they still would end up hurting each

other. Even if Anne testified and Riczini ended up behind
prison bars for the rest of his life, he was a vengeful man.
No one knew that better than Luke. Riczini wouldn't rest
until Anne was eliminated. To stay out of that evil man's
grasp, she'd be forced to spend her life in hiding. Moving
from one locale, one identity, to another.

And what about him? What if he lived through this?
What if there really was justice in this world and he appre-
hended Scorpion? It would be back to Washington for
reassignment. Then what?

No matter how optimistically fate stacked the cards, they
would never be stacked in their favor. The odds were too
high against them.

But Anne was right about one thing. They did have tonight.

He wanted to hold her in his arms, breathe in her es-
sence. Keep her safe. Whisper enough loving words to last
a lifetime. Whether that lifetime was another fifty years. Or
just tonight.

Slipping momentarily from her embrace, he pushed the
knapsacks aside, then lowered himself and pulled her next
to him.

Poising over her, he touched her hair. Her face. Ran his
fingers along the contours of her cheeks. Memorizing the
feel of her. Savoring the touch of her. Gathering enough
sensory experiences to take with him for later. When they
were both alone.

With each passing moment, their chances of survival were
ticking away. But for right now—for tonight—their love
shone brighter than any star in the universe.

Tomorrow would have to wait.

Chapter Fourteen

Anne woke up with a start. It was as dark as an Arctic night and just as cold. Her teeth were chattering uncontrollably, and a layer of goose bumps covered her body from head to toe.

A strange keening noise whistled over her head, and her back was aching. For a moment, she was disoriented, didn't know where she was, only that she was naked and freezing.

Then she felt Luke's warm arms pulling her into him, providing shelter from the frigid wind.

"Here, wrap this around you," he whispered, disengaging himself from her shivering body. "I found an old saddle blanket in one of the backpacks."

The thin, scratchy rug felt as luxurious as cashmere. She felt his hands gently rubbing her chilled flesh, warming her. As they lay still, nesting like spoons, he asked, "Better?"

"Mmm. Much. Thanks."

Reaching behind his back, he fumbled in a knapsack and pulled out a candy bar. Breaking it in two, he offered half to Anne. "Eat this. It'll give us some energy. And we're going to need it."

Anne slowly munched the nutty chocolate. Normally, she was a chocoholic, but tonight the candy tasted like cardboard. Not for one moment could she forget the lethal stalker waiting for them just a few yards away.

For a while, neither one spoke as they drifted in that gentle twilight between sleep and wakefulness. He knew neither of them really wanted to awake, to face the realities of daybreak. Luke knew the moment of truth was approaching. He only hoped his years of training would overcome his personal involvement. That he would be able to put his disturbing feelings aside and concentrate on the job at hand.

"Anne? I've been thinking for hours and, unless you can come up with a miracle, we only have one option—we have to tackle Scorpion head-on."

"No!"

"We don't have any choice. The only thing we've got going for us is the element of surprise."

Anne thought for a moment. "Do you really think we can sneak out there and overpower him?"

"Not 'we'—me."

"Don't give me that macho crap, McCullough. We're in this together. Granted, you're stronger—"

"And don't forget extensively trained for this kind of thing."

"But I can still create a diversion," she insisted.

Luke pressed his lips against her hair, breathing in her faint, womanly fragrance. She was a woman to die for. "I don't think we'll need a diversion if we can catch him deep asleep."

He lifted his arm and looked at the luminous face of his wristwatch. It was nearly four in the morning. Whatever they decided to do, it would have to be soon. Another hour until dawn. Lifting his arm from her shoulder, he sat up.

"Are we going now?"

He brushed the glorious tumble of copper curls from her face and lightly kissed her temple. "I'm afraid so."

"In the dark?"

"I think he'll be in a deeper sleep while it's still dark."

"Maybe," Anne said. "But there's also a good chance that you might trip over a rock or something and wake him up. I think we ought to wait until just before the sun comes up. When that predawn glow will give us a little bit of light."

Luke considered her suggestion. "You may be right, Annie. As usual. Is your nickname Wonder Woman, by any chance?"

Turning over in his arms, she reached up and took his face in her cupped hands. "I want to tell you something. No matter what happens today, I want to thank you for what you've done."

"Only my job, and not very well."

"That's malarkey and you know it. But I wasn't just talking about keeping me alive. You've given me a lot more. You've given me back a sense of *having* a life, instead of staying on the outskirts, watching other people live. You've taught me to take chances, to care again. I'm not so afraid anymore. I have you to thank for that, Luke Mc-Cullough."

Lowering his face, he pressed his lips to hers. Her naturally sweet mouth was redolent of chocolate, and she hungrily returned his kiss. Luke had to exercise all the willpower he still possessed to pull away from her, but their very lives depended on him now. It was almost time.

"Anne, thanks for listening to me last night. No one wants to hear about their lover's old flame, but I needed to unload."

For a moment, she didn't speak. "I'm sorry Glenna was killed, Luke. But I'm not sorry that I'm here now."

"Me, neither."

He kissed her again. A kiss filled with the solace of old wounds now laid to rest. A kiss of tender promise for an uncertain future. A kiss of ultimate perfection.

When they drew apart, Luke said, "There was one thing I didn't tell you last night."

"Oh?"

"We never found the hit man who killed Glenna, but the word from our informants was that it was none other than our friend, Scorpion."

"Oh, my God! Luke, you shouldn't have taken this assignment. This must have been absolute hell for you."

"Yeah, well, after Glenna died, I vowed to get that murderer if it took the rest of my life. Looks like that might be the case. Anyway, let's see if we can come up with a plan."

She sat up and wrapped her arms around her knees while they developed a simple strategy: Anne was to remain hidden in the other chamber of the cave while, using the covering darkness, Luke was going to try to take Scorpion by surprise.

At first, she argued that the two of them would stand a better chance of overpowering the killer, but Luke eventually convinced her that Scorpion would go after her, maybe use her as a shield against Luke.

In the end, she was going to stay out of sight, coming into the open only if it looked as if Luke was running into trouble.

Leaving their backpacks in the inner chamber, Anne followed behind him as they crawled back to the outer section of the cavern. The first pale rays of dawn had lightened the small enclosure, dusting everything with a powdery gray cast. The same shimmery color of Luke's eyes when he laughed.

She closed her eyes, saying a silent prayer. Asking for another time to enjoy Luke's laughter. Another chance at life.

Grasping at slender hope, she inched forward. Once more following Luke.

Lying on his stomach, with Anne behind him in the linking tunnel, Luke gingerly parted the yucca branches and peeked out. Scorpion's campfire had almost died. Only a few flickering embers sparked occasionally. In the predawn murkiness, he could just make out the bulky shape of the killer's body, still huddled on the far side of his campfire.

"Anne, no matter what happens, I want you to stay here until it's over. Until I tell you it's safe. Do you hear me?"

"Yes, Luke."

"And if something happens to me—"

"Nothing's going to happen to you!"

"But if it *does,* he's going to come looking for you. So I want you to watch. If he manages to take me, I want you to fly out of here and smack him on the head with the biggest rock you can find. Here, take this one."

He grabbed a heavy piece of granite that weighed about five pounds and was still small enough to fit easily in her hand. "I mean it, Anne. Don't wait for anything. Surprise is the only advantage you'll have. Just smash him as hard as you can and run like hell. Don't stop until you get back to the truck. There's a pistol behind the driver's seat. Ernie uses it for target practice. There are a couple of spare bullets in the glove compartment. Are you listening to me? Will you do exactly what I say?"

"Yes, Luke." Her whisper was as soft as a teardrop.

"Good."

Cupping her face between his hands, he took a long, steadying look at Anne's trusting face. Although it was still too dark to see her clearly, his memory filled in the details: the tiny creases at the corners of her eyes, that one miniature dimple at the edge of her mouth, her smooth straight forehead, the intelligence mirrored in her gaze. If Luke had to die, Anne's face was the image he wanted to take with him.

Quickly, before his courage flagged and he couldn't leave her, Luke scrabbled forward, heedless of the brush and cactus needles scratching his face.

As soon as his feet disappeared out the opening, Anne scrambled to take his place. Her heart in her throat, she watched as he rose slowly and moved toward the sleeping man with the stealthy grace of an Apache.

Not a sound broke the silence. No warbling call of morning birds. No rustling of small creatures emerging from their dens to forage for food. Only the whisper of Luke's boots as he padded cautiously across the clearing.

Keeping wide of their pursuer, he circled around, approaching him from the rear.

Luke stopped about a yard from the killer.

Tension crackled through the air like an electric charge. Only three more feet. She saw the long barrel of the rifle inches from Scorpion's hand.

With agonizing slowness, Luke took another step forward. Stopped. Waited. Then, lifted his right leg for another step.

At that moment, the man roared like a wounded moose and grabbed for the rifle.

Lurching to maintain his balance, Luke kicked, his foot catching the rifle butt and lifting it off the ground. Like a javelin, the weapon sailed through the air above the campfire and came to a clattering stop near the base of the mountain where Anne was hiding in the cave.

With a bellow of long-pent-up rage, Luke pounced on the killer.

Anne clutched her rock to her breast. She was afraid to watch and afraid to turn away. Each blow Scorpion landed on Luke struck a responsive pain in her own body. But she had to keep watching. Luke might need her help.

As the men rolled in the dirt, pummeling and grunting, Anne looked at the gun lying so close. All she had to do was crawl out of the cave and grab it.

But Luke had told her to stay inside.

She'd promised to follow his instructions.

But if she could get that gun . . .

Her eyes flew back across the clearing. The first pink light of dawn had risen above the lip of the plateau, illuminating the arena where the two men fought. They rolled. Punched. Arms flailing wildly, it was hard to tell them apart.

Then Luke raised his head, and she saw Scorpion's fingers wrapped around his throat. Squeezing. Luke's face was suffused with red, his teeth gritted with strain. He was choking!

Anne made her decision.

Throwing aside the rock Luke had given her, she scooted out of the cramped opening on her hands and knees. As soon as she was completely outside, she jumped up and sprang for the rifle.

The assassin must have seen her movement. Releasing one hand from Luke's throat, he patted the ground, his huge, bony hand scraping along the sand. She could see he was searching for something, a rock, a stick, a clump of earth. Something he could use to knock Luke out. Then Scorpion would be free to direct his assault on Anne.

Luke jerked away, and leaned forward on his knees, gasping. Filling his starved lungs with oxygen.

The killer's hand reached the edge of the camp fire and grabbed one of the rocks he'd gathered for a fire ring. Raising the heavy stone, he swung around where Luke was doubled over, still trying to catch his breath, and aimed for the side of his head.

At the last minute, Luke jerked aside and the rock glanced off his shoulder just as Luke swung his arm. His shoulder separated with a popping noise loud enough that Anne heard it across the clearing.

A searing pain immobilized him for a moment. Sweat popped out on his forehead as a wave of nausea rose from his churning stomach. Before Scorpion could take advantage of Luke's momentary frailty, Luke gritted his teeth and growled like a mighty grizzly. Ignoring the blazing pain shooting down his arm, he lunged for the killer. He held his right arm close to his body, and swung with all his strength with his left.

Scorpion easily deflected the blow.

Anne cocked the rifle and raised it to her shoulder. But she couldn't get a clear shot. She inched forward, covering them with the rifle.

With a furious growl, the killer rolled over and kicked Luke in the temple, stunning him. Then, lifting the heavy rock high in the air, the hired murderer rose to his knees, gathering force to smash Luke's head.

She couldn't let him kill Luke!

Before she had time to think, Anne aimed at the man's bulky chest and fired. Immediately, a red bloom seeped through the sleeve of his jacket as the impact of the bullet wrenched his body around. He took two staggering steps before his hands fell, the stone dropping from his grasp, striking Luke.

A trickle of blood dripped down Luke's face, then his eyes rolled and he sank to the ground. Still.

Anne lowered the weapon as wave after wave of horror swept through her. She'd killed Luke.

Scorpion was still alive, though. Before she fully realized what was happening, the man swiveled around. Bleating with pain and rage, he charged Anne.

With a trembling hand, she jammed the bolt action forward, cocking the gun. The man was almost upon her.

Closing her eyes, she fired again.

The second shot caught him in the shoulder and he staggered backward. Spinning on his heel, he continued to weave like a punch-drunk fighter.

Anne watched, paralyzed with shock as the wounded man lurched and stumbled across the clearing. Then, teetering on the edge of the embankment, he made a dreadful gurgling noise deep in his throat and pitched forward. Over the cliff.

A long, trailing scream followed his descent.

Then, abruptly, the scream stopped and a dire silence took its place.

Dropping the weapon, Anne ran to Luke's side and slumped to the ground beside him. Cradling his head in her lap, tears coursing down her cheeks, she murmured words of love. "Oh, Luke, please. Don't leave me. I...I need you."

A deep, wrenching sob tore from her soul. She could bear anything, even bear his leaving—just please, let him be alive!

With a soft moan, Luke twisted in her arms. Fresh tears, these of phenomenal relief, traveled down her chin, dripping onto Luke's precious face.

Raising his left hand with a groan, he reached up, reverently touching her as if she were a sacred object. "What happened? Scorpion?"

"Dead. I...shot him. Twice. He fell over...over the cliff."

Luke struggled to sit up, but her clutching embrace held him fast. "Anne, are you all right?" It seemed to Luke that he was always asking her that. But he didn't know how else to gauge her emotions. Sooner or later, the shock of having killed a man would rip through her. Luke knew that better than most. But for right now, he hoped the shock didn't set in until they were down the mountain.

Pushing up to a sitting position, he cradled his right arm and grimaced. She'd already saved his life. Now he was going to need her help along the narrow trail.

Within a half hour, Anne's quivering nerves had settled down somewhat. Using his belt, she was able to help Luke immobilize his arm. Finding a courage she couldn't have imagined yesterday, she crawled alone back inside the dark lair and retrieved the flashlight and their backpacks. She emptied Luke's of all nonessentials and folded it into hers. She didn't care how much he argued, that man wasn't going to try to strap that thing over his injured shoulder.

While they made their way back down the treacherous path, Anne tried to deal with the storm of emotions raging through her. She'd taken a man's life. That was a powerful thing. True, he'd been trying to kill her—and Luke. For a woman who couldn't bear to set a trap for mice, she knew that shooting Scorpion would torment her for a very long time—probably forever.

When she pushed that worry aside, another popped up to take its place. She'd almost killed Luke. Her interference had almost gotten them both murdered. Luckily, she'd been able to reach the rifle, but the situation could have ended worse. Much worse.

An unexpected burst of self-assurance swept through her. She wasn't a nitwit. Luke had been losing the battle. She'd used her own judgment. And it had been a good decision. They both were still alive. No, she wasn't going to waste another moment fretting about what might have been. There was too much else to worry about.

For instance, there were her newly recognized feelings toward Luke. She imagined as soon as she testified at Riczini's trial that the FBI would whisk her away to another state. Give her another identity. Where she would have to start over.

Without Luke.

How could she bear it?

In the daylight, it only took them an hour to reach the base of the mountain. While Luke walked out to where Scorpion had fallen, Anne made a discreet trip to the bushes before rejoining him.

"Go back, Anne," Luke said. "You don't want to see this."

"No," she admitted, "I don't want to, but I have to. I have to know if it's William."

Luke didn't argue. Motioning for her to stand back, he cautiously approached the body.

The killer was lying facedown, his bulky jacket flopped over his head. Luke wedged a toe beneath him and flipped him over.

Anne gasped.

Although his face was cut and bloody, she would have known that skeletal visage anywhere. "Dan Nevill, the attorney," she whispered, awed by the brutal sight.

Luke nodded. "Also known as Bernie Muldaur, aka Bernie the Blaster, aka Bernard Moon. He was Riczini's lieutenant, his right-hand man."

"Scorpion," Anne breathed. "He doesn't look so...so lethal now."

"Funny—" Luke shook his head "—I never had Muldaur pegged as Scorpion. Never figured he had the nerve. Bernie was famous for his stomach ailments. Always popping antacids. Just goes to show you, I guess."

"What do we do now?"

Luke looked up at the sky. It was only a little after six, but already the sun's burning rays were beating overhead. They were more than a mile from their truck, and there was no way they could tow Muldaur/Scorpion's body across the sand. Even if they trekked to the truck, it was out of gas.

The killer must have left a vehicle somewhere along the trail. But if it wasn't a four-wheel drive, it wouldn't traverse this rugged terrain with the dips, gullies and rock beds. They'd have to leave the body here for the authorities.

Luke went through Muldaur's clothing, pulling out his wallet and a set of keys. He slipped the wallet into his pocket. "For identification," he said to her raised eyebrow. "In case some prospector stumbles across the body before the authorities get here, I don't want to leave this behind. No telling what kind of notes or phone numbers the police might find tucked inside."

Pulling off the dead man's jacket, they covered his face and piled all the rocks and debris they could find on top of his body. When Anne asked about all the elaborate preparations, Luke simply shrugged and muttered, "Coyotes."

Finally, Luke slipped his left arm around her waist. "Come on, honey. Let's get the hell out of here. Or should I say, let's get out of hell."

Anne nodded. This desolate place had indeed been their hell, at least for a night. It had also been the place where she'd found her heart. Found the man she would always love.

Yes, Pima Trail would always engender mixed emotions for her.

They reached Muldaur's vehicle first—a large, shiny black truck now covered with a film of dust. Apparently, he'd carried the dirt bike in the truck bed and cast it aside closer to the mountainside.

Anne was surprised when Luke climbed into the passenger seat. "Can you drive a stick shift?" he asked.

"Sure."

"Good, my arm's killing me."

Anne climbed into the driver's seat and plucked the car keys from his hand.

Luke leaned back, relaxing against the headrest. Anne could see the pain etched in the furrowed lines of his forehead, in the tautness of his compressed lips. She had to get him to a hospital.

Luke insisted they telephone the Yuma police first.

Eventually, much to Anne's relief, they pulled into the emergency-room entrance. A half-dozen FBI agents waited for their arrival. To Anne's dismay, a pair of them kept her in the waiting room answering questions, while another pair accompanied Luke down the hall.

The other two headed for a bank of pay phones on the wall.

Finally, an intern, after taking one look at Anne's exhausted face, took pity on her and chased away the two agents, saying that she'd be available for questions later.

X rays confirmed Luke had dislocated his shoulder. After giving him a local anesthetic, the doctor manipulated his shoulder into the socket. Almost before he knew it, the emergency room personnel had encased his arm in a comfortable sling. The doctor gave him a few pills for pain, and, at last, they were ready to go home.

By noon, they were released. Piling into the rear of an inconspicuous tan sedan, they were silent while two agents drove them back to Anne's house. At Luke's firm direction, the two agents agreed to wait until later in the afternoon before subjecting Anne to more questioning.

Arms linked, the bruised couple tromped wearily into Anne's house. Although she was starving, the first thing she wanted was a bath. Or a shower. Or maybe even both.

Luke followed her down the hall where she stopped only long enough to turn on the air conditioner before going directly into her bedroom. She flopped across the bed while he perched at the side.

"Well," he said, "looks like it's all over."

"Finally. So what do you think will happen now?"

"I managed to stall them for a couple of hours, but sometime this afternoon, you'll be visited by so many G-men it will look like a convention."

Anne propped up on an elbow. "What about you?"

He sighed. "As soon as I have a shower—"

"But the doctor said—"

"I don't care what the doctor said about getting this thing wet, I want a shower!"

"Okay, okay. You can have a shower. Then what?" She held up a hand, her doe-soft eyes sympathetic. He deserved to be grumpy.

He drooped over, leaning his head on her hip. "Then a nap. Definitely a nap. Then, after the biggest, juiciest porterhouse steak that money can buy, *then* I'm going to call my office and check in."

"What about Ernie's horses—what do we do about them?"

"Shoot!" Luke sat up. "You go ahead and take your shower, honey. I'd better call the sheriff and see if somebody found them."

With a groan, she rolled off the bed and pulled off her filthy cotton top. Ugh. She should just throw this entire outfit away. It would probably never come clean, and even if it did, she'd never wear it again. It would remind her too much of their ordeal.

Taking a light, flowered sundress from the closet and clean undies from her bureau, she kissed Luke on his heavily stubbled cheek. "Feel free to use my shower when you're finished on the phone. I'm going to use the other bathroom—the one with the Jacuzzi tub. I may soak until this time tomorrow. No, that's not true. I do want to be awake for this fettuccine you've been promising."

Plumping a pillow behind his head, he leaned back. "Are you telling me that you expect me to cook? With one arm?"

"You've been telling me that you're a man of many talents, but I guess you're right. Maybe I should fix our dinner—"

"What's your specialty?" Suspicion glittered in his eyes.

Anne laid a finger against her temple. "Uh, guacamole and baked potatoes."

He waved a hand in dismissal. "I'd have to have both arms broken and be in a full body cast before I'd let you cook. Fettuccine's on. Tonight."

WHEN ANNE CAME back into the bedroom nearly an hour later, a note was pinned to her pillow saying that Luke had gone to fetch Ernie's horses. The animals were safely penned up at a rancher's house only a few miles from where they'd wandered off.

Apparently, Officer Diaz had stopped by to take Luke to retrieve the truck.

Roaming around the empty house, Anne felt a sense of disorientation. Everything had changed. Even though Scorpion was dead and the danger finally past, she still felt as if she were walking on eggshells—still waiting for something to happen. The sense of relief she'd anticipated had not yet appeared.

It was only because Luke was gone, she told herself. For the past few days, he'd constantly been with her. In spirit, if not in fact. A warm, mindful shadow in the night watching over her. The house felt hollow, empty without him.

She wandered into the kitchen. The room that had been a sort of command center during the past few days. Her imagination placed Luke everywhere. Straddling that chair. Checking the patio door. Filling the coffeepot.

Anne decided she liked having a man around the house. At least, one special man. But she better not get used to having him around. Because before long, her memory of Luke would be all she had to keep her company. Their time together was almost over.

Deciding that she'd better find something constructive to do until Luke returned, she phoned the hospital.

To her relief, Nurse Oliver told her that although Mr. Farmer was still comatose, he was holding his own. She thought that by tomorrow the doctors might consider easing his medication dosage. Try to bring him back to consciousness.

"Did anyone ever contact his son?" Anne asked.

"Yes, as a matter of fact. He phoned this morning. He'll be in sometime tonight to stay with his father. He seems like an awfully nice young man," Nurse Oliver added. "After his father is released from the hospital, he's going to take him father back to Colorado. So the old gentleman won't be alone anymore."

"That's…that's very nice. Could you let me know when Mr. Farmer is able to have visitors?"

"I'll do that."

Anne laid the receiver on the hook and sank onto a chair.

She exhaled deeply, a mixture of relief and encroaching loneliness. It was truly all over.

She was safe.

Auggie Riczini was back in custody and Scorpion was dead.

She should be jumping for joy. Celebrating.

But the bad news overshadowed the good.

Luke would be leaving soon, and all she'd have left was her empty life with a few, precious memories to fill it.

Chapter Fifteen

When Luke came home, he found Anne lying on a chaise longue on the patio, dozing peacefully. His first impulse was to wake her up and give her holy heck for being so careless. Falling asleep out in the open where she'd be an easy target. Then he remembered. It was truly over. The last loose end had been tied. William Gardner's body had finally been recovered. At least enough of it to make a positive identification.

First thing in the morning, Luke had to catch a flight out of San Diego for Washington. Worse, the last flight out of Yuma for San Diego had already departed. That meant he still had a three-hour drive ahead of him.

Stifling a sigh of regret, he tiptoed back into the kitchen. Halfheartedly, he filled a pot with water for the fettuccine noodles. The bureau wanted an in-depth debriefing of the Scorpion incident ASAP. In person.

Luke had hoped he and Anne would have at least a brief period of normalcy to sort out their relationship and figure out where they were going.

Yet, he still felt more lighthearted than he had in years. Cleansed. He'd carried his hatred for Scorpion like a yoke around his neck for so long, that he felt almost physically lighter now that the load was gone. Luke wasn't sorry Scorpion was dead. He just wished he'd killed the cold-blooded monster himself. With his bare hands.

Right now, though, he had to concentrate on dinner before the noodles overcooked. Forcing his mind away from their uncertain future, he carried plates and silverware into the dining room.

Someone whistling in the background and a luscious aroma enticed Anne to wakefulness. Rising to her feet, she walked to the sliding glass door and stopped. Luke was standing at the stove, stirring a pan of something heavenly. He'd put a vase of flowers on the table.

Her heart pounded in her chest at the sight of him, so at home in her kitchen. Luke was truly a gem. Unlike any man she'd ever known, he was fierce warrior, protector, frustrated comedian, incredibly sexy lover and short-order cook all in one. She adored every facet of his complex personality.

She would miss him terribly.

As if he sensed her watching him, Luke turned from the stove and grinned. "Hi! Hope you're hungry."

"Starving."

Anne closed the sliding glass door behind her. "Can I give you a hand?"

"Yeah. You got an extra?"

Grabbing an oven mitt, she took the saucepan from the heat. "This smells ready to me." She sniffed the air appreciatively.

Luke nodded. "Pour it in slowly."

Anne stuck out her tongue at his fussiness, but raised the lip of the pan. "Stop being so bossy and open the wine."

He pulled the corkscrew from the junk drawer, seated himself, and wedged the raffia-wrapped bottle between his knees. Then he worked it into the cork.

How incredibly *normal* it seemed, working together in her cozy kitchen, their hips bumping at every turn. There was a peculiar intimacy, she discovered, in sharing small household tasks. An intimacy she could learn to enjoy. A lot.

"Hurry up, McCullough. I'm hungry."

"You're always hungry. It's ready. Let's go to the table."

Anne carried the wine while Luke used his good arm to tote the large bowl of pasta. At the table, he made an effusive production of dishing out the best fettuccine she'd ever tasted.

True gourmands at heart, their conversation was limited to a few grunts and slurps while they devoured the exquisite meal. At last, Anne held up her hand and patted her stomach. "Enough! I'm going to burst."

Pushing their plates aside, they leaned back, lingering over their wine.

Anne looked up. "Oh, I forgot to ask you! Did you get the horses all rounded up?"

"Yeah. They're safely back in their stalls. Officer Diaz is going to—" He broke off and sipped his wine. He'd almost told her that Officer Diaz had agreed to keep an eye on Ernie's house until Luke's ex-partner returned home. Luke wanted to savor a bit more of their evening before he told Anne he was leaving.

"Officer Diaz what?" Anne asked curiously.

"He took me out to pick up the horses. We got the truck towed in. Someone had punctured the gas tank with an icepick. Gave us a nice slow leak. They also found a bug in Ernie's phone. That's how Scorpion knew we'd be going for a long drive."

"My God, the man was absolutely diabolical."

Luke shook his shaggy dark head. "Never would have given Muldaur the credit for being that smart. Did you talk to the hospital? How's Mr. Farmer?"

Anne briefly repeated the conversation she'd had with Nurse Oliver. "Anyway, if he goes to Colorado with his son, it's kind of like a final chapter to this saga. All the loose ends tucked neatly into place."

Except for one, she thought. *Her broken heart when Luke left.*

She saw him watching her, an anxious look on his face. Not wanting to spoil the mood, she forced a cheeriness into her voice. "Everything was just wonderful, Luke. The food. The flowers. Thank you."

"You're welcome. Did you get a good nap?" he asked. "You certainly look well rested."

She frowned in chagrin. "Not as long a nap as I wanted. Your colleagues were here most of the afternoon."

"Did they tell you what their plans are—for you, I mean?"

Anne shook her head. "Not exactly. I think they're going to move me out of Yuma in the next few days. Put me in a temporary safe house until the trial. Just because Scorpion/Muldaur is dead, doesn't mean Riczini can't put out another contract with somebody else. Sometimes, I don't think this nightmare will ever truly be over."

He reached across the table and patted her hand. "Hang in there, honey. Something will work out. Do they have a trial date yet?"

Anne took a sip of the dry, red wine and nodded. "It's set for later this month, so I'll have to go back and testify. After that, I guess they'll give me another identity."

Luke polished off his glass and poured another. "Something will work out, Anne, I just know it."

She said nothing.

They sat quietly for a moment, lost in their own morose thoughts. Finally, to dispel the gloomy mood that threatened to spoil the evening, Anne stood up. "Why don't you go into the living room and relax? I'll rinse off these dishes and bring in our wine.''

He pushed back from the table. "Sounds good to me.''

Anne carried the plates into the kitchen, then stopped back at the dining-room table to pick up their goblets. As she was walking down the tiled entryway toward the living room, she stopped. A cold chill settled in the pit of her stomach.

Luke's suitcase was parked just inside the front door. This morning it had been in her bedroom.

A scalding knot formed in her throat as hot tears pooled behind her eyes. He was leaving her. Today.

She'd imagined how this moment would feel, but the reality was worse than any pain her mind could conjure up. Why hadn't he told her right away? She deserved at least that much. They'd spent an hour over dinner making inane conversation and, all the time, he'd known he was leaving.

Anne straightened her shoulders. She'd get through this. She'd survived worse. Much worse. But she couldn't stand to sit through the rest of the evening, pretending she wasn't dying inside. A quick, clean amputation was easier than ripping her heart out chunk by chunk.

Luke turned away from the mantel as she entered. Anne's stiff, haughty posture and halting gait were a dead giveaway.

With slow, deliberate steps, she crossed the room and handed him his Chianti. Holding her own goblet in tense, cupped hands, she stood facing him. Her chin was thrust forward, her head tilted back. "So when were you planning on telling me?"

"Anne, believe me, I was going to tell you—"

"When?" she cut in coldly. "After dinner? After you'd made love to me? Or maybe you just planned to leave a note on my pillow."

"It's not like that! I just found out this afternoon that I have to go back to Washington right away. I...I didn't want to spoil our dinner and—"

"Well, dinner's over. Your obligation to me is done, so have a safe trip."

He set his glass on the mantel and grasped her upper arms. "Don't do this! Please, listen to me. Let me explain. I didn't want to hurt you."

She didn't want him to feel sorry for her. Not that, please God. Not his pity. She was already humiliated by her own need. If begging would make him stay, she would have fallen to her knees. But he had to go. And she had to let him.

A sudden fury filled her.

She was angry at Luke, at herself and at the venal fate that was forcing their separation. Her arms were burning from his touch. Unable to stand his closeness a moment longer, she jerked away. Red droplets of wine spattered on the beige carpet. She didn't care. Nothing mattered any longer. Nothing.

"Listen, Luke, we had some good times. A few laughs. But let's don't draw it out into a melodrama, okay?"

Luke's hands fell to his sides. His gray eyes shot with sparks like a fire out of control. "Is that all we were to you, Anne? A good time? A few laughs?"

She stood unbowed, unspeaking.

"You're making a mistake, Anne. Why won't you listen to me?"

Finally, she raised her eyes and met his fierce, unwavering gaze. "Please, Luke, let's don't spoil everything by fighting. Just go."

After staring at her for a long, searching moment, he turned on his heel and stalked out of the room. A moment later, the front door closed gently behind him.

ANNE DIDN'T LEAVE her house for the next two days. She'd refused to answer the phone, leaving the answering machine on all the time. After two days, there was still no message from Luke.

The FBI finished their investigation. She would be relocated within the next two days. The nightmare was over; yet, Anne felt this growing sense of impending doom. In two days, she would disappear and become someone else. In two days, no one, not even Luke, would be able to find her.

Anne stood up and unplugged the answering machine. It was time to get on with it. Walking into the living room, she drew open the curtains. The sidewalk shimmered with heat. The streets were deserted, as if the whole world were on hold, waiting for the summer to end and the unmerciful heat wave to pass.

Even with the swamp cooler on high, it was hot. Fire-breathing hot. Hell hot. Even the cactus in the yard looked wilted.

In the distance, a jagged flash of lightning sizzled across the sky. A chill chased up her spine.

A raucous peal of thunder caused her to jump. In a matter of moments, storm clouds would steal across the vast skies, sending down bolts of lightning.

There was a feeling of dread in the air. Impending doom. Anne couldn't remember the last time she'd been so edgy. It was as if she'd stuck her head in a guillotine and was waiting for the executioner to release the blade.

No wonder, really. With everything that had happened the past few weeks, it was hard to believe that she was safe now. If only for the time being.

Another thunderous crash and Anne jerked the drapes closed. At that moment, there was a knock on the door. Grateful for the distraction, she raced to the front door.

Her next-door neighbor, Elaine Bittner, stood on the porch carrying a pizza box and a six-pack. "Thought you might be free for a few hands of cribbage."

Anne reached out and pulled her inside. "Am I ever glad to see you. I've been about ready to crawl up the walls."

"Why? What's up?"

Anne shook her head. "Nothing really. I...I just have this creepy feeling that something awful's going to happen."

Elaine chuckled. "You're just missing Luke McHunk, that's all. Come on. Dig out the cribbage board and find the hot pepper flakes. This pizza won't keep much longer."

Somehow, though, Elaine's steady stream of bawdy humor didn't distract Anne as it usually did. As the evening progressed, so did her sense of a looming catastrophe.

Her fear was enhanced by the dark, starless night. Anne opened the kitchen window to let some of the heat escape into the slightly cooler night.

"Come on, Annie, your deal. Where's your mind? Back with Lu—never mind. Forget I said that, just deal."

Looking at the board, Anne saw that she was once again on the verge of getting beaten.

"So, where's your guard dog tonight?" Elaine asked.

Anne shrugged. "Now that Scorpion's dead, they really couldn't justify keeping a full-time watch on me. One of the agents went back to Phoenix this afternoon."

"That seems awful risky. For you, I mean. Hand me those hot peppers."

"Not really. The police are putting extra patrols on the street for the next two days and I still have one agent assigned to me." She passed the container and watched as Elaine liberally sprinkled the red flakes on her fourth slice of pizza. Anne was truly amazed at the woman's capacity for food.

"My play?" Elaine asked as she took a deep draft of beer.

Outside, the wind had picked up and was beginning to howl, sounding like a pack of marauding coyotes. Anne shivered despite the heat.

For a few moments, the women concentrated on the intricacies of counting points. Despite all odds, Anne won and Elaine threw her cards down in disgust. "You lucky devil!"

Anne stood up, glad the game was over. "Luck? That was skill. You're just a sore loser. I'm going to get some chips and dip, want anything?"

"Skill my foot," Elaine grumbled. "I'm telling you the truth, Annette, you're the luckiest woman this side of Las Vegas."

Anne's hand was on the refrigerator door before Elaine's careless words sunk in. She froze, as the implications became clearer. Slowly turning on her heel, Anne faced the older woman. "You...you called me Annette. How...how did you know my real name? Except for my mother and the FBI, no one knows my real name."

Shrugging nonchalantly, Elaine reached for her handbag. "I *didn't* know it was your real name. Slip of the tongue, I guess. You just look like an Annette. Mind if I smoke?"

Anne shook her head in complete bewilderment. "That was no slip of the tongue—you've never called me that before."

"Actually, you're right, that wasn't a slip. I just wanted to see the look on your face. It was priceless." Elaine chuckled. But her laugh was lacking humor. "Oh, come on, Anne. Can't you guess? Deep inside, don't you really know who I am?"

Anne's confusion was slowly evolving into a dark, horrible suspicion. Her voice, thin and wavery, asked, "Why, Elaine? Who are you? Really?"

Elaine threw her handbag aside and rose to her feet. In her right hand was a black, lethal-looking revolver. Pointing directly at Anne. "Surprise, surprise. Did you really think that you'd killed Scorpion? Don't make me laugh."

The full impact of Elaine's confession suddenly plowed into Anne like a low blow. Muldaur wasn't Scorpion.

Dear God, Elaine was her dreaded nemesis. Elaine was Scorpion.

Before the shock could take control and paralyze her, Anne took a step away from the fridge, edging toward the arch between the kitchen and hallway.

"Don't do anything stupid, Anne. Move over here, away from that door."

Anne hesitated, then took two halting steps toward Elaine. "But I...I don't understand. You...Muldaur...both of you?" A sob caught her throat. She'd *trusted* this woman. Did Anne have such poor judgment that everyone she cared for was bound to betray her?

"You really *are* a little fool, aren't you? I can't believe you thought that wimp Bernie Muldaur was Scorpion!" Elaine sneered contemptuously. "He wasn't man enough to clean my gun. Come back over here and sit down. Right where you were."

Anne forced her wobbly legs to move forward, toward the kitchen table. Her mind was whirling.

As her trembling hands pulled out a chair, she stared, unbelieving, into Elaine's frigid blue gaze. "But why?"

"Why?" Her husky voice broke into a hideous laugh. "Money, sweetheart, money. A hundred thousand dollars."

"Why...why did you wait so long? Why didn't you just shoot me a month ago? When you first came here."

Elaine snorted. "Oh, that idiot Riczini had some idea that if we made it look like an accident, no one would question your death. But he wanted your old boyfriend, Gardner, taken care of first.''

Anne shook her head in confusion. ''But you were here, in Yuma, when William was killed. I remember.''

''Give me a little credit, kiddo. I set that whole thing up a week before I moved here. I rigged plastic explosives to the bilge pump. That way he was sure to be out to sea before the charge was activated. How was I supposed to know Gardner wouldn't take his precious yacht out for nearly six weeks? It still worked,'' she added defensively.

Anne closed her eyes, an inner voice telling her not to accept defeat. To fight.

Elaine flipped off the safety. ''Anyway, kiddo, looks like it's your turn now.''

Anne tried to think of something—anything—to keep her talking. The longer the woman talked, the greater Anne's chances were of finding a chink in Elaine's armor. Some way to escape.

If she didn't, Elaine—Scorpion—was going to kill her.

Nodding, encouraging Elaine to keep talking, Anne carefully slipped her hand under the edge of the table. Maybe if she flipped it over—distracted Elaine for just a minute...

A sudden metallic click from the patio sounded as loud as a bomb detonating in the tense atmosphere.

Elaine instinctively turned toward the sound. Taking her split-second advantage, Anne took a deep breath, summoned all her courage and overturned the kitchen table.

At that moment, the lights went out.

Chapter Sixteen

Acting out of pure instinct, Anne plunged behind the fallen table. A deafening boom resounded in her ear as the muzzle of Elaine's gun spit fire into the darkness.

The patio door exploded like a fragmentation bomb. Shards of glass flew, showering the room with millions of silvery razors. As the splinters of glass crashed around her, Anne instinctively dropped to the floor.

She had the impression of something large, something man-size flying through the broken door just before she tucked her head under her arms for protection.

Her breath coming in frenzied pants, Anne gritted her teeth and soundlessly began crawling along the edge of the room, skimming her hand along the wall for support. Her only plan was to somehow make it to the doorway.

"Anne?"

She gasped aloud. Luke! Her heart pounded so hard in her chest that it hurt. Luke was here. He'd come back.

"Anne?" To hear him calling her name again was like a special gift from heaven. "Just stay where you are. Don't move."

"I have your girlfriend covered, McCullough. She can't get away from me. This time you're dealing with the real Scorpion. No one escapes from Scorpion," Elaine threatened, her voice as hard as a tempered steel sword—and just as cutting.

A shudder rippled through Anne's body. The woman was completely amoral. Lacking any semblance of a conscience. And that lack made her totally unpredictable.

Luke had said not to move, but it didn't matter. Anne had reached the end of her wall. She couldn't go any farther. She'd boxed herself into a corner.

"Oh, Annie? Little Annette-Annie, where are you?" Elaine's voice sliced through the room like a whip.

Luke's voice shot back. "I'm warning you, Elaine. You're in my sights. Drop your gun."

Anne's pulse raced. She had to make it to the foyer. If she could just get to the door—

She heard Elaine's footsteps crunching on broken glass as she came closer. Closer.

Anne knew Luke couldn't shoot in the darkness. Knew he wouldn't take a chance on hitting her by mistake. She had to do something, but she couldn't think. Couldn't move. She was too terrified for Luke.

Those horrid steps bit through the glass again. As her eyes adjusted to the darkness, Anne could make out Elaine's silhouette moving into her line of vision. Any second now, Elaine would spot her. Any second and Elaine would pull the trigger and—

Her fingertips found a glass cylinder rolling on the floor. Holding her breath, Anne picked it up. It was a glass bottle. She unscrewed the top. The crushed red peppers!

Elaine was directly in front of her now, Anne could see the outline of her revolver. If Luke had taught her anything, it was not to be a victim. Gathering her courage, she jumped to her feet and emptied the shaker of red peppers in the direction of Elaine's face.

The woman shrieked, flailed her arms, twisted swiftly away from the peppers and struck Anne across the cheek with her gun.

Anne staggered away just as another sharp report filled the room. Elaine gasped and spat out a vile curse.

Anne raised her head. She could vaguely see Luke and Elaine, shadowy figures, scuffling in the darkness. She heard grunts. Elaine cursing. Another odd clicking noise.

For a long moment, the room shivered with the sudden silence, then Elaine's shrill scream pierced the air. "You bastard!"

Then, miraculously, Anne heard the wonderful sound of Luke's voice. "Just shut up, Elaine. Anne? Are you all right?"

She choked back a peal of hysterical laughter. Luke *did* spend half his time asking her if she was all right! Her face was stinging where Elaine had struck her, but she didn't feel any blood.

The glass crunched again and Anne saw Luke dragging Elaine with him outside. An instant later, sudden dazzling light stung her eyes as he turned the power back on.

Luke came into the room. His hair was damp with perspiration, his shoulder sling was hanging uselessly, his shirt was spotted with dirt and blood. No man had ever looked more bedraggled. But no man, anywhere, anytime, had ever looked more splendid.

He dragged a snarling, bleeding Elaine back into the kitchen. She'd been shot in the shoulder, and although her face was pale and strained, her eyes still glittered with hatred. Anne was relieved to see Elaine's hands were cuffed behind her back.

Luke pushed the assassin into a chair. Grabbing a tea towel from the drawer, he used his good arm to shove it inside Elaine's blouse; staunching the flow of blood. With his other, Luke reached for the wall phone and dialed 911.

When he hung up, he checked Elaine's wound again. "You'll live," he pronounced.

Now that his duties were almost complete, he rushed to Anne's side and helped her to her feet. He pulled another chair across the room, far from Elaine's glaring eyes, and guided Anne into it.

With a hand as soft as a summer night's breeze, he caressed her cheek. "God, I love you."

Luke loved her. That thought kept her company throughout the following long, tiresome hours.

It only seemed like seconds before the house was lit up with the blinding glare of searchlights. Officer Diaz was the first through the patio door. Within minutes, it seemed to Anne that a full battalion of officers were swarming through her small house. Police. Sheriff's department. FBI. Even the Highway Patrol was represented.

Luke loved her.

She hardly noticed when the officers flooded into the room, weapons drawn.

An ambulance was called for Elaine. After reading Elaine her rights, Luke leaned over her. "I have just one question for you. Off the record. A question that goes back a long time. Almost five years."

"What the hell are you talking about, McCullough?"

"You know. That job you did in Las Vegas five years ago. Glenna Glaser."

"Oh, yeah. Your hooker."

"Cocktail waitress."

"Whatever. What about her?"

Luke drew a deep breath. "She opened the hotel door for you that night. I've never understood that."

Elaine rolled her eyes. "First of all, I don't know what you're talking about, but theoretically..."

Luke nodded his agreement. The prosecutor would have to make his own case against Elaine. It shouldn't be difficult. But this... this was a private matter. Between him and Scorpion. "Theoretically speaking, of course."

"That was a cinch, speaking only in the abstract, you understand. Everyone thought Scorpion was a man. That made my job a lot easier."

"So she opened the door to you just because you were a woman?"

Elaine shook her head. "I wasn't even there that night, remember, but if I had been, I would have been *very* clever. Maybe I would have put on a maid's uniform. Maybe I would have carried an extra pillow and told her that you had called the desk and asked for it. Maybe that's what I would have done—if I'd been there. Which I wasn't, of course."

"Of course."

Luke walked away as the paramedics rushed into the room and swarmed around Elaine. So it was as easy as that, he thought. And the witch was right—*everyone* had thought Scorpion was a man. They'd never, in all these years, imagined otherwise. No wonder Glenna had bought her story. Hell, he might have opened that door himself. In fact, almost anyone would have opened that door to a slender uniformed blonde, carrying a pillow.

While the emergency medical technicians attended to Elaine, he gazed at Anne. The woman was absolutely incredible. Sitting there speaking with the officers as calmly as if she'd invited them to tea. Where did she get her inner strength? Her stamina? He didn't know, but he intended to spend the rest of his life finding out.

Anne looked up and saw Luke anxiously watching her. She smiled reassuringly. *He'd said he loved her.* Nothing else mattered. With his love to sustain her, she could go through this nightmare a dozen times over.

Luke ambled over and draped his good arm around her shoulder. Addressing Officer Diaz, he said, "You guys sure got here quick. That's one of the best response times I've ever seen."

Officer Diaz smiled. "Wish I could say we always get onto the scene that fast. Truth is, like I've been telling Ms. Farraday, here, we were already on our way when your call came in."

"Oh?"

"Yeah. You know that old man in the hospital? Farmer?"

Luke nodded.

"Seems young Mr. Farmer finally convinced somebody at the hospital to listen to his father. The staff had been brushing him off every time he started talking about a neighbor-woman bashing him in the head. My partner and I had just left the hospital and we were on our way over here to have a little chat with the neighbor-lady."

When the ambulance driver brought a stretcher into the already crowded kitchen, the other officials started to disperse. After the ambulance left and the last policeman closed his notebook and departed, Luke shut the door behind them and ambled back into the kitchen where Anne was still sitting in the wreckage.

At last, her ordeal was truly over.

With his thumb, Luke pointed to the shattered patio door. "Am I going to have to spend the rest of my life calling glaziers and locksmiths?"

"Not if you'll start opening doors instead of smashing through them."

He offered his good hand, and helped her to her feet. Arms wrapped around each other's waists, they slowly walked into the living room.

"That was a pretty clever trick, McCullough."

He tightened his hold on her waist. He didn't want her a single inch away from him ever again. "Which trick was that?"

She looked up at him, her brown eyes twinkling. "The old turning-off-the-power trick."

"Oh, yeah." He laughed, guiding her toward the over-stuffed easy chair. "Well, it worked pretty well for Scorpion once, I mean Elaine, so I figured why not give it a shot."

He dropped into the huge chair and propped his feet up on the ottoman. "Here," he said as he patted his lap, "sit down."

"Best seat in the house," she murmured as she lowered herself onto his lap and laid her head on his chest. "Oh, Luke, I've never been so glad to see anyone in my whole life!"

"That makes two of us, honey. I'll tell you one thing, though."

"What's that?"

"You are one stubborn woman. I must have called twenty times in the last two days, but you never answered your damn phone."

He'd called her twenty times. He did love her. "Why didn't you leave a message on the recorder?" she teased.

"Because I didn't want to talk to a machine. I wanted to talk to you. Besides, I figured you'd never call me back."

She sighed. "I'd have called you back."

"Anne, about the other night..."

She sat up and lightly pressed the tips of her fingers to his soft, incredibly sexy lips. "Shh. I don't want to talk about the other night. I don't want to even *think* about my temper tantrum. I'm really sorry, Luke.''

"I'm the one who should be apologizing. I really handled that poorly.''

"It doesn't matter," she said softly. "We won't mention it again.''

"No, we *have* to talk about it. It's important. You see, when my boss insisted that I return to Washington on the next available flight, we got into quite a wrangle. I wanted—no, needed—some time alone with you. Anyway, he wouldn't budge and I came this close—'' he held his fingers a scant inch apart ''—to telling him exactly what he could do with his job.''

"I think I can fill in the . . . uh, details.''

"Yeah, I imagine you can. Well, then I got to thinking. I know the bureau would like to squeeze a few more years of service out of me—they invested quite a tidy sum in training me. So I figured I might have enough leverage to make a trade.''

"What kind of trade?''

"The kind that couldn't be discussed on the telephone. See, old Alonzo—that's my boss—Alonzo's been hassling me for the past year or so to come in.''

She frowned in confusion. "Come in?''

"Spy-speak for get out of the field. Take an office job.''

"Oh.''

"Anyway, up until now, I couldn't imagine anything more boring than a nine-to-five office job. But you know, a man's got to grow up sometime. Can't play cops'n'robbers the rest of my life. And, suddenly, the idea of coming home every night didn't sound so bad. Not bad at all.'' *Not if he was coming home to Anne.*

She snuggled closer. "So what's the trade you were talking about?''

"I wanted the head honcho to have you relocated in the D.C. area. So we could be together."

Anne sighed. "I think Washington would be fine. Cherry blossoms in April. Fourth of July fireworks over the nation's capital. Sounds nice. But . . . I'll still have to be undercover, won't I?"

Suddenly, the thought of living yet another lie was repugnant: always having to think carefully before she divulged any personal information, afraid to make friends because she might let something slip. No, Anne didn't want to live that kind of life; but her circumstances compelled it. But she couldn't let Luke join her in exile. She loved him too much for that.

As she opened her mouth to tell him, he touched her lips with his fingertips. "Save it. I wouldn't care if they renamed you Bertha Buffalo and moved you to Outer Mongolia, I'm going to be with you."

"But—"

"But I don't think it's going to be necessary. It looks like your hiding days are over."

"What! But Riczini will put out another contract. You told me he would. The other agents agreed and—"

"That was before last night," he said quietly.

Anne's eyes darkened in perplexity. "Why? What happened last night?"

"Last night, in the D.C. Federal Correctional Center, inmate August Emilio Riczini, aka Auggie Riczini, was killed in a prison knife fight. Seems an old enemy finally got revenge. That's one mobster who won't be putting out any more contracts."

Anne's heart leaped into her throat. "You mean . . . you mean I'm free? To go wherever I want? To be myself again?"

A broad smile on his face, Luke gloried in giving her the news. "Free as a bird, Anne—I mean, Annette. Which should I call you?"

"Annette," she said shyly. Somehow, it was important that he like her real name. That he like her real self.

"Annette," he repeated, tasting the name on his tongue. "Nice. Kind of soft and sexy. Like you."

In response, she wrapped her arms around his neck and drank in the wonder of his face. The events of this evening had turned from a nightmare into a fantasy. One she had every intention of indulging.

"Yeah," Luke whispered. "That's a very sensuous name. What's your middle name? I don't remember seeing it in the file."

She bit her lip. "I, uh, don't really use my middle name. It's kind of, well, unusual."

"Oh, come on. It can't be that bad."

"Yes, it is. Trust me."

"Tell me. I'm a grown man, I can take it.

"Okay, but don't say I didn't warn you. My full name is Annette Irish O'Toole."

"Irish? What kind of name is that?"

Anne giggled. "It's Irish, silly."

Luke groaned.

"No, seriously. That's my legal name. My father wanted to make sure I never forgot my heritage."

"Like O'Toole wouldn't be enough of a clue?"

"In case I married a man named Martinez. Or Smith. Or DuBois. Or—"

"I get his point. I think. Well, Annette Irish O'Toole, I have a question for you of some import."

She felt a warm glow in her heart, and a flush of excitement crept up her cheeks. "Yes?"

"What would you think about being the wife of a desk jockey?"

Her pulse raced like a runaway freight train. Looking deep into his silver gaze, she focused on the key word. "Wife?"

"Uh-huh. If you'll have me, that is?"

Have him? "Are you kidding, Luke McCullough? If you try to leave me again, I'll buy a pack of bloodhounds and track you to the ends of the earth."

"Think your dad would approve? I mean, McCullough is a foine ol' Irish name, begorra."

"Your accent needs serious work," she teased. "But I think my dad would have approved. Definitely."

Lacing her arms around his head, she curled her fingers into his thick, midnight-black hair and pulled his lips to hers.

Her kiss told him everything. Told him of her abiding love, her wracking pain while he was gone. Shouted of her utter consuming need for him. When she pulled her lips away, he burrowed his face in her neck, drinking in the sweet nectar of this woman who'd given him a new life.

"So what do you think, Irish? Want to storm the capital with me?"

For her answer, she unbuttoned his shirt and slipped her hands inside, luxuriating in the warm, hard feel of his flesh. This was how they'd spend their nights. In front of a roaring fire. Snow falling quietly outside while they spent a lifetime exploring the wonder of their bodies.

Proving his remarkable versatility, Luke had managed to unbutton her blouse without her noticing. And with one hand, yet. The man was truly incredible.

After a long while, she stirred in his arms. Her nimble fingers worked at the snap of his jeans. "I like roses. And ivy is nice. But..."

"But what?" His tongue teasing at her earlobe was slowly driving her to distraction.

"But I want a white picket fence, too."

"You got it."

"And fettuccine once a week."

"You'll get fat."

She chuckled and slid to the floor, pulling him down with her. "Not if we get plenty of exercise."

"Irish, you're one hell of a woman."

My Valentine 1994

Celebrate the most romantic day of the year with
MY VALENTINE 1994
a collection of original stories, written by
four of Harlequin's most popular authors...

MARGOT DALTON
MURIEL JENSEN
MARISA CARROLL
KAREN YOUNG

*Available in February, wherever
Harlequin Books are sold.*

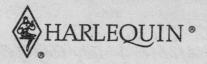

HARLEQUIN ®

VAL94

Valentine's Day was the best day of the year for
Dee's Candy and Gift Shop. Yet as the day drew closer,
Deanna Donovan became the target of
malicious, anonymous pranks.

A red heart was pinned to her front door with a dagger.

Dead roses adorned her car.

Soon, she was being stalked by her unseen admirer.

Suspicious of everyone, Deanna has nowhere to turn—and no
way to escape when she is kidnapped and held captive by her
Valentine lover....

#262

Cupid's Dagger
by *Leona Karr*
February 1994

You'll never again think of Valentine's Day without feeling a
thrill of delight...and a chill of dread!   CUPID

HARLEQUIN®

Don't miss these Harlequin favorites by some of our most distinguished authors!
And now, you can receive a discount by ordering two or more titles!

HT#25409	THE NIGHT IN SHINING ARMOR by JoAnn Ross	$2.99 ☐
HT#25471	LOVESTORM by JoAnn Ross	$2.99 ☐
HP#11463	THE WEDDING by Emma Darcy	$2.89 ☐
HP#11592	THE LAST GRAND PASSION by Emma Darcy	$2.99 ☐
HR#03188	DOUBLY DELICIOUS by Emma Goldrick	$2.89 ☐
HR#03248	SAFE IN MY HEART by Leigh Michaels	$2.89 ☐
HS#70464	CHILDREN OF THE HEART by Sally Garrett	$3.25 ☐
HS#70524	STRING OF MIRACLES by Sally Garrett	$3.39 ☐
HS#70500	THE SILENCE OF MIDNIGHT by Karen Young	$3.39 ☐
HI#22178	SCHOOL FOR SPIES by Vickie York	$2.79 ☐
HI#22212	DANGEROUS VINTAGE by Laura Pender	$2.89 ☐
HI#22219	TORCH JOB by Patricia Rosemoor	$2.89 ☐
HAR#16459	MACKENZIE'S BABY by Anne McAllister	$3.39 ☐
HAR#16466	A COWBOY FOR CHRISTMAS by Anne McAllister	$3.39 ☐
HAR#16462	THE PIRATE AND HIS LADY by Margaret St. George	$3.39 ☐
HAR#16477	THE LAST REAL MAN by Rebecca Flanders	$3.39 ☐
HH#28704	A CORNER OF HEAVEN by Theresa Michaels	$3.99 ☐
HH#28707	LIGHT ON THE MOUNTAIN by Maura Seger	$3.99 ☐

Harlequin Promotional Titles

#83247	YESTERDAY COMES TOMORROW by Rebecca Flanders	$4.99 ☐
#83257	MY VALENTINE 1993	$4.99 ☐
	(short-story collection featuring Anne Stuart, Judith Arnold, Anne McAllister, Linda Randall Wisdom)	

(limited quantities available on certain titles)

	AMOUNT	$
DEDUCT:	**10% DISCOUNT FOR 2+ BOOKS**	$
ADD:	**POSTAGE & HANDLING**	$
	($1.00 for one book, 50¢ for each additional)	
	APPLICABLE TAXES*	$ _____
	TOTAL PAYABLE	$ _____
	(check or money order—please do not send cash)	

To order, complete this form and send it, along with a check or money order for the total above, payable to Harlequin Books, to: **In the U.S.:** 3010 Walden Avenue, P.O. Box 9047, Buffalo, NY 14269-9047; **In Canada:** P.O. Box 613, Fort Erie, Ontario, L2A 5X3.

Name: _____

Address: _____ City: _____

State/Prov.: _____ Zip/Postal Code: _____

*New York residents remit applicable sales taxes.
 Canadian residents remit applicable GST and provincial taxes.

HBACK-JM